D1221598

PATCHWORK MYSTERIES

A MOTHER'S LOVE

KELLY ANN RILEY

Guideposts

New York

Guideposts.org
(800) 932-2145
Guideposts Books & Inspirational Media

Cover design by Wendy Bass
Cover illustration by Joyce Patti
Interior design by Lorie Pagnozzi
Typeset by Aptara, Inc.

Printed and bound in the United States of America
10 9 8 7 6 5 4 3

This book is dedicated to my father Larry Leiske and my son Austin Riley. Thank you for believing in me. I also wish to thank my editors Beth Adams and Sarah Baar for all their hard work on this series. They have been a joy to work with.

PATCHWORK MYSTERIES

 CHAPTER ONE

S arah Hart hummed along softly with the radio as she drove out of the small town of Pleasant Valley on a narrow country road. White farmhouses and red barns dotted the rolling hills. Ancient oak trees lined drive-ways, stretching their budding branches to the blue heavens adorned with wispy clouds. Although most of the fields they passed lay bare, waiting for seeds, green sprigs of grass and wildflowers poked their heads out of the rich earth along the endless white fence lines.

"Gram, watch out for the horse!" Audrey Hart exclaimed from the backseat of the silver Grand Prix.

"Don't worry, sweetie. I see it." Sarah braked gently as a buggy pulled out of a driveway. The information packet the school tour director had given Sarah before she set off on the field trip to Amish country had warned about watching for buggies and people on foot.

"This is so cool!" Amy, who sat in the passenger seat, rolled down her window, and air laden with scents of plowed earth and mowed grass rushed in. Springtime had arrived in northern New York State. "It's like living in the olden days."

"That's for sure." Audrey leaned over the back holding up her cell phone. "I get only one bar and it keeps disappearing. Do you get anything, Emma?" she asked her classmate.

"Nope. Same thing," Emma said.

"You're supposed to put your phone away while we're here." Amy looked over her shoulder. "Mrs. Hiland said so. You're going to get in trouble."

"We are not," Audrey said. "She didn't say we couldn't use them in the car."

"We're almost there anyway. You can put your phones in the glove compartment with Amy's or keep them in your backpacks. Just don't use them while we're visiting," Sarah said, maneuvering to the center of the road to put some distance between the car and a young boy herding two cows down the lane.

"I like his hat, but I wouldn't want to wear a bonnet or whatever they call the girl hats," Emma said.

"I think they're called prayer caps." Sarah glanced in the rearview mirror at the petite, redheaded eighth grader. Emma had once worked on a school project with Amy, and Sarah was glad someone familiar had been assigned to their group. "We can check in the handout the teacher gave us."

"I have one in my backpack," Emma said. Paper rustled as she pulled out a packet and flipped through the pages. "Yep, the ladies' hats are called prayer caps, and this says the women wear dresses with full skirts and a cape over their bodice, which is fastened with snaps or straight pins. No buttons. And they can only wear solid colors, no patterns. Wanna bet this will all be on the quiz?"

"Weird," Audrey said. "How come they have to wear those boring clothes anyway?"

Amy sighed. "Weren't you paying attention to anything Mrs. Hiland said? They have to wear them if they want to be part of the group."

"The community," Sarah corrected. "Dressing plainly is their way of not being worldly. They've been doing that for hundreds of years. It's a choice they make."

"Boring," Audrey repeated as they passed two boys in slacks, blue shirts, and suspenders. Their broad-brimmed straw hats shaded their faces as they whitewashed a fence.

"Just because they dress differently doesn't make them boring," Amy said.

"I wasn't calling the *people* boring, just the clothes."

As the sisters continued to bicker, Sarah glanced at her trip counter, estimating they had another half mile to go. It had taken two hours to drive from Maple Hill to Pleasant Valley, New York, and with the speed of the horse in front of them, the last leg of the trip was going to take a while. She could try to pass, but there wasn't much room on the narrow road. The clock on the dash indicated they were slightly ahead of schedule, so she relaxed against the seat.

The Amish experience was part of the eighth grade social studies curriculum, and as Mrs. Hiland emphasized, a once in a lifetime opportunity. A small group of Amish families outside the town of Pleasant Valley agreed to host students in their homes once or twice a year to help the students learn about their ways. The children slept overnight in the Amish home and participated in the family chores and activities.

After the whole class met briefly in the town park where they had again been lectured on behaving properly and showing the utmost respect for their hosts, they had split into groups and headed to their host homes for the evening. Each chaperone was matched with two to four children, depending on how many people their Amish host was able to accommodate. Sarah, her granddaughters, and Emma were assigned to stay at Abram and Annie Fisher's farm. Abram Fisher ran a harness business and they were to look for the sign.

Inconspicuous as the sign was, Sarah almost missed the small white placard with "Harness Repair" on it.

Sarah braked and turned right into the yard that surrounded the Fisher house. Thick-trunked trees shaded the long graveled driveway and yard. A woman with a basket in her lap sat on a rocker on the wide porch of the white, two story farmhouse. She set the basket down and rose gracefully. She came to the steps and gestured toward a corner of the house.

"You can park over there in the shade." She pointed and Sarah followed her direction. A large red barn towered over a dusty, flat area lined with farming equipment including a plow and scythe. As Sarah got out of the car, she noted the wide barn doors were open and someone was moving about inside.

"Hello." Sarah waved, but the tall, thin figure melted into the shadows.

Amy came around the hood of the car to Sarah's side. "Who are you waving to, Gram?"

"The man in the barn," Sarah said. "Maybe it's Mr. Fisher."

Amy squinted against the bright sunlight. "I don't see anyone."

"Hello, I'm Annie Fisher," a soft, melodic voice said. "Welcome. You must be Sarah Hart."

Sarah turned to face a woman dressed in a navy skirt and cape over a white blouse. Freckles sprinkled her unlined face. Her smile seemed genuine and lit up her blue eyes. Sandy blonde hair, done up in the traditional Amish bun, was encased in a filmy white prayer cap.

"Hello, it's so nice to meet you. Please call me Sarah."

"Thank you, but only if you refer to me as Annie."

"Thank you so much for having us as your guests. This is Emma, and these are my granddaughters Amy and Audrey."

Annie clapped her hands together. "Twins. My cousin Hannah was blessed to have a pair, but they aren't identical like you two. Please, come into the house. My husband Abram is not home right now. He is tending to his harness repair business. In the afternoons he makes deliveries or attends to emergency repairs. He will fetch your bags when he comes home."

Sarah glanced back at the barn. "So that wasn't Abram in the barn?"

"No." Annie looked at the barn with a slight shake of her head. "No one else is here right now. Abram is not due back until later."

"Maybe I was mistaken. Shadows can play tricks."

"*Ja,* sometimes that happens." Annie nodded, but her smile seemed forced. "Would you like to come into the house and rest a bit? You must be weary after your long trip. As I said, Abram can fetch your bags later."

"We don't want to be a bother. We can get the bags and then you can put us to work. After all, that's why we're here—to experience how the Amish live," Sarah said, and the girls scampered to the car. They hadn't brought much luggage since it was just an overnight trip. They retrieved their backpacks and Sarah grabbed her small suitcase.

They followed Annie up the stairs, past the basket of peas she had been sorting and entered the house. The wood floor was scrubbed clean and neat and tidy furniture lined pale blue walls. "This is our sitting area. We take our turn at having church in here. The dining room is to the right and the kitchen is in the back."

They climbed more stairs to the second level. "This is my daughter's room," Annie said. "The girls may stay here, and Sarah you may have the room across the hall."

The spacious room had a high ceiling and two wide windows, letting in the afternoon sun. Like downstairs, the wood floor and simple, brown furniture gleamed with cleanliness. The only bright splash of color in the room was the quilt that covered the double bed.

"You three don't mind sharing a bed, do you?" Annie asked.

Audrey shot Amy a look. "Only if she doesn't kick me. Watch out Em, she kicks in her sleep."

"Well, Audrey snores," Amy said with a grin.

Emma rolled her eyes.

"Perhaps one of you would like to sleep with me?" Sarah asked. "I wouldn't want you to be too crowded."

The three girls exchanged glances. "We're okay," Audrey said and the other two agreed.

"I thought so," Sarah said with a smile. She turned to Annie. "They should be fine in here. It's a lovely room."

Annie nodded. "It's adequate."

Audrey looked at the dress hanging on a wall peg. "Where is your daughter?"

"She is away right now," Annie smoothed the quilt with a loving touch. "She won't mind your sleeping here."

Emma had wandered to the open window. "Oh, look! There are kittens playing in the grass." Audrey and Amy rushed to look over her shoulder.

"That would be Naomi and her babies," Annie said. "She lives in the hayloft, but she must've wanted some sun. If you approach her nice and quiet, she will probably let you play with her kittens."

"Can we?" Amy asked Sarah.

Sarah nodded and the three girls hurried out of the room and clambered down the stairs.

"They are so excited," Sarah said.

"It is good to hear young voices." Annie smiled. "I am glad you came to visit. It can be quiet around here."

Sarah lifted Audrey's backpack off the bed and set it on the floor. "This is such a beautiful quilt. Trip Around the World is one of my favorite designs. I'm in the process of planning a quilt for my new grandbaby. My daughter Jenna is due anytime now. I've been holding off starting it, not knowing whether the baby is a boy or girl."

"Babies are such blessed events," Annie said. "I'm thankful God granted me at least one."

Sarah stepped to the foot of the bed and studied the quilt. In traditional Trip Around the World quilts, small squares radiate from the center in colorful diamond-shaped bands, but in this case the quilter had done something different. A heart had been appliquéd onto a large center square, and it was surrounded by tiny, intricate stitching in a pattern Sarah didn't recognize. She examined the heart more closely. It contained some squirrelly stitches and loops that resembled a flower.

Sarah looked at Annie. "This center block design is unique. Whoever sewed it is very talented."

"My daughter and I worked on the quilt together. She designed it, and I picked the fabrics. I—"

Through the open window came the sound of wheels on gravel and the snort of a horse.

Annie turned away. Her shoulders trembled as if she might burst into tears any minute.

"I'm sorry. Did I say something wrong? Are you okay?" Sarah asked, growing alarmed.

Annie headed to the door and said in a choked voice, "That's Abram. He's back early." She left the room without looking back.

Sarah scanned the room. Other than the dress hanging on a peg, a set of colored drawing pencils on the desktop, and a doll on the beautiful quilt, very little revealed anything about Annie's daughter. Sarah wondered if something had happened to her.

Heavy footsteps and voices sounded from downstairs. Sarah hurried down and saw a tall man with muscular-looking arms and shoulders standing on the porch. His hair was a dishwater color that suggested he had once had blond hair like his wife's. A beard with gray streaks donned his chin below a tanned, weathered face. His blue eyes were piercingly direct as his gaze took in Sarah.

"Sarah Hart, this is my husband Abram Fisher," Annie said, not meeting Sarah's gaze. There were damp spots on her cheeks as if a few tears had been swiped away.

"Thank you so much for this educational opportunity for the children."

"This was not my idea." Abram glanced at his wife. "But you are welcome, Sarah Hart."

"Well, we're here to experience how you live, so just treat us like we're part of the family, and please feel free to put us to work doing chores or whatever you need," Sarah said.

"That I can do," Abram answered with a hint of a smile.

The late afternoon and evening sped by. Sarah accompanied Abram and the girls to the barn to assist Abram with chores. Abram taught them how to milk the cow by hand, although he informed them the bigger farms had milking machines powered by gas engines. They tossed feed to the chickens, cleaned out the horse stalls, and pulled weeds in the vegetable garden. As the girls went to feed the horses grain, Sarah returned to the farmhouse just in time to see Annie putting the food on the table.

"Is there a place I can wash?"

"Yes, there is a washroom down the hall."

"How nice. You have running water," Sarah said.

"*Ja*, about fifteen years ago, the county ordinances required all houses to have plumbing and septic tanks," Annie said.

Sarah found the small bathroom and scrubbed the barnyard dust off her hands and arms. There was a mirror in the bathroom so small it was difficult to discern the state her hair was in. She felt her head carefully for any lingering twigs of straw.

As she returned to the kitchen Abram and the girls came in the door. In the commotion of getting everyone washed up and to the table, Sarah didn't have a chance to speak to Annie alone. Although she knew it was none of her business, she was still concerned about Annie's reaction upstairs.

Maybe Annie just missed her daughter. Sarah knew what that was like. She wondered how long she had been away.

Audrey, Amy, and Emma, with hands and faces scrubbed, sat at the table drooping with fatigue. Sarah joined them.

"So what did you think about those chores?"

"Feeding the horses was fun," Amy said with a yawn hidden behind her hand.

"The chickens were cool. Even when the rooster chased us across the yard." Emma giggled.

"Audrey, do you think you would want to be a farmer?" Sarah asked.

"No way," Audrey said. "It's too hard." She leaned her head on her propped hand and nearly nodded off before obviously remembering her manners and sliding her hands onto her lap.

Abram pulled out a chair. "Hard, honest work is a blessing. We should be grateful."

Audrey's expression appeared dubious but she nodded.

Abram said a prayer and conversation ground to a minimum as they dove into the food. Annie had made a hearty stew loaded with beef and big chunks of potatoes, carrots, and onions. Fresh bread and home-churned butter rounded out the meal. For dessert Annie served a huckleberry pie with whipped cream that was so delicious that Sarah almost moaned with appreciation.

After they had helped Annie wash dishes and clean the kitchen, they moved to the front room. Sarah sat with Annie on the couch while Annie hemmed a black dress, and they talked about quilting. Abram played a board game with the girls until it was almost nine o'clock. He then read a passage from the Bible and prayed before they all retired to the bedrooms.

As the girls changed into their pajamas, Sarah's thoughts turned to Jenna. How was Jenna doing? Was she resting as she was supposed to? Had there been any contractions yet?

Sarah went to the dresser and retrieved her cell phone from her purse. Audrey was right. The service was lousy out here. Maybe Jenna had tried to call and couldn't get through. She padded quietly downstairs and went out on the front porch. The signal grew stronger as she crossed the yard to the driveway.

She pushed the speed dial on her phone and waited for a connection. Crickets sang in the fields and the air smelled of damp grass. A half moon hung overhead and without the usual benefit of streetlights, the stars seemed almost close enough to touch.

"Hello?" Jenna said, her voice low and gravelly.

"Hi, sweetheart. I'm sorry. Did I wake you?" Sarah glanced at the time on her phone. It was only eight in Texas.

"That's okay," Jenna said in a louder voice.

"How are you feeling?"

"Too pregnant. I'm tired all the time. My back aches. I'm not comfortable standing, sitting, or lying down. I'm just a big grump. I snapped at the kids tonight for playing the TV too loud and then at David for leaving his socks on the closet floor. Now they're all tiptoeing around me. I decided it would be safer for everyone if I just went to bed."

"I'm sorry it's so hard," Sarah said. "It won't be long now."

"Yeah, tell that to junior here. The kid doesn't want to budge."

"What did your doctor say this morning?" Sarah asked, knowing Jenna had an appointment every Monday at this late stage in the pregnancy.

Jenna sighed. "Same thing as last week and the week before. Everything appears perfectly fine. The baby will come when it's ready. I just wish..." Her voice trailed away into the sound of a yawn.

"Get some sleep, sweetie."

"Thanks for calling, Mom. I'm sorry I'm so grumpy." The connection clicked off. Sarah tucked her phone in her pocket and slowly headed back toward the house.

"Is anything wrong?" Annie's soft voice asked from the porch.

"No, not really." Sarah climbed the steps. "I'm just worried about my daughter. Her baby is due any day."

"I remember the days when I worried about my daughter all the time," Annie said in a wistful tone. "If I had known she would be my only child, I would've treasured those moments more, no matter how uncomfortable they got."

"What's your daughter's name?"

Annie didn't say anything for a long moment and then she almost whispered, "Katie."

"I've always liked that name. How old is she?"

"Nineteen." Annie gazed out into the moonlit yard. "People say she looks just like me except her eyes are darker blue and she has more freckles, especially on her nose. She likes to be outdoors. At least she did when she was here…" Her voice trailed away.

"Jenna took after me in hair and eye color, but lucky for her, she got her father's height."

"Do you see her often?"

"Not as much as I'd like to. Jenna moved to Texas after she got married. But we stay in touch by phone and e-mail. I've gotten used to her not being near, but it gets difficult at times. Like now. She's expecting her third child and I wish I were there. I'm going to stay with her for several weeks after the baby is born and help out."

"Surely she'll appreciate her mother's help," Annie said. "What's your Jenna like?"

Sarah leaned back against the porch railing and smiled as she thought about her daughter. "She's very bright and ambitious—she works in marketing right now. She has a good husband, David. He's a dentist. She's also very independent and stubborn, insisting I wait to come until after the baby's born. She doesn't want to inconvenience *me* any more than she has to. I don't think she understands that being with her is never an inconvenience."

"Someday she may realize that. And she has other children?"

"Two sons. Jonathan, who is the spitting image of his father with dark hair and eyes, is five, and his older brother

Thomas started first grade this year. Thomas got the light coloring. They're good boys but rambunctious."

"As boys usually are," Annie said with a sigh. "I wish Abram could have experienced a son, but after Katie, the doctor said there would be no more children."

"I'm sorry, Annie. That must have been hard."

"It is God's will, and Katie was all I could ask for in a daughter. I...always hoped someday, when she married, Abram would have someone he could relate to as a son." She took a deep breath.

"Where is Katie now? If you don't mind my asking, that is." Sarah gazed at the moon hovering behind the trees.

When Annie didn't answer right away, Sarah continued. "You mentioned she was away. I can understand how hard that is. I miss Jenna every day even though I know that she's fine. It's just..."

She looked over at Annie. She was using her apron to wipe her eyes. "Oh, Annie, I'm sorry. I didn't mean to upset you. Can you tell me what's wrong? Is there anything I can do to help?" Sarah asked.

Annie sank down on the top step and wrapped her arms around her knees. She buried her face in her skirt. The moment stretched and Sarah wondered if Annie was going to speak at all when she finally lifted her head. "My Katie left home over a year ago. I haven't seen her since."

"Oh, I'm so sorry." Sarah sat beside Annie on the cold wood.

"I pray about her all the time, but I can't find peace. If I could just know how she's doing, I could bear her absence more bravely."

"Do you know where she went?" Sarah pressed her hand over her heart. "She wasn't abducted, was she?"

Annie shook her head. "No. She sent a note after she left saying good-bye and not to worry. I do not believe harm came to her. At least not then. I don't know about now." She took a deep breath. "Katie was having some problems and ran away. I thought maybe she would write again, but she hasn't. If I just had an address, I would feel better."

Annie sighed. "Seeing those young girls in her room brings back so many memories." She took several shaky breaths. "I apologize. I am not being a good hostess. I am keeping you from sleep." She started to rise, but Sarah put a gentle hand on her arm.

"Would you like me to try to find her?"

Annie blinked rapidly. "I-I really could not ask."

"I'd be happy to. I can search for her address on the computer and make some queries," Sarah said, although it would be difficult narrowing the search down, not knowing the direction Katie might have gone. She was going to need more information.

"I would be so grateful, but ..." Annie stood. "Enough for tonight. Would you like me to say a prayer for your daughter Jenna?"

Sarah nodded, and Annie took Sarah's hands in hers. "Our mighty Lord, guardian of all life, please grant Your blessings on Sarah Hart's daughter and her baby. May her difficult time be short and the baby healthy. Grant Sarah peace and comfort and safe travels for her to be reunited with her daughter. Amen."

Sarah squeezed Annie's fingers. "And please be with Katie, wherever she is, and bring Annie peace also. May they be reunited soon. Amen."

"Thank you, Sarah Hart," Annie said with a glimmer of a smile.

"And you," Sarah said as Annie stepped back. "Now, about Katie—"

"Annie, are you down there?" Abram called.

Annie's shoulders jerked upward and she spun toward the door. "Yes, Abram, I am coming."

"Maybe we can talk in the morning," Sarah said.

Annie nodded. "Good night."

Sarah waited for several minutes after Annie went inside, reluctant to leave the fresh night air. Talking about Annie's missing daughter had left her feeling shaken. What a terrible thing not to know where your daughter was.

A movement under the trees caught her attention. Was that a deer or some other animal? Whatever it was, it stood still in the shadows as if waiting. She went inside, shut the door behind her, and then darted into the dark living room.

A man, wearing an Amish-style hat, strode along the edge of the barnyard. Sarah blinked, trying hard to focus on the man's face, but the lanky silhouette turned down the driveway, slipping in and out of the shadows.

Sarah wondered if she should get Annie and Abram. But really, what would that accomplish now? The man reached the bend in the drive and disappeared. She would mention the incident to them in the morning.

She went upstairs to the guest room and set out her night-gown and toiletries before she checked on the girls in Katie's bedroom. Amy was stuffing her clothes in her backpack. Audrey sat cross-legged on the bed, and Emma sat behind her braiding Audrey's hair.

"Grandma, this has been so fun," Audrey said with a big yawn. "It's like living like a pioneer."

Sarah smiled. "It is, although we're lucky to have plumbing in the house or you'd be heading to the outhouse in the backyard."

"Ew," Emma said as she wound a rubber band around Audrey's braid. "I'm glad they have a bathroom."

Amy tossed her backpack in the corner and climbed on the bed. "Tomorrow, Mr. Fisher is going to teach us how to put a harness on their horse and then he's going to take us for a ride in his buggy."

"Sounds like fun. Now we need to get to sleep. We have to get up early," Sarah reminded them.

Amy groaned. "How early is early?"

"Mrs. Fisher says they get up at five."

"Will it even be light then?" Audrey asked.

"I don't think so."

Amy groaned again and flopped on her pillow.

"Why doesn't Katie's doll have a face?" Emma picked up the doll in the middle of the bed and handed the toy to Sarah.

"I'm not sure." Sarah examined the doll with the pretty calico dress. The fabric was soft and worn, suggesting Katie had played with the doll a lot.

"I know," Amy said, lifting her head. "It's because they don't want to have anything that looks like an idol."

"Probably has to do with it being perceived as a graven image," Sarah added. "That's why they don't like photographs taken of them either." Sarah gave the doll back to Emma who set it between her and Amy. Audrey climbed into bed and they all snuggled under the quilt.

"Ready for me to turn off the lantern?"

"Yeah," Amy said as Audrey and Emma scooted around to get comfortable.

"I'm right across the hall if you need me. Try not to giggle all night, okay?"

"Okay." Audrey glanced at Emma and started to giggle.

"Don't start." Amy popped her pillow over Audrey's face.

"Hey!" Audrey said, snatching the pillow away and rolling into Emma who was between the twins.

"Girls," Sarah said gently. "Settle down. Morning will be here too soon."

Audrey let out a big sigh and tossed the pillow back to her sister. "Night, Gram."

"Sweet dreams." Sarah turned down the lantern on the dresser until the flame flickered out. She paused in the doorway, gazing at the moonlit room, wondering about Katie. A girl who had grown up here, sewn that beautiful quilt, and played with her doll. A daughter whose mother missed her desperately. Just like Sarah missed and worried about Jenna. She couldn't even bear to imagine the agony she would go through if she didn't know where Jenna was or how she was doing.

She shivered, trying to shake off the chill that had washed over her. Quietly closing the bedroom door, she walked to her room with the reassuring thought, "Even if I can't be there right now to help Jenna, I can at least help another mother find her daughter."

CHAPTER TWO

"That was a wonderful breakfast, Annie," Sarah said as she picked up the plates from the table and carried them to the sink. "I can't believe I ate so much. And I don't think I've ever seen the girls clear their plates so fast." Breakfast had consisted of scrambled eggs, hash brown casserole, homemade turkey sausage, cinnamon rolls, and great coffee.

"The country air deepens the appetite." Annie dunked the plates in sudsy water as Sarah went back for more dishes.

Sarah took a deep breath of the fresh air wafting in from the open doorway. Birds sang in the oak trees and the cloudless sky promised a beautiful day. Getting up at five and doing chores for an hour and half had also contributed to Sarah's and the girls' big appetites. They had milked the two cows with Annie, brushed the horses, searched for eggs in the henhouse, and helped prepare breakfast. Abram was now giving the girls a lesson on harnessing a horse in the barnyard.

"This has been a great experience," Sarah said, already regretting they would have to leave soon to meet up with the school group.

"I enjoyed our time together," Annie said.

"Me too. And I want to thank you for letting me talk to you about Jenna last night. It helps to share with someone who understands about being a mother," Sarah said. "I'll try to return the favor by finding your daughter."

"Thank you for being so kind, but maybe I was hasty." Annie stared out the window. "Acceptance of God's will is difficult at times."

Acceptance of what? Losing one's daughter? How did she know that was God's will? Sarah wanted to protest, but she held her tongue. There were things she didn't or couldn't understand about Annie's simple way of life.

When she had spoken to Annie and Abram about the man she had seen in the yard the previous night and how there might have been someone in the barn when she had arrived at the farm, neither one seemed overly concerned about anyone trespassing on their property. Neighbors dropping by without notice was common in their Amish community.

Sarah put the milk and the butter back into the propane-run refrigerator. "I saw some colored pencils upstairs. Did Katie like to draw?"

"Oh yes, ever since she was a little girl. She used to create pictures in the mud. Oh, she would get so dirty." Annie laughed. "I found it annoying then, but now I find the memory endearing."

Sarah smiled. "My late husband had a workshop and loved to create with wood. Jenna and my son Jason would sometimes get in there and start all kinds of projects too. Such a mess sometimes. I remember once they decided to make a tree house. Unfortunately they got into Gerry's cherrywood planks rather than the scrap wood. Cut it all to pieces before Gerry or I noticed. Let's just say we had the most expensive tree house in the neighborhood. But then we couldn't blame them. The wood was stacked beside the scrap pile. They were only eight and ten."

"Is the tree house still there?"

"Unfortunately not. Lightning struck the tree during a storm. Split the trunk and Gerry had to cut it down."

"That is sad."

"It was, but luckily the kids had outgrown the tree house by then, although Audrey and Amy might have enjoyed it." Sarah picked up a bowl from the rinsed pile and wiped it dry. "Amy likes to draw too. She's always sketching something. I've wondered if she'll pursue art when she gets to college."

Annie dropped a plate on the floor. Her fingers trembled some as she picked it up.

"Are you okay?" Sarah asked.

"I have slippery fingers this morning." Annie wiped her hands on her apron, her face tipped down so Sarah couldn't see her expression. "Katie took some art lessons for a time. She loved them. Her teacher said she had talent, especially with paints."

The sound of the girls chattering came nearer and the screen door swung open. Audrey bounded into the room followed by Amy and Emma. "Grandma, I got to drive the buggy!" Audrey said.

"We all did!" Emma said breathlessly. Dust smudged the freckles on her nose above her wide grin, and wind had painted her cheeks pink. "It's not hard."

"I got the horses to trot," Audrey said. "It was so cool."

"You were so scared," Amy said with a laugh.

"Was not!"

Sarah raised her hand. "Girls—"

"Mr. Fisher gave us a lesson," Audrey said. "We learned to turn the horses and everything, and I didn't even crash into anything."

Sarah smiled, although a wave of apprehension crashed over her at the sudden image of her granddaughters careering down the road in a runaway buggy. She blinked the image away. They were perfectly safe and, right now, very excited. "Sounds like you had fun."

"Yeah, and you don't need a license to drive a buggy," Amy pointed out. "Course, Mr. Fisher made sure we didn't do anything wrong. He had his hands on the ends of the reins. He said the children here start handling horses when they're really young."

"That's so," Annie said. "My Katie started working with our horses when she was five. She had a favorite mare named Esther and—" She abruptly turned back to the sink.

Abram stood in the doorway. He hung his hat on the wall peg and crossed the kitchen to the sink. Annie placed the last dish in the drying rack and moved to the side so Abram could wash his hands.

"I wish I could have a horse. Brittany Foster keeps one out at Slater Stables." Amy slid onto a chair. "It'd be fun to ride on the trails and maybe learn to jump."

Emma nodded. "It'd be awesome!"

"Not me." Audrey said. "I like horses, but I'm saving money for a car. I can't wait to get my driver's permit."

Abram wiped his hands on a towel and leaned back against the counter. "Some think a driver's test should be required for Amish youth too. The county has a manual for our young ones that teaches road laws, but they aren't required to take an exam."

"Are there many accidents involving buggies?" Sarah asked.

"Sometimes. There are a few winding roads where cars travel too fast and it becomes dangerous, especially at night. But we've been traveling this way for hundreds of years and will continue to do so," Abram glanced at the three girls and then back at Sarah. "Would you and the children like to take a buggy ride while I deliver a bridle to the Stoltzfus farm?"

Emma clapped her hands together and sprang up from the table. "Sweet!"

"Come on, Gram. You're going to love this," Amy added.

Sarah looked at her watch. They still had two hours before they were due to reunite with the school group in town. "We have time."

Audrey and Amy bumped shoulders as they tried to get outside at the same time. Emma laughed and ran out after them.

Sarah smiled. It was great seeing the girls so enthusiastic. She was thankful she had gotten to share this experience with them. Keeping busy took her mind off her other worries.

Sarah hesitated by the door. She really wanted to ask Annie more questions about Katie. "Are you coming too?"

"Annie has things she needs to do," Abram said, holding the screen door open for Sarah to go through.

Annie nodded, her gaze not meeting Sarah's eyes. "Best I tend to things." She reached for a sweater hanging on the peg by the door. "Here, take this in case there is a chill."

"Are you coming, Grandma?" Audrey called.

Abram closed the screen door behind Sarah and as they strode down the steps, Sarah glanced over her shoulder at Annie standing alone in the doorway. Annie gave her a wave, but she didn't smile.

It wasn't right that Annie was so alone, especially when family was so important in the Amish culture. Even if Katie wasn't home, knowing where her daughter was and being able to communicate with her would bring Annie comfort. Just as Sarah's phone conversations and text messages with Jenna made Sarah feel closer to her daughter. Every mother deserved to know her children were safe.

As Sarah followed Abram around the corner of the house to the barnyard, she felt frustration for Annie rise.

"This one is called a pickup." Amy's hand rested on the back of a buggy with a flatbed behind the covered driver's seat. It did look like a pickup truck.

Amy and Audrey climbed in the bed and settled with their backs against the driver's compartment.

"We won't travel fast," Abram said as if reading Sarah's thoughts about no seat belts. "They would have to be pretty determined to fall out."

She climbed up into the driver's compartment on the passenger side and settled on the upholstered seat. The dash had a button to turn on lights and what Sarah assumed was a brake pedal poked up from the floor.

Abram swung up beside Sarah and took the reins in his large hands. He clucked to the horses, and they were off down the road. A cool breeze swirled through the compartment, but the morning sunshine tamped down the chill that rose from the fields.

The sound of the horse's hoofs on the asphalt created a pleasant, rhythmic sound, and Sarah gradually relaxed against the seat.

"We really appreciate your welcoming us into your home. This has been such a good experience for the girls and for the other school children that are visiting families. It's such a great way for them to exchange ideas and learn about other ways to live."

Abram grunted a reply that Sarah couldn't quite catch.

"That's a beautiful horse. Does he have a name?"

"Amos."

"He's not as big as the horses you had in the barn." Sarah gazed at a field where a farmer was using a team of four horses to plow. The rich scent of moist soil wafted over them.

"Amos is a quarter horse. We use the Belgians, as those are out there, for farm work. Some have mules, but I find them too stubborn for my taste."

"Annie mentioned how much your daughter liked horses and that she started working with them very young," Sarah said.

"That she did." Abram brought the buggy to a stop at an intersection. Several cars roared by and some of the passengers turned their heads to stare. Abram appeared not to notice.

"She said that Katie had a special mare."

Abram frowned. "What else did my wife say?"

Something in his tone warned Sarah to tread lightly. "Not that much, but I did admire your daughter's quilt. She's very talented."

Abram grunted as if it didn't matter.

After a moment, Sarah added, "Annie seems to miss her very much."

"Sometimes sacrifices have to be made for the benefit of the whole." Abram's hands gripped the reins so hard his knuckles turned white. "Please do not speak of Katie anymore."

The Stoltzfus yard was teeming with activity. Two girls dressed in blue with black aprons hung wash on a line with a pulley between the house and a large oak. A man and two young boys wearing straw hats and the traditional slacks and short-sleeved shirts shoveled soiled straw out of a large red barn, and in the distance another young man and a team of horses plowed the field.

The man with the pitchfork walked out into the sunshine and raised a hand in greeting. "Abram, greetings!"

The buggy slowed to a stop. "Good morning, Seth. I've brought the mended bridle." Abram stepped out of the buggy. He helped Sarah down and introduced her and the girls. "They are with the school group from Massachusetts."

"Ah yes, I'm glad Father allowed the visit to continue after all." Seth's smile widened. "Maybe there will be more in the future."

"I hope so. This has been so educational and so much fun," Sarah said, wondering what Seth meant by his father allowing them to visit after all. Had there been some attempt to veto their visit? She knew that the Amish preferred to keep the world at bay, but surely they didn't see a group of young school children as a risk.

"These are my sons, Daniel and David," Seth said, gesturing to the two boys in the barn. The boys smiled and turned back to their shoveling. "Miriam and Ruth are hanging the wash."

A young girl, with braids but no cap, bounded out of the house's front door and down the steps to stand by Seth.

"And this is Mary." Her father affectionately rubbed her head. "She is my youngest."

Mary smiled, revealing a missing front tooth.

"Abram, I have another harness I'd like you to take a look at. I'm debating whether to buy a new one or try to repair it again."

Abram turned to Sarah. "Is there time?"

Sarah nodded. "We're still ahead of schedule."

"My wife is in town buying supplies, but Mary can show you around if you would like," Seth turned to the three teens standing by the wagon wheel. "There are baby goats over in yonder field."

"Cool!" Audrey said.

"Please come this way." Mary straightened her shoulders and marched in front of them, obviously taking her duty seriously.

Sarah followed Mary and the girls across the yard to a fenced pen. Inside were two mother goats and half a dozen babies. Mary opened the gate. The mother goats turned their brown-eyed gazes on the girls. Amy and Emma sidled inside the gate, but Audrey hung back.

"The mothers won't hurt you." Mary grabbed a bucket by the gate. She took it over to a corner and poured out grain. The mother goats turned their wary gaze from the girls and ambled over to the corner and began eating, their short tails wagging.

Sarah leaned on the fence and watched the girls play with the tiny goats. Soon Mary and the teens were laughing and chatting up a storm. Too soon Sarah noticed Abram standing by the buggy. "I think it's time to go."

Mary brushed grass off her skirt. The girls did the same with their jeans and T-shirts. "I wish you were here longer," Mary said.

"Me too," Audrey said. "We stayed over at the Fishers' farm."

"Oh, we used to go over there a lot when ... well, before."

"Did you see Katie often?" Sarah asked.

Mary nodded. "Every Sunday, and my sisters went to school with her. You can see the school over there." She pointed to a small structure on a knoll. "That is going to be my school too."

"If I went to the school here, I'd graduate this year and be done with school forever," Amy said.

Emma grinned. "That would be awesome."

Audrey shook her head. "I wouldn't want to miss high school."

"You sound like Katie," Mary said and then clamped her hand over her mouth, her face reddening as if holding her breath.

"Are you okay?" Sarah asked.

"I forgot. I am not to talk about her."

"Why not?" Emma whispered.

Mary glanced over to where her father conversed with Abram. "Because she did something wrong."

"What was it?" Audrey asked.

"Audrey, if Mary isn't to speak of it, we shouldn't ask," Sarah said, although she wanted to hear Mary's answer too.

"I don't know what she did," Mary said with a shrug, "but it was bad."

Sarah opened her car trunk so Abram could load her suitcase. She hadn't had a chance to speak privately with Annie since returning to the Fisher farm. Abram had avoided talking to her too. On the way home, she had sat in the back on the pickup bed so the girls could take turns holding the reins again. Then Abram had hovered in the kitchen while they retrieved their things.

Annie came down the steps clutching a folded piece of fabric and a pie plate. "I have some gifts for you. Here is a huckleberry pie." Annie handed the pie to Audrey and gave Sarah the fabric. "And this is something Katie and I made."

Sarah unfolded the square and examined the pillow cover with a Log Cabin design pieced from rich blue and pink floral fabrics. Intricate stitching created a flowery pattern on the border. "This is so beautiful, Annie. Thank you."

"You are welcome." Annie lowered her voice to a whisper. "The stitching was another design of Katie's."

"I'll treasure it." Sarah held Annie's gaze and whispered back. "And I'll still do what I can to find her, okay?"

Annie gave her a brief nod, her eyes growing wet. She backed up the steps. Abram shut the trunk and stood stoically watching, his arms over his chest, as they got in the car.

"Thanks again for everything," Sarah called. The girls waved good-bye until the car turned on the road that led to downtown Pleasant Valley. Soon they drove onto Main Street where charming shops lined both sides. Sarah parked in front of the Tiny Stitches Quilt Shop that nestled next to the Amish-owned restaurant, Plain Pleasant Eating, where the class was meeting for lunch. Sarah cast a longing gaze at the quilt shop as she followed the girls into the noisy restaurant. Students were already seated at the long tables where food was served family-style.

"Hey, Audrey and Amy, sit with us," a girl with curly hair called from across the room. "You too, Emma."

"Go ahead," Sarah said. "I'll sit over there with the teacher and chaperones." She walked to the table closest to the door, and settled between Mrs. Hiland, the teacher in charge of the Amish field trips, and one of the six other parents who had volunteered to drive.

Tantalizing aromas from the mashed potatoes, green beans, and fried chicken tempted the appetite, and sturdy silver pitchers of iced tea, milk, and water sparkled against the crisp, white cloth.

"How was your visit with the Fishers?" Mrs. Hiland asked, passing Sarah the bread basket as the other parents continued their chatting.

"Very nice. The Fishers were very hospitable. I think Audrey, Amy, and Emma had a great experience."

"That's good." Mrs. Hiland smiled, a tinge of relief in her voice. "They're such a nice family. I met them about five years ago when we were setting up the first visitation program. As I was telling the others, I have an aunt and uncle who live in town and know just about everyone."

Sarah selected a warm roll and passed the basket. "That must be a big help when it comes to coordinating the visits."

"Oh, it is. I'm not sure if I could've pulled this off without them," Mrs. Hiland said as she cut her chicken. "Some of the Amish around here, especially those with young children, discourage letting outsiders stay in their homes because of the outsiders' worldly influence. Don't get me wrong, they're the nicest people in the world, but they try hard to maintain their special way of life. I was surprised Annie Fisher wanted to participate again, considering what happened with their daughter. Annie's such a sweetie and she's been through so much."

"Annie made us feel right at home. Did you ever meet their daughter Katie?"

"A couple of times, although I didn't get to know her very well. She seemed very bright and inquisitive."

"Her mother misses her."

"I can imagine. I thought it was strange that she ran off like she did. But then…" Mrs. Hiland sighed. "Amish life has rigid rules and customs. Sometimes their young people leave the church."

"Have you heard anything about where she might have gone?"

Mrs. Hiland shook her head. "No, but someone must know. My aunt said that Katie was almost seventeen when she left. From what I understand, she's safe or the police would've been involved."

The door opened and a frazzled-looking mother staggered in followed by three excited boys. She shooed them toward the other tables and headed for Mrs. Hiland. Sarah scooted over on the bench to make room.

"Sorry we're late," she said, smoothing her flyaway auburn bangs. "Bradley wanted to feed the pigs, of all things, and then fell off the fence into mud." She let out a squeaky laugh and plopped down beside Sarah.

"It's quite all right," Mrs. Hiland said. "We're just beginning to eat. I believe everyone's here now."

Sarah helped herself to a generous serving of chicken and mashed potatoes. After the breakfast she had eaten, she was surprised at how hungry she felt. The delicious meal continued as everyone related their adventures.

When the children had finished their food, Mrs. Hiland announced they were going to walk to the county historical museum down the road. The chaperones were welcome to come along or do some shopping along Main Street for the next two hours. They would meet back at the park in the center of town at two o'clock.

Audrey, Amy, and Emma appeared content with their friends and enough chaperones chose to visit the museum that Sarah opted to duck into the quilting shop next to the restaurant.

"Good morning." A middle-aged Amish woman stood by a table of fabric scraps. Her doe-colored hair was gathered up in a bun, the same way Annie wore hers, and covered by a snowy prayer cap. She wore a lilac-colored blouse under the traditional Amish black cape that went over her shoulders and was attached to her black apron with straight pins. Sarah had read that in some communities the pins indicated that a woman was baptized and married. What Sarah could see of her legs and feet was clad in black stockings and sturdy black shoes.

Sarah smiled at her. "Good morning." Her gaze took in the racks of quilts displayed along one side wall and the back. "You have such a lovely shop."

"Thank you. The quilts are sewn by women in the community. They are all of the highest quality. Please take your time to look around and let me know if I can assist you," the woman said as she turned to help two other customers in the shop.

Sarah moved closer to the quilts, feeling like a kid in a candy shop. It was wonderful. She marveled at the fabric choices in the traditional Log Cabins and Double Wedding Rings, the vibrancy in the Star patterns, the delicacy of an Ohio Star, and the fun color combinations in the Tumbling Blocks quilts. The details were superb and boasted of fine workmanship. Obviously labors of love.

She checked the prices and barely kept from gasping. The more hand-sewing, the higher the price. Worth every penny but a bit out of her price range. Besides, she had more fun creating her own.

As she neared the end of the rack she came across a white quilt with an intricate quilting pattern similar to the one on the quilt on Katie's bed.

She gestured to the shopkeeper and asked, "Does this pattern have a name? I like the intricate stitching."

"That's a variation of Turkey Tracks. You don't see it very much anymore. It used to be called Wandering Foot, but there was an old superstition associated with that. Some said that if a boy slept under a Wandering Foot quilt, he would eventually leave home and wander aimlessly for the rest of his life. So the name got changed."

"Interesting. The stitching looks difficult," Sarah said. "I saw something similar to this back at Annie Fisher's place. It was in the center of a Trip Around the World quilt. Annie said her daughter Katie designed it."

"Annie is a wonderful quilter, although she doesn't wish to sell any of her work right now."

"What about Katie? Was she ever interested in selling her quilts?"

"The Turkey Track quilt or *any* of the quilts can be put on layaway," the woman continued. "You can send money each month and when it's paid for, we'll mail it to you." She gave Sarah a small smile and backed away.

"Thank you," Sarah said, wondering if she had somehow offended the woman. "I'll think about it."

She went back to look at the quilts, but the sense that she had done something wrong plagued her, dampening her previous enjoyment. Why didn't the storekeeper want to answer her questions about Katie? Surely if she knew Annie, she knew her daughter. Mary's words at the Stoltzfus farm suddenly echoed in her ears.

I don't know what she did, but it was bad.

She glanced around the shop, and one of the customers, a gray-haired woman dressed in bib overalls, caught Sarah's eye and gave her a big smile. Sarah smiled back, her spirits lifted, and she continued to browse for a while longer. She settled on a couple of handmade baby bibs and a set of quilted place mats in colors she knew Jenna liked. She got five place mats instead of the usual four in honor of the new member of her daughter's family.

She cast another longing gaze at the quilts and promised herself she would attempt some of the more elaborate patterns. She paid for her purchases and stepped outside, trying to decide which shop to try next when a voice said, "Couldn't help but eavesdrop."

Sarah looked down to see the gray-haired customer who had smiled at her earlier sitting on a bench outside the quilt shop door. "Hi there, I'm Gertie Hamilton."

"Sarah Hart."

"Are you a quilter?"

"Yes, I am," Sarah said. "And I have a quilt restoration business."

Gertie's smile widened. "You don't say? How rewarding that must be. I dabble at sewing myself, although I'm nowhere near as skilled as those ladies in there. Anyway,

I heard you asking Rebecca about the Fisher girl. Rebecca won't talk to you about it. In fact none of the Amish around here will. Not unless they want to get in trouble."

"Why is that?"

"From what I've heard, and I hear a lot, she's been shunned."

"Shunned?" Sarah sank down on the bench beside Gertie. She had heard the term before. "What did Katie do to be shunned? Is that why she ran away?"

The woman shrugged. "I don't know the details. I'm still an outsider, although I've lived here twenty years. My Amish friends are friendly and kind, but very private when it comes to sharing personal matters with *Englishers*."

Sarah wondered why Annie had omitted such an important detail. Was she ashamed about the shunning? Would she think that Sarah wouldn't look for Katie if she knew? That explained Abram's reluctance to discuss his daughter or allow his wife to. And why little Mary had said she couldn't talk about Katie.

"The thing is," Gertie continued, "they can't talk to you about Katie because they risk being shunned themselves, which means no social contact and being ignored by all. Even their own families. It's like Katie doesn't exist."

"Well, thanks for telling me. That explains the reactions I got from people," Sarah said with a deep sigh. Poor Annie.

"What's your interest in all this?"

"I stayed at the Fishers' last night and was intrigued by a quilt Katie made," she said, deciding to keep her other reason to herself. She didn't want Annie to get in trouble for wanting to find Katie. "I'd like to talk to her if possible."

"Wish I could help," Gertie said. "I could try asking around again and if I hear anything let you know. Are you visiting for long?"

"We're leaving today. I'm here with my granddaughters' school group on an overnight trip. That's how we ended up at the Fishers'."

"I'm glad the bishop still allows it," Gertie said more to herself than to Sarah.

"The bishop?"

"Samuel Stoltzfus. He's the bishop over this community. He would've been the one to impose the shunning on Katie Fisher."

CHAPTER THREE

S arah found an empty picnic table in the park where the students and chaperones were supposed to meet after the history museum. She set her packages down, glad to rest a bit.

After she had given Gertie her card with her phone numbers, she had canvassed most of the shops on Main Street, popping into a clothing store and two craft shops, and window-shopping the rest. She had found an apron with a quilted star pattern on the bodice that she was contemplating saving to give to Martha for Christmas. In that same store, to her delight, she had spied a book on Amish quilts, which she had purchased to add to her quilting library.

Her wanderings took her to another store where she bought a local herb blend for grilling chicken and some unique handcrafted barbecue gloves for Liam, the handsome owner of the Spotted Dog Café and Bookstore and, more important, someone who was becoming increasingly special in her life.

As much as she enjoyed the shopping, she couldn't get Katie Fisher out of her mind. She had tried asking a few of the other storekeepers about Katie, but either they didn't know her or they politely redirected the query to something else.

The balmy air smelled like freshly plowed earth even in the middle of town. Birds twittered in the branches of the large oak that cast a cooling shadow over the picnic bench. She still had twenty minutes before she was to meet up with the school group.

She dug into her large purse and pulled out a notebook and a pen. She had been using the notebook to keep track of quilting supplies and other items she wanted to pick up. She flipped past those lists and poised her pen over a fresh page.

She jotted Katie's name at the top and listed what she knew about the young woman. She was nineteen. She had gone to the Amish school they had seen down the road on the way to the Fisher farm. Katie liked to quilt, draw, and paint and took some art classes. She had left home just before she turned seventeen, and so far no one seemed to know where she was located.

Sarah began listing everyone she had talked to: Annie, Abram, Gertie, the shopkeepers, and little Mary Stoltzfus, who most likely was the bishop's granddaughter.

She wrote down Bishop Stoltzfus's name and circled it. This was the man who had the authority to have Katie shunned. The man she probably should avoid to keep Annie out of trouble.

She tapped her pen on the notebook. She didn't have any leads other than that Katie had done something "bad" and she loved art.

Sarah had passed a gallery that had a sign informing the public it sold art supplies. She grabbed her bags and hurried back down the street to Sunrise Gallery.

Door chimes rang as she entered the shop. Several customers roamed the store, gazing at the paintings on the walls or the sculptures on their pedestals. Some of the paintings depicted local nature scenes, others featured the Amish and buggies, and there were a few abstract pieces mixed in. She moved to the back of the store and waited for a chance to talk to a short, wiry man dressed in a gray suit and black tie. He passed a credit slip for a customer to sign and his pale gray eyes shifted toward Sarah.

"Can I help you, ma'am?" the gentleman asked, shoving his round spectacles up his long, thin nose.

"I was wondering if you offered art classes."

"We don't here, although there are several places in the county that do." He gestured toward the far wall. "There are some brochures and business cards on the table behind that bronze bust." He turned back to the other customer.

Sarah hurried over to the table and scooped up a brochure, a paper flyer, and some business cards, all advertising art classes. She ducked out the door. In the distance Mrs. Hiland and the students gathered in the park.

Audrey ran up to her. "Grandma, what did you buy?"

"You want to look?" Sarah held out the bags and Audrey took them back to the bench where Amy and Emma waited.

"Oh, I like the apron," Audrey said. "Do you think I could get one for Mom?"

"Sure, sweetie, but in a little while. I thought someone was coming to talk to us about Amish history," Sarah said, pulling out the printed agenda Mrs. Hiland had given her.

"Oh yeah, I forgot." Audrey sighed and plopped down on the bench next to Sarah.

Mrs. Hiland moved to the middle of the group and lifted her hand signaling for silence. "I want to introduce you to Timothy Jones. He grew up here in Pleasant Valley and has come to share with you some history about the Amish faith."

The stocky, balding man had a warm smile and disarming sense of humor as he greeted the kids. He became more serious as he discussed how the Amish had migrated out of Europe in the 1700s to escape persecution and seek religious freedom and then settled in Pennsylvania, Ohio, Indiana, Illinois, and other states such as New York.

"Can anyone tell me why the Amish do not use electricity?" Timothy asked.

A lanky teenage boy with glasses answered, "Because the electric lines are like connecting people with the world."

"Ah, so you did your homework." Timothy beamed. "That's right. The Amish value simplicity and being like strangers or pilgrims in the world. They don't want to be connected to the world through electric lines, phone lines, or even television antennas. Sometimes technology can interfere with family closeness and involvement in one's community. The Amish value people over machines and strive to keep things plain and simple."

Sarah looked over the group of children and imagined most of them probably thought they couldn't survive without their cell phones or computers for a day, let alone a lifetime. She knew she would miss hers.

"Now, having said all that," Timothy said. "I must mention that they *do* use phones for business and emergencies. Neighbors will share a phone, but it is not allowed in the home. You may have seen the little phone shacks along the road. A phone might also be in a barn. They are usually in places where you wouldn't like to spend hours gossiping or being kept from your work for long."

Amy leaned against Sarah and whispered. "That's what that building was."

Sarah nodded. When they had been on the buggy ride with Abram, they had seen a little brown building about the size of an old-fashioned phone booth out by the road near the Fisher farm.

Timothy continued the question-and-answer period until the students' attention spans seemed to be shortening. Mrs. Hiland thanked him and informed the group that it was time to go home.

Since Emma was riding home with Mrs. Hiland, Sarah had only her granddaughters to transport and they didn't need to leave with the group. They walked back to the car so Emma could get her backpack and Sarah could deposit her packages.

After the girls had said good-bye to Emma and some other classmates, Sarah asked, "Do you want to buy some souvenirs now?"

"I want to see the aprons," Audrey said, gazing down the street.

"Aprons?" Amy asked, wrinkling her nose. "Why?"

"I want to get one for Mom," Audrey said.

"I got an apron for Martha." Sarah showed Amy the one she had bought. "Was there anything in particular you wanted to look for?"

Amy lifted a shoulder. "I'll know it when I see it."

"Okay, let's go by the store where the aprons are first." Sarah closed the trunk and they descended on the shops. Audrey found an apron in Maggie's favorite colors and Amy offered to split the cost with her. Then they picked out a brass pencil sharpener fashioned into a horse and buggy for their father Jason.

While the girls set out to find some souvenirs for themselves, Sarah looked over the papers she had picked up at the art gallery. The brochure advertised an art school that appeared to be a chain throughout the Northeast. The flyer was for after-school art classes at a local high school. The art teacher listed was Rachel Jackson and there was a phone number. Sarah glanced at her watch. Almost three thirty. School would probably be dismissed by now.

"I'll be out front," she told the girls. She stepped outside and fished her cell phone out of her purse. She dialed the number from the flyer.

"Rachel here," a friendly voice said.

"Hi, Rachel. I'm Sarah Hart, and I saw your flyer for art classes in the one of the art galleries."

"Oh yes, we have a wonderful after-school program for ages thirteen to eighteen. How old is your child?"

"Actually, I wasn't calling about classes. I was hoping to get some information about Katie Fisher."

"Katie? She's all right, isn't she?" The voice rose with alarm.

"I think so." Sarah's heart thumped with excitement that the teacher knew Katie. "That's what I'm trying to find out. I'm a friend of her mother's. She hasn't talked to Katie in a long time and is worried about her."

"I . . ." Rachel paused, and Sarah could hear young voices in the background. "Now isn't a good time for me to talk. I need to get the students going on their projects. Perhaps you could stop by in an hour or so. I'll be here until five."

"That should be fine. Thank you." Sarah would stop by on their way back to Maple Hill. She got directions to the high school and then rejoined Audrey and Amy to help them pick out a souvenir. Audrey chose a quillow, a combination of a quilt and a pillow. The narrow Log Cabin quilt folded neatly under a flap and formed a colorful pillow. Amy discovered a small wood hand carving of a horse that resembled Amos on the Fisher farm.

Happy with their purchases they piled back in the car. Sarah headed for the high school and possible answers about Katie Fisher.

The high school, set on several acres of land, was quite a stately structure for such a small town. The aged bricks on the three story building gave it a dignified air. A brass plaque on a sign indicated the building had been erected in 1940. Newer construction could be seen in the back, one building obviously a gymnasium.

According to Rachel's instructions, the after-school art classes were in a one story building between the gym and the ball field.

Sarah parked the car in the student parking area. She had explained to Audrey and Amy that she wanted to ask the teacher some questions about Katie.

"You don't have to come in if you don't want to." Sarah turned off the engine. "I shouldn't be very long."

Amy pushed the back door open. "Nah. We can help you find Katie." Audrey scrambled out of the front seat, determined to participate too.

They crossed the asphalt and entered the long, narrow building through a glass door.

"This is really cool," Audrey whispered as they surveyed the interior.

The air hung heavy with the scent of a mixture of paint and wet clay. One shelved wall displayed clay jars and sculptures. Watercolors lined another. Six students were working about the room—three girls around the twins' age were drawing on easels with charcoal pencils. A younger-looking boy worked beside a wooden box of tiles at a table where he was creating a mosaic picture. An older teen worked a potter's wheel, his brow furrowed as his nimble fingers guided the clay lump upward into a vase.

At the far end of the room, a petite woman strolled through a door that looked like it led to an office. She spied Sarah and the girls and started toward them, her full, mid-calf skirt swirling out behind her. Her multicolored peasant blouse, cinched in with a tooled belt, brought out the gold streaks in her chestnut hair that was scooped back in a messy bun. Narrow rectangular glasses perched on her nose and framed brown inquisitive eyes.

"Hello!" she said with a warm smile. "You must be Sarah. I'm Rachel Jackson."

Sarah shook her small, cool hand. "These are my grand-daughters, Amy and Audrey. Thanks for taking the time to see me."

"My pleasure. Anything to help one of my students." She turned her gaze to the girls. "Do either of you like art?"

"I do. I draw," Audrey said.

"Excellent," Rachel said. "How about you, Amy?"

Amy shrugged. "I like it okay."

"She's more into sports," Audrey said.

"Well, tell you what, while I talk with your grandmother, feel free to jump right in. Our classes are casual. We let students explore their creativity."

"Cool!" Audrey said with such enthusiasm Sarah smiled.

"Have you ever tried charcoal?"

"Nope, but I'd like to."

"Come on over here. This is Jessica and Shanna." Rachel led the way over to the easels, introduced Audrey, and set her up with an easel and charcoal. She turned back to Amy whose attention was captured by the tile box on the table.

"Jeff, why don't you show Amy how to make a mosaic?" Rachel said. "She can make something small to take home with her."

Jeff glanced at Amy and moved over, gesturing her to come closer to share the table.

"Let's talk in my office," Rachel said to Sarah.

"That was nice of you to let the girls participate," Sarah said as they walked across the room.

"I like to see if I can spark interest. You never know when it can lead to a fire of creativity. With budget cuts of music and art programs during school hours, I try to encourage art whenever I can." She pulled out a folded metal chair from behind the door in the tiny, cluttered office. "Please excuse the mess. When it comes to paperwork, I tend to get overwhelmed." She set the chair by the desk for Sarah.

"I understand. I taught high school history for four years."

"Ah, a fellow teacher." Rachel smiled and leaned back in her wooden office chair. "So how can I help? You said Annie Fisher sent you here."

Sarah set her purse on the floor. "Not exactly. I spent some time with Annie and, confidentially, Annie is missing her daughter. I'm trying to help her track her down, just so she knows Katie is safe."

"Poor Annie. I haven't seen Katie in over a year and a half, although I think about her often. Such a beautifully talented child. Smart too. Such a shame that their lifestyle permits schooling only to eighth grade. I was surprised that she was allowed to take the art classes, but then Katie had a lot of drive—a lot of creativity to express. Before you go I'll show you some of the work she left behind. Extraordinary raw talent."

"I'd like to see it. How long did she take lessons here?"

"Almost a year. It was during her *Rumspringa* and parents are lenient."

"*Rumspringa?*"

"Yes, when Amish teens are allowed to explore the *Englishers*' world. When they finish sowing their wild oats, so to speak, they're expected to get baptized and married. Most return to the Amish ways."

"So Katie wanted to continue school?"

Rachel nodded. "I must confess I encouraged her. I even got her a GED study book. Maybe that was wrong, but I wanted her to have options. I suppose in a way I contributed to her problems at home."

"Annie didn't give the details of what happened, but I assumed something must have caused Katie to run away," Sarah said.

Rachel rubbed the back of her neck. "Well, I don't know exactly what happened, but yes, she was getting pressure to quit her other activities and get married like Amish women are expected to. She never confided in me, but she did have a couple of close friends here."

"Are they still around?"

"They left for college, but Kevin e-mails me occasionally. He might know where Katie is. Maybe you can talk to him."

"That would be great." Sarah reached into her purse for her notebook. "What's Kevin's last name?"

Rachel tapped her chin and then after a long pause said, "You know what? I'll get in touch with him and see if he wants to talk to you. I don't feel right giving out his personal information without his consent. You know how it is, being a teacher and all. I can pass on your contact information to him."

"I appreciate it." Sarah gave Rachel her business card. "My e-mail address is on there too."

Rachel set the card on her desk and scooted back her chair. "Wish I could've been more help. I liked Katie a lot. If you do find her, please let her know that I'm thinking about her and wishing her well."

"I will." Sarah picked up her purse as a thought occurred to her. "You mentioned that most Amish children return to the Amish ways. So why was Katie getting so much pressure? Did she act like she might be thinking of leaving her faith?"

"I don't think so, although ... I heard the girls teasing her about a boy once. I got the impression it was an Amish boy."

"Did you ever see her with any boys?"

"Only Kevin. Katie, Madison, and Kevin stuck together most of the time they were here. I didn't get the impression that Kevin was anything more special than a friend who shared her love of art, but remember I only spent a few hours of the week with her." Rachel walked through the door. "Let me show you some of Katie's work. I suppose I should ask her mother if she'd like to have it. But between you and me, I just didn't want to part with it yet."

She showed Sarah a set of canvases of Katie's drawings and watercolors. Sarah wasn't an art expert but she could see there was something energizing and a little unusual about Katie's technique.

"She has an eye for color," Sarah said.

Rachel nodded. "She knows how to work the hues to contrast slightly and yet work together in a cohesive flow. Note her form. Like that painting there. You see a house, but if you look closer at the detail you notice things are slightly off. She draws what your eyes don't expect so it catches you at a subconscious level."

Sarah leaned closer to the painting. "Amazing. Did she experiment with other art media?"

"She did a few sculptures too, although she didn't put a lot of work into them." She showed her a clay tile. "But she did like making these."

"Oh, it's a quilting square," Sarah said with delight over the design carved into a clay square. The square even puffed up in areas like fabric would around quilting stitches.

"And here's one that she painted." Rachel handed Sarah another tile painted with a classic starburst design. "She wouldn't try animals or people because they might be construed as graven images. She was already pushing the boundaries of what was acceptable."

"I really like this," Sarah said, imagining it on a shelf in her office.

"So do I," Rachel said. "Katie could turn these out quickly. She sold a few of them at the local shops. Some of her paintings too. This was right before she withdrew from class."

Sarah turned the cold clay tile over in her fingers, wondering where Katie was now. Was she still painting and making these delightful tiles?

Rachel joined Audrey and the girls drawing land-scapes. "You all are doing such fantastic work. Jessica, you should try smudging the horizon a tad more. Shanna, you need to be a little bolder in the foreground, but it's really coming along. Audrey, I like your style. Great mountain."

Audrey's smile widened. "I like using charcoal."

"You're good at it," Rachel said. "Here, let me spray it before you go. That way the charcoal won't smudge while you take it home." Rachel reached for a can of adhesive and sprayed the paper as Sarah went over to where Amy and Jeff were still hunched over a table.

Amy coated a walnut-colored glass piece with glue and placed it on the board. Sarah studied the picture they were creating "Race cars?"

"Indy five hundred," Jeff said. "My dad took me last year."

"You're getting a great sense of movement there, Jeff, which can be difficult with mosaics," Rachel said. "Thanks for the help, Amy. I'm sure Jeff appreciates it."

Jeff shot Amy a shy smile as Rachel reached into a drawer and pulled out two small plastic bags with tiles and small boards. "Here, take these, and you can finish your mosaic design at home. You'll have to provide your own glue. The white powder in the little bag is grout. Just follow the instructions on how much water to use."

The girls thanked the teacher as Rachel walked them to the door. She promised Sarah again that she would pass on the message about Katie to Kevin.

Audrey carefully set her drawing on the backseat beside Amy and then got in the front with Sarah. "That was way cool!"

"I'm glad you had fun, sweetie."

Amy yawned noisily. "Where are we going now?"

Sarah pointed the car north. "Home."

The sun had set by the time Sarah and the girls rolled into downtown Maple Hill. Lights glowed from the windows of Maggie's store, Magpie's Antiques, indicating Maggie was working late. Sarah parked in front and the girls scampered inside. They had been gone only one night but by the excited way they talked over each other to their mother about all they had done, it seemed like a week.

"Thanks for taking them," Maggie said to Sarah after the girls' torrent of information slowed to a trickle.

"It was an adventure," Sarah said. "I'm glad I got to go."

"Grandma has another mystery to solve," Amy said before following Audrey to the back of the store where Maggie sometimes kept cookies.

Maggie raised her eyebrows. "We can't send you anywhere, can we?" she said with a laugh.

"I can't help it. These things just seem to fall in my lap." Sarah briefly told Maggie about Annie and her missing daughter Katie.

"That poor mother!" Maggie said. "I can't imagine how horrible it would be not to know where one of my children was."

"Me either, which is why I want to find her. Someone must know where Katie is," Sarah said.

She declined the offer of supper at Maggie and Jason's house. She was tired from the drive and wanted to call Jenna when she got home. She drove past the Spotted Dog. Liam might still be working, but feeling frazzled, she decided she would drop by in the morning to give him his gift.

Her familiar Queen Anne seemed to welcome her as she pulled into the driveway. She dropped the suitcase at the bottom of the stairs and took her purchases to the kitchen with her.

The house was extra quiet since she was in between boarders. With the uncertainty of the timing of her trip to

Texas, Sarah preferred not bringing someone new into the house until she came home.

She had left a container of homemade chicken and wild rice soup in the refrigerator. She set the bowl in the microwave to heat and then hit the play button on her answering machine.

There were a couple of hang-ups and Sarah assumed that the calls were from telemarketers. She decided to have some iced tea and was reaching into the cupboard when her son-in-law's voice nearly had her dropping the glass.

"Sarah, it's David. I tried your cell phone, but you must be out of range. I just wanted to tell you we're heading for the hospital. Jenna's contractions are about eight minutes apart. She's doing fine, so don't worry. I'll call when I have some news."

Sarah raced to the machine and hit replay. The message had come in when she had been in the store talking to Maggie and had left her cell phone in the car. She reached for the phone and then with tremendous effort set it down. No, she wasn't going to bother them right now. This was a special time for the young couple. David had said he would call, and she would wait for that call.

Suddenly she wasn't hungry, her stomach in knots. Too excited to eat, she grabbed her suitcase and took it up to the bedroom. She needed to empty it and repack. If all went well, she would be heading to Texas soon. She quickly sorted clothes out of the suitcase that needed to be washed. She packed some lightweight slacks and shirts, choosing comfortable shoes for pacing the floor with an infant. She would take one of her dresses for church too.

All too soon, the packing, except for her toiletries, was done and she wandered back downstairs. The soup had cooled in the microwave. She reheated it and settled at the table with her notebook. She would work on finding Katie to keep her mind from getting stuck on the fact that her fifth grandchild might be born any minute.

She added Rachel's name to the list of people she had talked to and jotted down a summary of the information gleaned from the young teacher. Katie had attended art classes for a year and a half. She had been friends with Madison and a boy named Kevin. Sarah wondered where Kevin had gone to school. Surely he still had family in the Pleasant Valley area. She started a list of things she would start to investigate tomorrow. *If* she was still in town.

One of her notes caught her eye. Who was this Amish boy that the girls had teased Katie about? She left a blank spot, hoping Kevin or Madison might be able to provide a name. If Katie had been close to this boy, maybe *he* knew where she was.

Sarah kept glancing at the clock. It was after nine now. Why hadn't David called? She tapped her notebook with her pencil. She needed to concentrate on Katie. Not being able to talk to the Amish community really narrowed down her options. She went into her office to retrieve her laptop when the phone rang. She spun and dashed back to the counter and grabbed the handset.

"Sarah? It's David. We're still at the hospital but heading home. Another false alarm." His low voice dragged with fatigue.

"How is she?" Sarah said.

"She's doing fine but a bit worn out. I need to get her into bed. She's supposed to rest. Doctor's orders."

"The boys doing okay?"

"They're pretty bummed they don't have a brother or sister, but my parents are spoiling them rotten, so they're fine. Hold on a second." There was the sound of a hand muffling the receiver and then David came back. "The nurse is here to discharge Jenna."

Sarah was dying to ask more questions and talk to Jenna, but she needed to do what was best for her daughter. "I'll let her rest then and call her in the morning."

"She'd like that," David said. "Get some rest yourself. Sorry about the false alarm."

"Nothing to be sorry for. I'm just glad everyone is okay." Sarah set the phone back on the counter and, feeling suddenly deflated, returned to her office. She sat in the chair for a moment, letting her heart rate return to normal and then booted up the computer. She brought up the White Pages. If Katie was living on her own now, she might have a phone.

She started the search in Pleasant Valley, but no Katie Fisher popped up. She tried just Fisher. Abram Fisher was listed. That must be for the shared neighborhood phone. There was also a David Fisher and a Matthew Fisher who shared the same number. Possibly relatives of Abram, since it was a small community.

Sarah jotted this information in her notebook just in case she needed it later. She widened the search to include the state of New York, and over a hundred names with Katie or K. Fisher popped up. She groaned and rubbed her temples with her fingers. She really needed some idea of the direction Katie would have gone. She wished she could have asked Annie more questions, but there was no way to contact her unless Annie happened to be in the phone shack. Abram certainly wouldn't approve if he knew she was looking for Katie.

She printed out both lists and picked up a highlighter. The online White Pages gave an age range on some of the names and she highlighted all those in the eighteen to twenty-four range and those that didn't list any age. The list narrowed to nine. Much more manageable. She set the list by her computer for the morning.

Maybe she would learn more from Katie's friend Kevin. Sarah respected the teacher's desire to protect his privacy, but she desperately hoped Kevin would contact her. Tracking down Katie might prove to be difficult, if not impossible, if no one would talk to her.

Her gaze shifted to the clock on the computer. A half hour had passed. She wondered if Jenna was home yet. At least she knew that her daughter was being well taken care of. David was an excellent husband and father, but still ... a mother couldn't help worrying. If Sarah were Annie, she would be frantic not knowing how Katie was. Frantic and unable to do something about it without the risk of being shut off from her husband and her community. No wonder Annie had reached out to a stranger.

To Sarah.

She stood and tucked the notebook under her arm to take upstairs with her in case an idea popped into her head during the night. The search had proved futile tonight, but tomorrow she would start fresh.

Katie Fisher was out there somewhere, and Sarah was going to find her.

CHAPTER FOUR

S arah awoke to gloom. Spring rain came down in
earnest, slicking up the window, drenching the trees,
and turning her backyard into a bog. They needed
the rain, so Sarah knew she should be thankful, but it would
be easier to bolster a sagging mood on a sunny, bright
day.

She hadn't slept well the night before, so around 1:00 AM
she had retrieved the book of Amish quilts she had purchased and took it to bed with her. She flipped through
the pages trying to get inspired about the baby quilt, but
her mind kept wandering back to Katie and her quilt block.
What had inspired Katie to create that design? Did it have
special meaning? She had finally fallen asleep and was
plagued with dreams about Jenna needing her.

Determined not to let the gloomy day darken her mood
any further, Sarah decided to do a bit of spring cleaning
while she waited until it was late enough to call Jenna. She
dressed in jeans and a soft, oversize blue T-shirt and tennis

shoes. She tackled cleaning her kitchen, straightening the cupboards, scrubbing the refrigerator shelves, and getting the porcelain and floor to shine.

Finally she picked up the phone.

Jenna answered on the fourth ring. "Hey, Mom."

"I hope I didn't wake you."

"No, I'm awake. Have been for hours. I couldn't have slept in if I wanted to. I must've had six calls, all well meaning, and I appreciate people caring, but the baby will come when it wants to. Talking about it isn't going to hurry things along. I'm tired of rehashing every little detail. You know what I mean?"

"I understand," Sarah said and bit back questions of her own.

"I'd take the phone off the hook, but the kids are at school. What if they need something? And David might call and worry. I made him go to work this morning. No sense having him here pacing and asking me if I'm okay every two minutes. He'll be home for lunch though."

"Sweetie, I can fly out today if you want me too."

"So you can stare at my stomach too?" Jenna asked. "Oh, I'm sorry. I didn't mean to snap at you."

"It's okay. I understand. But if I was there I could answer your phone calls and try to keep everything quiet for you until the baby comes."

There was a long sigh. "I appreciate it, Mom, and I can't wait to see you, but everything's fine. Really. It's just me being cranky. You'll be here soon enough when I *really* need help. I don't want to be a bother and—oh, it's call-waiting. It's the doctor's office. Got to go."

"Okay. Just remember you're never a bother to me," Sarah said hastily. "And if you change your mind about my coming early, please let me know."

"Love you, Mom."

"Love you too." Sarah reluctantly hung up the phone. Jenna sounded miserable. She was tempted to just ignore her daughter's wishes and head on over to Texas. But, then, Jenna had always been the independent sort, and Sarah's presence might actually cause her more stress. Pregnant women could be difficult at times with hormones running rampant.

Gerry had treated her with utmost tact when she was in her third trimesters and kept quiet or disappeared whenever she tried to pick a fight. But it had been worth all the stress and high emotion. Jason and Jenna had been great kids and were now strong, well-adjusted parents themselves.

Sarah decided she just needed to keep busy. She got her laptop from the office and set it on the kitchen table so she would have more room. She opened her notebook and placed it beside the keyboard. Now, where was she?

The front doorbell rang.

Martha stood on the porch shaking out an umbrella as Sarah hurried to unlock the dead bolt.

"Hey, good morning! Did you have a good trip?" Martha's smile beamed in sharp contrast to the gray, wet world behind her.

"It was great, definitely worth it. The girls had a blast on the farm," Sarah said as she stepped back to let Martha in. "Would you like some coffee? I was just thinking of making some."

"Sounds great." Martha slipped off her rubber boots and shrugged out of her pink raincoat.

Sarah led the way to the kitchen and grabbed the new bag of French roast she had bought the week before. She put the coffee pot in the sink and turned on the water. "How's Ernie?"

"Doing fine. He's content working on one of his junkers in the garage. Something about a faulty gizmo in the carburetor."

"That's good," Sarah said, her mind roaming back over her conversation with Jenna. Why had the doctor's office called? Surely if there was a concern about the baby, Jenna would call her. Or would she?

"Okay, what's wrong?" Martha's voice penetrated her musing.

"*Hmm?*" Sarah paused in her measuring of the coffee into the filter basket. Martha stood beside her, her hands placed on her hips.

Martha raised her eyebrows. "Either you've developed a liking for extra, extra strong coffee or something's bugging you."

Sarah looked down at the grinds overflowing the filter and laughed. "Sorry. I'm distracted. I just got off the phone with Jenna."

"Oh! Is the baby on its way?" Martha's hands fluttered over her heart.

"Not quite yet." She invited Martha to sit at the kitchen table with her and explained about David's call and then her conversation with Jenna. "I wish Jenna would let me help her now."

"Like mother, like daughter. Strong and independent." Martha patted Sarah's hand. "She'll be fine."

"Logically I know that, but I can't help worrying. I'm sending up frequent prayers," Sarah said. "The field trip was a good distraction, but now time seems to be passing so slowly. I don't have any current repair jobs, and I've been putting off starting a new quilt thinking I'd be heading for Texas any time now."

"What about the quilt you're making for the baby?" Martha asked.

"I decided to wait until I knew if it was a boy or girl but...maybe..."

"You could start now," Martha finished the thought for her. "Just make the colors unisex, and with the baby due anytime, you can always change it. Or even make another."

"I could." Sarah thought about it, the familiar excitement of starting a new quilting project beginning to give her goose bumps. "You should've seen the wonderful quilts in Pleasant Valley. The hand-stitching was amazing, so uniform and skillful. I could've spent a fortune buying quilts, but I just bought a book so I can drool over the photos. You know what? I'd like to try something different on this baby quilt. A version of one of the patterns I saw."

"Now that's more like it. I say go for it."

"You want to come with me to pick out some fabric?" Sarah glanced out the window at the pouring rain. "Maybe after the rain lets up some?"

"Love to," Martha said. "I need to pick up some yarn while we're out. I'm going to crochet Sylvie a poncho," she said, referring to her three-year-old grandchild. Martha's ten grandchildren kept her busy with crocheting projects, and she loved it. "I saw the cutest pattern with lady bugs on it. It was knitted, but I think I can do it with crochet."

"Coffee's done." Sarah went to the cupboard and got them each a mug. She grabbed the milk and the sugar canister and placed them on the table. Martha was studying the notebook Sarah had left open.

"Who's Katie?"

Sarah stirred milk into her coffee. "She's the daughter of the people we stayed with on the field trip. Katie ran away over a year and a half ago. Her mother Annie asked me if I could help find her. She just wants to know she's okay." She told Martha about the shunning and what the school teacher had told her.

"That's really rough. Poor woman!" Martha shook her head. "But surely Katie didn't go far."

"That's what I'm thinking. Katie didn't drive, at least not then. I'm hoping her friend Kevin will have some answers. I ran a White Pages search on Katie Fisher in New York and there were over a hundred references for a Kate or K. Fisher, but I was able to narrow those down to nine possibilities."

"If you want help, count me in. I can make phone calls," Martha said in an eager tone.

Sarah smiled. Her best friend loved getting involved in Sarah's sleuthing. "Some of the listings give an age range as well as a phone number and the town, but not all. And of course this is assuming Katie has a published phone number or a phone, for that matter. I'm not holding out much hope we can find her this way."

"Nothing ventured, nothing gained," Martha said with a big grin.

"Clichéd but true," Sarah giggled at Martha's enthusiasm. Her spirits buoyed as she retrieved the copies of the White Pages' list of phone numbers.

Martha took her cell phone into the living room so they wouldn't have to talk over each other.

Within half an hour they had called all the names. Two didn't answer the phone. One was a disconnected phone, and the rest said they weren't from Pleasant Valley and didn't know the girl they were asking about.

"It was worth a shot. Thanks for helping," Sarah said. "I'll try the ones that didn't answer later tonight."

"Well, I'm disappointed that we didn't get a hit, but I know a way to cheer us up." Martha grinned. "Ready to go shop for fabric?"

Sarah shoved her cell phone and notebook in her purse. "You don't have to ask twice."

Sarah loved her local fabric store, Wild Goose Chase, especially when inclement weather gave her an excuse to linger even longer than usual. The owner, Vanessa Sawyer, had tea brewing and the warm, cinnamon scent beckoned. The variety of colorful fabric bolts and the selection of sewing tools would make any serious quilter stop in her tracks.

Martha went immediately to the yarn section and Sarah stopped at the newest fabric display by the door.

"Aren't those lovely? They came in yesterday."

"I really like this one with the yellow roses." Sarah rubbed the fabric between her fingers.

"Me too. Reminds me of summer. What project are you working on now?" Vanessa hopped down from her stool behind the counter. The petite woman was dressed in soft blue jeans and a peasant blouse. Her welcoming smile made her customers feel at ease.

"I'm going to do a quilt for Jenna's baby," Sarah said. "So I need to pick out some fabric."

"That's going to be fun. How is Jenna doing?" Vanessa asked.

"Hard to tell. The baby's due any day now."

"Those last days can be tough. With Terrance I was in labor for forty-eight hours. Worth every minute of course, but during the ordeal I had my doubts about going through with it." She laughed. "But it's not like you can change your mind at that point. Luckily Lena was easier. I barely got to the hospital in time."

"Since this is Jenna's third, I'm hoping the labor will be short," Sarah said. "But not so short that she doesn't get to the hospital in time. Luckily it's not far from their house."

"That's good." Vanessa cleared a bolt of fabric off the cutting table. "Is it a boy or a girl?"

"A surprise." Sarah smiled.

"Okay, so you probably don't want to make your color scheme all blue or pink. What pattern are you going to use?"

Sarah pulled out the Amish quilt book and flipped it open. "I'm thinking of doing something like this one." She showed Vanessa the Trip Around the World design.

Vanessa took the book from Sarah. "Pretty. Those small squares create all kinds of possibilities for color."

Sarah nodded. "I'm going to vary the traditional pattern a bit and leave an area in the center to either appliqué or create a new block," Sarah said thinking of Katie's quilt. She wished she had a photograph of it. Vanessa turned the book over and read the back cover. "Where did you get the book?"

"It was in one of the shops in Pleasant Valley. The girls and I were just there for a field trip and stayed with an Amish family."

"What fun! I didn't know they did that." Vanessa handed the book back.

"This was a special arrangement for the school children. I think it really opened their eyes to a different culture and also gave them a glimpse of how their ancestors lived when they came over to this country."

"I hope Terrance and Lena get to experience something like that," Vanessa said.

"I hope so too," Sarah said, thinking about what Seth and Gertie had said about the bishop considering stopping the trips. Terrance and Lena were only nine and seven. Could the program be canceled before they reached eighth grade?

"So do you know what colors you're leaning toward?" Vanessa asked as Martha approached the counter with an armload of skeins.

"I think I'll browse a bit and see what strikes me."

Sarah moved between the bolts and fabric pieces. Martha finished her purchase of yarn, settled on a chair near the counter, and promptly started crocheting the poncho. Vanessa brought out tea and the ladies chatted. After spending half an hour perusing the shop, Sarah chose a cream-colored fabric for the quilt's center and for the squares, colors that reminded her of spring, varying patterns in green, blue, burgundy, rose, and pink. She would decide on the border fabric later. She carried her choices to the counter.

Martha looked up from counting her loops. "Those are pretty."

"Jenna once mentioned they might do garden colors in the nursery, but I'm not sure what theme she finally decided on. She kept changing her mind."

"This will look lovely no matter what she's done." Vanessa flipped over a bolt and began measuring out the yardage Sarah specified. She grabbed her shears and made a neat cut. "Speaking of garden colors, have you heard about the memorial garden they're putting in at the historical society?"

"I remember there was some talk years ago, but I thought the idea got vetoed," Sarah said.

"Well it's on again," Martha said, her crotchet hook flying. "I heard Irene proposed the idea again as a fund-raiser to help upgrade the computers and software, but I don't know any of the details."

"I ran into Irene at the market, and she told me all about it." Vanessa picked up a bolt of green fabric. "It just got approved by the board. Between their building and the CPA's office, they're going to replace that strip of lawn with a brick patio, add a water fountain, and put in some benches and planters." She lifted her shears. "How much?"

"One yard of each of the rest, please," Sarah said. She was probably buying more than she needed, but the extra fabric could be used in future projects.

Vanessa made a snip and then guided the scissors across the fabric. "People can donate a brick in memory of someone who lived in Maple Hill and have the name engraved on it or pay for a plaque on one of the benches or planters."

"Like they did in the park with benches?" Martha asked.

"Yes, but on a smaller scale," Vanessa said. "Irene was also hoping to maybe get a small version of Nathaniel Bradford's statue or other busts of our more famous citizens."

"Oh boy, I can see Irene out there right now talking to the statues," Martha said with a giggle.

Sarah smiled. Irene had an endearing habit of talking about historical characters in the present tense. It could be startling to those caught unaware of her tendency.

"It'll be a nice, quiet place to read or have a sack lunch," Vanessa added with a smile. "Irene also suggested providing wireless Internet for people who want to do research or surf the Web outdoors."

Research! Irene loved research. Sarah wondered if Irene might give her more ideas on how to track down Katie.

"Martha, would you be interested in visiting the historical society after this?" Sarah asked.

Martha looked up and smiled. "You don't have to ask twice."

CHAPTER FIVE

Martha parked her green minivan in front of the hitching post at the Maple Hill Historical Society. The hours varied without warning, so Sarah was glad to see the front porch light beaming through the mist. Martha grabbed her umbrella, and Sarah pulled a raincoat hat over her head and dashed through the rain up the sidewalk to the porch. She stomped her boots on the doormat as Martha set her umbrella on the porch.

The pleasant scent of parchment, leather, and aged cedar greeted her as she stepped inside. A fire was lit in the stone fireplace. Irene Stuart, the historical society's historian, sat in one of the overstuffed chairs and looked up from a large book she was studying. "Sarah, Martha, what brings you out on such a miserable day?"

"Shopping." Martha grinned and quipped a variation of the USPS creed, "Neither snow nor rain nor heat nor gloom of night will keep us from buying fabric or yarn."

Irene smiled faintly at Martha with a puzzled expression in her brown eyes.

"We were just over at Wild Goose Chase," Sarah explained. "Vanessa mentioned the new memorial garden and we thought we'd stop by."

"Oh yes! Isn't it exciting? Come over here, and I'll show you where it's going to go." Irene popped up from her chair and led the way to a large window overlooking the side yard. "We're going to put a patio in right there. I wanted cobblestones, but we're going with bricks so people can put on them the names of people they wish to remember. See the stakes? That's where the patio will go. Benches and raised planters will go around the perimeter."

She pulled a large sheet of paper off a filing cabinet by the window. "Here are the blueprints."

Sarah looked at the drawings and then back at the drenched landscape. "It'll be lovely."

"I think so too. I'm also asking if we can do an arbor or gazebo for days like this. Not that anyone would want to be out there during the winter necessarily, but during the warm weather it would provide shade and shelter. It all depends on how much money we bring in. It needs to pay for itself and whatever is left over will go toward upgrading our system."

"When are you starting?" Martha asked.

"This week. We finally got approval from the board and some initial funding. We're going to put out advertisements on how people can be part of the project. It's a great way to raise money while at the same time honoring the citizens of Maple Hill. A nice, tangible memory."

"I may be interested in contributing," Sarah said, thinking about her parents and grandparents. They had been a part of Maple Hill's history.

"Me too," Martha said.

"Here's the brochure. They're not very fancy. I had to design them myself with some help at the Copy Shop." She gave them each a folded sheet. "You'll probably get another one in the mail."

Sarah skimmed the brochure that gave a brief history of Maple Hill from its incorporation in 1786. Irene's passion for preserving the history of Maple Hill evoked a feeling of hometown pride and an enthusiasm for the memory project. "This is really well done, Irene."

"Very professional," Martha added.

"Thank you," Irene beamed with a pretty blush on her pale cheeks. She smoothed back a brown strand of hair that had escaped her French twist. "So is there anything else I can help you with?"

"Maybe. And only if you have time," Sarah said. "I'm trying to locate someone and was wondering if you might have some ideas. She doesn't live here in Maple Hill. She's Amish and she was living in Pleasant Valley, New York, with her parents. She could be anywhere now, though I suspect she didn't go too far. I've tried the White Pages, and so far no luck. Being Amish she may not even own a phone."

"*Hmm.* She may not be in the usual search databases either, especially if she doesn't own property or hasn't held a job outside the Amish community," Irene said. "Let me see what I can find out. This will be interesting."

Sarah gave Irene the names of Katie and her parents and their address.

"Fisher," Irene repeated. "That's a common name, but let me do a bit of research on Amish records and see what I can find."

"Where there's a will, there's a way." Martha caught Sarah's eye and grinned. "Sorry, Ernie and I have been reading a book of quotes before bed. It's supposed to help with motivation."

Sarah laughed. "No problem. We can use all the help we can get."

The rich scent of brewing coffee and fresh muffins greeted Sarah as she and Martha entered the Spotted Dog Café. The lunch crowd was there, and they had to take a small round table in the far corner by the window.

Karen Bancroft hurried over, whisked away the glasses left by the previous customers, and swiped a rag over the table. She whipped her order pad out of her pocket and smiled. "Always nice to see you ladies. The special today is homemade cream of asparagus soup and chicken salad with ranch vinaigrette on herbed foccacia bread."

"That sounds very springlike," Martha said, unfolding her napkin. "I'll try that."

"Me too," Sarah said. They ordered iced tea and Karen hurried off to the kitchen.

Martha looked toward the bookstore. "I don't see Liam. Is he working this morning?"

"I don't know," Sarah said feeling a twinge of disappointment. It had been a couple days since she had seen him, and she had brought in the gift she had bought at the Amish store.

"Here's your tea." Karen set two tall glasses on the table. "Your order will be up soon."

"Is Liam around?" Sarah asked.

"He's running an errand, but he'll be back soon," Karen said and turned to a customer who was holding up a finger to get her attention.

Martha took a sip of the tea and added some sweetener as the door opened and Liam's dog Murphy bounded in followed by Liam. He was dressed in a blue long-sleeved shirt and jeans. His green eyes brightened when he saw Sarah. Sarah's cheeks warmed as he strode toward them.

"How was Amish country?" he asked.

"Amy and Audrey loved it and we learned quite a bit. The girls even drove a buggy."

"Now that's something I'd like to try sometime. Caitlin wanted a horse when she was young," Liam said, referring to his daughter who had gotten married the previous fall.

"Amy's caught the bug now and wants to take horseback riding lessons too."

"There used to a riding stable north of town," Liam said. "I wonder if it's still there. Does Audrey want to ride too?"

"Audrey's more interested in cars and shopping." Sarah reached under the table and grabbed the paper bag. "I saw something in Pleasant Valley I thought you might like."

"A present for me?" The paper crinkled loudly as Liam opened the bag and extracted the extralong oven mitts and the jar of herbs. "Thank you. Is this a hint you'd like me to cook?"

Sarah's cheeks flooded with heat. "They were advertised as barbecue mitts."

Liam held them up. "Well now, these are great, almost too nice to use. Thank you. And I was teasing. Now that the weather is getting warmer, we should have a cookout."

Martha eyed the design. "I bet Ernie could use some of those too. They'd protect his arms more." Martha's husband was suffering from Parkinson's disease and although the tremors were still mild, Sarah knew Martha worried about Ernie injuring himself.

Karen arrived, carrying the tray with their soup and sandwiches. "Liam, good thing you're back. The bread delivery just arrived, and they brought the wrong kind of bun. You'll need to call the bakery."

"Duty calls. Enjoy your lunch, and don't leave without saying good-bye," Liam said with a wink. He took the tray from Karen so she could place the food on the table before he went behind the counter and picked up the phone.

The green soup was smooth and warm, which contrasted nicely with the cold sandwich. The grapes in the chicken salad added a sweet crunch. Sarah and Martha chatted about Martha's grandkids and plans for their spring break. "Are Maggie and Jason planning a trip or doing anything special?"

"I don't think so. At least they haven't mentioned it to me. I'll probably still be at Jenna's," Sarah said, resisting the urge to check her cell phone again for messages.

Martha pushed back her chair. "I'm going to go wash my hands before we leave."

Sarah took her check over to the cash register and was taking change from Karen when Liam came back out. "Bun crisis averted," he said.

"That's good." Sarah dropped her change into her wallet. She dug out her cell phone and glanced at it. No calls or new texts.

"How's Jenna?" Liam asked.

Sarah looked up. "She says she's doing okay. I'm just being a nervous wreck for her. This is my fifth grandchild. You'd think I'd be calmer."

Liam smiled. "I don't think it ever gets easier. Worrying as a parent is a lifelong job."

"I just wish I was there now."

"Why don't you just go down?"

"I would, in a heartbeat, if Jenna gave me the okay. She doesn't want to be a bother," Sarah said. "She wants me to rest up to be available when they bring the baby home. There may be some long nights ahead."

Liam smiled. "No doubt. Caitlin had colic as a baby. I almost wore a groove in the floor walking with her."

"I'm sorry. Jason had colic too, but Gerry and I were lucky. Jason settled down quickly, and Jenna took to sleeping for hours on end from the time we brought her home. Come to think of it, they were both good sleepers as teenagers too."

Liam laughed and the sound warmed her from the top of her head to the tips of her toes. "Caitlin as a teenager could be challenging at times, but...there are times I miss those days."

"Uh-oh. Is this a sign you're ready to be a grandpa?" Sarah teased at his slightly wistful tone.

Liam blinked as if startled by the thought. "Maybe it is." A slow smile spread over his face. "*Grandpa.* I think I could handle it."

"Are Caitlin and Trevor thinking about having kids soon?" Sarah asked.

"There's been some talk about maybe in the next few years, but you never know. These things sometimes have a way of surprising you." Liam winked.

"I think they'll make great parents, and you'll be a terrific grandpa." She looked down at the corgi chewing his bone by the counter. "I bet Murphy would love a little kid to play with."

"That he would," Liam said.

Sarah spied Martha heading her way. "Time for us to be going."

"You going to be okay?" he asked. "Worrying can wear one out."

Sarah smiled, touched by his concern. "I just need to keep busy."

"Well, I'd be happy to oblige there. I was thinking I really don't want to wait until we have a barbecue. How about dinner later this week? Assuming you're not in Texas by then."

"I'd like that. How about coming over to my place on Saturday? Annie Fisher sent home a huckleberry pie that I stuck in the freezer for a special occasion," Sarah said.

"Pie? You twisted my arm." Liam leaned closer. "Not that *you* ever have to."

Sarah set down her bags of groceries and her bag from Wild Goose Chase on the kitchen counter. She had gone with Martha to run some errands to the local pharmacy and then to the market. She had bought fresh fruit and bread. Dinner with Liam was still three days away so she would pick up more items for salad on Friday.

Sarah placed the fabric she had bought in the washing machine and set it for a light cycle. The fabric was a hundred percent cotton and she didn't want it to shrink after she had quilted it.

She turned on her laptop and scanned her in-box. Nothing from Jenna or Kevin. Audrey had forwarded her a trip photograph she had taken on her phone of Amy and Sarah in the park. There were two advertisements, which Sarah sent to the spam file. And another one from someone in-quiring about quilt restoration and costs. Sarah sent her standard list of services and fees, which were tentative upon inspection of the quilt.

She was about to sign off when a ding sounded and an e-mail popped into her mail box from TheDude@DNA.com.

She clicked it open.

Don't know where K is. Try Madison.

And he listed Madison's e-mail address. Sarah stared at the short, curt message and considered e-mailing him back. Surely he knew something about Katie. Rachel had men-tioned they had been friends.

Maybe Madison would be more communicative. She copied her address to compose a new e-mail.

Dear Madison,

I'm Sarah Hart. Kevin gave me your address. I have an important message for Katie Fisher from her mother. Please contact me ASAP.

Sarah typed in her phone number and sent it off with a quick prayer she would get a reply.

She moved the fabric to the dryer and straightened up the kitchen before she went into her office to retrieve her cutting mat and rotary cutter. She checked her computer again. Still no new e-mail. With a sigh, she picked up the laptop and took it to the kitchen.

The dryer buzzed and she retrieved the warm fabric and spread it out on the kitchen table. The green ivy material had wrinkled so she quickly ironed it and then played with the various pieces for a while, trying to decide which combinations of fabric patterns and colors would be best.

Grabbing some graph paper, she blocked out an idea for the order of the fabrics. An hour flew by and Sarah suddenly realized that Jenna still hadn't called. She hoped everything was okay.

Sarah decided to start with the ivy-patterned fabric and lined up the material on her cutting board. She checked the quilt book and the instructions for Trip Around the World. She needed to cut one-and-a-half-inch strips from each of the fabrics. The cutter sliced through the fabric with ease.

She had cut two strips when she realized she had cut them from the length of the fabric, not the width. Not a huge mistake, but she needed all the strips from the different fabrics to be the same length. She wasn't concentrating. Worry about Jenna and thoughts about Katie competed for her focus. She set the cutter down and ran her hands over her face.

What was wrong with her? Jenna was a sensible woman who was already raising two children. David had a good head on his shoulders. If something went wrong with the pregnancy, they would make wise decisions on how to proceed. So why the intense worry? Could it be empathy with Annie and her situation that was increasing her anxiety? They both missed their daughters and worried due to lack of communication.

How did Annie deal with it? She thought back to the prayer Annie had said with her. Annie's faith ran deep, despite her despair over her daughter.

Lord, You know I'm worried about Jenna. Please be with her and protect her and her baby. And if You had me meet Annie for a reason, please guide me on how to help her.

Feeling calmer, Sarah picked up the cutter again. The quilt was something she had control over, and she imagined how much Jenna was going to like it. After the boys had outgrown the baby quilts Sarah had made for them, Jenna had had them professionally cleaned and then packed them away in a cedar trunk for when the boys had their own babies someday. Sarah loved the idea of great-grandchildren enjoying her quilts.

Sarah hummed one of her favorite hymns and was almost done cutting all the strips she needed when her e-mail indicator dinged once again. She glanced at the screen and recognized Madison's e-mail address.

Hi, Mrs. Hart. I haven't seen Katie. Is this urgent? Is her mother okay?

Sarah tapped her fingers on the tabletop. After her curt response from Kevin, she really wanted to talk to Madison in person.

Thank you for responding so quickly. Annie is okay, but I need to speak to Katie. Would it be possible for us to talk on the phone? She listed her phone numbers again and went back to cutting the fabric. She was almost done with the greens when the phone rang.

"Mrs. Hart?" a young woman with a slightly nasal voice asked.

"Yes it is. Are you Madison?"

"Yeah. Is everything okay with Katie's mom?" Madison's voice sounded worried above the beat of music playing and a murmur of voices in the background.

"I'm sorry. I didn't mean to scare you. She seemed fine when I saw her yesterday."

"Oh, I'm glad she's okay," Madison said with a whoosh of air. "I haven't seen her in ages. Have you had her cookies? She makes the best!"

"No, but I've had her pie."

"Awesome!" The music grew louder. "Glad she's okay. I gotta go—"

"She's really worried about Katie," Sarah interjected hastily before the girl hung up. "Do you know where she is?"

"Nada. Katie and I said good-bye before I left for college." There was a banging noise and after a few moments Madison came back on the line. "Oops! Sorry! I dropped the phone."

Sarah pulled her notebook closer and made a note. "Do you have any idea why Katie left home?"

"Beats me. We had a blast while she was on her *Rumspringa*," she replied and then called, "I'll be there in a sec." She lowered her voice. "Nice talking to you Mrs. H. Hope everything works out okay."

"Do you know anyone else who might know where Katie is?" Sarah said. "Another friend of Katie's?"

"You already talked to Kev, right?"

"He e-mailed and said to contact you."

"Can't think of anyone else right now. You could try the art school."

"I talked to your teacher there."

"Sorry I'm not more help. If you find Katie, tell her to give me a call, 'kay?"

"Sure. I appreciate your talking to me, Madison. One last thing. Did you know that Katie is shunned?"

"Yeah, but what does it matter? She's not even there, right?"

Sarah hung up thinking the same thing. She needed to talk to Annie again.

She picked up the phone and called Martha. "Would you like to go to Pleasant Valley? I'm heading there tomorrow."

CHAPTER SIX

T he rainstorms had moved east by morning and scattered showers were forecast. Sarah's Grand Prix plowed through puddles as Sarah and Martha headed for Pleasant Valley. Martha had attended a church committee meeting that morning and they left after lunch for the two-hour drive, bringing overnight bags just in case.

Sarah updated Martha on the previous evening's conversation with Madison. "She seemed like a nice girl and was worried about Annie, but I got the feeling she was being evasive."

"Kids tend to stick together," Martha said. "But Madison did have a good point about the shunning. Why punish someone who isn't even there?"

"Good question. I'm hoping I can talk to Annie without Abram being around. I just hope this isn't a waste of time."

Martha looked up from the poncho she was crocheting and gazed out the window at the passing farms. "I hope so too, but I'm just glad you called. Ian volunteered to stay overnight with Ernie."

"That was nice of him," Sarah said. Ian, a gangly eighteen-year-old, was closer to Martha than any of her other grandchildren. Ian's love of painting and Martha's creative design work with her crocheting forged a special bond.

"Actually it works out great for all of us. Ian needs some work on his car, and Ernie loves a challenge when it comes to mechanical mysteries," Martha said with a grin. "And I've been wanting to visit Pleasant Valley. There's a farm there where they raise alpacas and spin yarn from their wool."

"Alpaca yarn?"

"I read about it in one of my craft magazines. The yarn is very warm and soft. Their fleece doesn't contain lanolin which makes it hypoallergenic, so it's great for allergy sufferers."

"That sounds great for someone like Maggie. She tried learning to knit once but found she was allergic to mohair," Sarah said as she turned into the Fisher barnyard. The doors to the harness shop were closed and Abram was nowhere in sight. She parked the car by the house. Annie came out the door and met them on the porch.

"Mrs. Hart? Did you find Katie?"

"Not yet. I'm sorry," Sarah said gently. "Annie, this is my friend Martha Maplethorpe from Maple Hill."

Annie took a deep breath before she smiled gently at Martha. "Pleasure to meet you, Martha Maplethorpe. Won't you come in?" Annie stepped back.

Martha stepped into the house. "What a lovely home."

"Thank you." Annie gestured to the chairs in the living room. "Please be seated. May I bring you something to drink?"

Sarah and Martha declined politely and waited until Annie had settled on the wooden chair opposite them.

"I ran into some problems while I was asking questions about Katie," Sarah said. "You didn't tell me she was shunned."

Annie's face colored. "I...I apologize. I thought people might talk to you since you didn't know. You're not Amish so the *Ordnung* doesn't apply to you...if that makes any sense."

Sarah smiled. "It does. I'm an *Englisher* but unfortunately that didn't make a difference. People in your community would not discuss her. I did talk to her art teacher though, and she referred me to some of Katie's friends, Madison and Kevin? Both of them denied knowing where your daughter is."

"I've never met Kevin, but Madison visited a couple of times. She seemed like a nice girl, although Abram worried about their friendship." Annie took several deep breaths and looked at the floor. "You know, Mrs. Hart, I've been thinking since you left that I should not have accepted your kind offer to look for Katie. It goes against my husband's and the bishop's wishes."

"I see." Sarah glanced at Martha. "But you *do* want to find her."

Annie nodded and tears spilled over. Martha reached into her purse and pulled out a tissue for Annie. "Can you tell us why Katie was shunned?"

"She went against the direct counsel of her elders."

"Did this happen before or after she ran away?" Sarah asked.

"They talked to her before she left but the shunning was imposed after." Annie's attention shifted toward the window.

Gravel crunched and a buggy pulled up to the porch. A woman held the reins. Annie stood, wiping her cheeks. "Mrs. Yoder is here. We are going to the market."

"We won't keep you," Sarah said as they stood. Martha stepped out onto the porch as Mrs. Yoder climbed down out of the buggy. The older Amish woman's sharp gaze swept over Martha and Sarah.

Annie placed her hand on Sarah's arm as they walked outside. "Please come back for supper. You came all this way. That is, if you're going to be in the area."

Sarah glanced at Martha, who nodded. "We were thinking of getting a motel in town."

"No, please stay here. It would make me feel better for inconveniencing you in coming all this way."

"This wasn't an inconvenience," Martha said. I've wanted to come out to Pleasant Valley for years."

"Still, please oblige me." Her gaze met Sarah's.

Sarah nodded, although she was puzzled by Annie's insistence. Perhaps Annie had something she still needed to share with her.

"What time shall we come back?"

"Six o'clock." Annie went down the stairs. "Mrs. Yoder, these are my new friends, Sarah Hart and Martha Maplethorpe."

Mrs. Yoder nodded a greeting to them but didn't crack a smile. Her gaze followed Sarah and Martha to the car.

Sarah fired up the engine and turned the car down the driveway. Martha looked in the side mirror as they pulled onto the road. "I feel like we got caught by the teacher for passing notes or something," Martha said with a little laugh. "Did you get the feeling Annie's friend doesn't approve of us?"

"Maybe she heard that I've been asking questions about Katie," Sarah said.

They drove into Pleasant Valley and visited several of the shops. From one of the storekeepers Martha got directions to the alpaca farm.

"We must be almost there." Martha gazed at the alpacas grazing in the fields. "Aren't they cute?"

Sarah slowed the car so she could get a better view of the tan and white animals that resembled llamas.

"The shop is supposed to be near the barn," Martha said. Sarah turned into the driveway and drove past a white two story farmhouse with a large wraparound porch. Parked cars by a squat square building suggested they had found the shop. Sarah parked as thunder rumbled overhead. Big droplets fell as they dashed through the wide double doors into the Amish shop.

"Hello," a young Amish woman said from behind a table. Beneath the protective gray apron, she wore a soft purple blouse and traditional dark skirt, cape, and shoes. Her prayer cap covered glossy auburn hair and freckles sprinkled her nose. A child of about three years old played with a faceless doll at her feet.

"Hi," Martha said. "I'm looking for alpaca yarn."

"You came to the right place." The woman smiled and gestured for them to follow her to the back of the shop where skeins of yarn, sorted by color, were displayed on shelves. "All our yarn is made from our own animals and hand-dyed. We have several blends to choose from. What are you going to use the yarn for?"

"I thought I'd make some slippers, but I may do some mittens and hats too."

"Any of our yarns would work well for those projects, but I'd recommend the seventy-percent alpaca, thirty-percent Merino wool blend."

As Martha continued to ask questions and study the wool selections, Sarah explored the shop. She paused by a table of knitted sweaters made from alpaca blends. She lifted a blue cardigan. The wool felt silky and soft and she could see why Martha was excited about trying out the yarn.

Several quilts were displayed, featuring variations of the Double Wedding Ring and Log Cabin designs. A large quilt hung on the wall with an index card fastened to it saying it was not for sale. Sarah took a closer look. Each of the squares offered a different design, including flowers, houses, and a covered bridge, and some of the squares were embroidered with names or initials.

"Is there anything I can help you with?" the young woman asked quietly as Martha sorted through various yarn rolls, comparing colors.

"This is beautiful," Sarah said. "It's a Friendship Quilt, isn't it?"

"Yes. It was a wedding gift."

Sarah studied the squares and found what she was looking for. "Oh, there's a block from Katie Fisher. I stayed with her parents the other night while my grandchildren were on a field trip. I'm Sarah Hart. What's your name?"

"Eva Miller."

"Did you go to school with Katie?"

"*Ja.*"

"How nice." Sarah turned to the displayed quilts. "I saw one of Katie's quilts on her bed. I thought it was a wonderful blend of old style with a contemporary twist. Do you quilt too?"

She nodded. "I did the Log Cabin ones, though I like making scrap quilts best. I like taking old fabrics and making something new."

"I like those too. Did you ever quilt with Katie?"

Eva shook her head. "I really need to get back to work."

Sarah lowered her voice. "I understand if you can't talk about her. I was hoping to find someone who might know where she may have gone. I'm not a part of your community, so maybe the *Ordnung* rules don't apply to me." Sarah paraphrased Annie's words to her.

Tears filled Eva's eyes and she blinked them away. "I miss her," she whispered. "When we were in school, we would talk about getting married and raising our children together. It is hard to pretend she doesn't exist." She cleared her throat. "I do not know where she is. She wrote me one letter saying she was safe and to look after her mother. I threw the letter away before my Jacob found it."

"Was there a return address?"

"No, but the postmark was from Sunnyvale." Her lips trembled and she turned to refold sweaters that were already in perfect order.

"Do you know why Katie was shunned?"

"She did not obey, but I do not know the details. The bishop made the decision."

"Maybe I should talk to him."

Eva's face paled. "If the bishop finds out that Mrs. Fisher is looking for Annie, she could be shunned too. And me for talking to you."

"I understand. I'm sorry I upset you," Sarah said. "I'm just learning about your ways. I hope I didn't get anyone into trouble."

Eva lifted her chin, her eyes dry now. "My fault for speaking of things I should not." She moved back to the table where Martha had stacked fifteen rolls of yarn.

"Aren't these lovely colors?" Martha said to Sarah.

"They're all beautiful, but I especially like the royal blue."

"Me too. I'm going to crochet Ernie a blue sweater for Christmas. And with the green and pink yarns I'm going to make the grandkids some caps."

"What are you going to do with the red?"

"I don't know yet, but it was too pretty to leave behind," Martha said with a merry laugh. "Did you find anything?"

"There's lots I'd love to take home," Sarah said as she noticed a pair of sand-colored gloves. It didn't get as cold in Texas as it did in New England, but Jenna might appreciate the soft, lightweight gloves.

They paid for their purchases. Eva thanked them but kept her gaze down.

"She seemed upset," Martha said after they had run through the rain and jumped into Sarah's car.

"My fault." Sarah tossed her package on the backseat. "I asked about Katie. They went to school together and were friends."

"She doesn't know where Katie is either?"

"No, but she did get a letter from Katie postmarked from Sunnyvale about a year ago saying that she was okay."

"Great. A clue!"

Sarah smiled, although she still felt terrible about causing Eva distress and guilt over potentially breaking the *Ordnung*.

But surely a mother's concern was forgivable. If they were risking such severe consequences, Sarah just hoped it wasn't in vain.

"It smells so good in here," Martha said as she rolled out dough. "I love the smell of baking bread, especially cinnamon rolls."

"This was my mother's recipe and Katie's favorite. We will put the rolls in the refrigerator and then bring them out in the morning to rise and bake."

"I can't wait to taste them, although right now I couldn't eat another bite. Supper was wonderful, Annie," Sarah said as she washed the last plate and placed it in the rack. She rinsed her hands, picked up a towel, and proceeded to dry the plates.

Sarah and Martha had arrived at six and supper had been on the table. Fresh green beans, chicken and dumplings, and mashed potatoes rounded out the meal with apple cake and caramel sauce for dessert.

Abram had been pleasant but said little, and Martha kept the conversation lively by discussing crafts and recipes. After they had finished eating Abram relaxed in his chair at the table and read a newspaper while the ladies cleaned up.

"I am glad you met Eva Miller. She started the yarn business when she got married. She is ambitious for a twenty-year-old and she is doing well."

"She will not make much profit if the price of feed continues to go up this winter," Abram said, shaking the paper as he flipped a page.

"I think she is planning on stocking up now," Annie said. "She is also thinking of hiring on another helper.

Abram looked at his wife. "We have discussed this. You have work here."

Annie's smile faded. "Yes, Abram."

"What do you want me to do next?" Martha asked, patting the flat rectangle of dough.

Annie handed Martha a canister and a bag of walnuts. "You can add the raisins, and I will chop the nuts."

Martha took a handful of raisins and sprinkled them over the dough. Annie chopped a large knife over the walnuts and added a large portion of the nuts to the rolls. She passed Martha the cinnamon and brown sugar.

"How much should I add?" Martha asked.

"Whatever looks good to you," Annie said with a smile. "It is hard to make a mistake with those ingredients."

"I like your style of baking." Martha laughed. She generously sprinkled the cinnamon and sugar, then rolled up the dough. Annie handed her the large knife. Martha cut the roll into discs and placed them on a baking sheet as Sarah finished drying the dishes and helped Annie put them away in the cupboards. After the rolls were covered and placed in the refrigerator, they cleaned up the mess and wiped the counters down.

"Your kitchen is cute," Martha said with a sigh. "I bet it's really cozy in the winter."

"It is the warmest place in the house which is a blessing in the cold season," Annie said. "But in the summer we use a stove outside. It can get very hot in here."

"I can imagine." Martha eyed the large cast-iron stove. "My kitchen can get stifling in the summer when I run the oven, even with the AC going."

"Some of our neighbors have summer kitchens added onto their houses." Annie glanced at Abram again. "But we get by just fine."

"We used to barbecue a lot in the summer when my children were young," Sarah said. "Those were fun times."

Abram set the paper down on the table and stood. "I need to check on Nell."

"Our mare was blessed with a filly this afternoon," Annie said to Sarah and Martha.

"Oh, can we see it?" Martha asked. "I love baby animals."

"*Ja*, if you wish." Abram picked up his hat and settled it on his head. As they crossed the barnyard, the sun was starting to set, covering the distant clouds with a warm peachy glow. In the barn, Abram stopped by a stall and Sarah peered over the door. In the dim lighting she could make out a small horse lying in the straw. The large, Belgian mare looked at the visitors with wide eyes, planting her body between the people and her baby.

"Isn't she sweet?" Martha cooed, scooting over to get a better look at the filly. "It's hard to imagine that something so small will grow up to be as big as her mother."

"They grow quickly." Abram smiled and rubbed Nell's muzzle. "Easy girl, we are just taking a look."

"She's out of grain, Abram," Sarah said. "Can she have more tonight?"

"*Ja*, she deserves it."

"I'll get it." Annie went to an empty stall that contained covered barrels. When she opened the door the cat and four kittens trotted out.

Sarah reached out to touch one and it spooked, darting away from the group on wobbly legs. "I'm sorry, little one. I didn't mean to scare you." She followed it behind a stack of straw bales that didn't appear too stable.

"You better not get stuck back there." She scooped the kitten up in her hand. As she turned, her shoes slid on the slippery straw. She grabbed a board that rested against the wall. It fell away from the wall, but she was able to push herself up. As she shoved the square board back, a flash of bright blue caught her attention. Cuddling the kitten under her chin, she pulled the board away from the wall. Brightly colored paint covered the other side. The pattern looked familiar. Could it be? It was. A quilt square made out of wood.

"Sarah, are you all right?" Martha called.

Sarah pushed the board back. "I'm fine," she called and made her way back out. "I scared this little one and didn't want her to get lost." She set the kitten back down by the mother cat.

Martha grinned. "You have stuff in your hair. What were you doing? Rolling in the straw?"

"Close enough." Sarah brushed the stalks out of her hair and off her shoulders. She wanted to ask Annie about the quilt block, but she had to wait until they were alone in case Katie had created it as she suspected. They went back to the house and settled in the living room. Martha got out her crotcheting and Annie her quilting hoop. Abram offered Sarah part of his newspaper.

"This is the *Budget*. It contains letters," he said.

"The Amish can keep in touch with each other," Annie said. "It is organized by different parts of the county."

Sarah scanned the columns of chatty letters that talked about weddings, crops, weather, visitors, church meetings, and other interesting day-to-day things.

Martha leaned over and read the back side of the paper. "It's like a printed form of Facebook."

Sarah smiled. "Only with longer entries and no photos."

Martha missed a loop and concentrated back on her crotcheting. Sarah continued reading the *Budget* and searched for a section with letters from Pleasant Valley, but either Abram had that part of the paper or no one had written letters from here.

At exactly nine o'clock, Abram set his paper down and stood. "Time to sleep."

Annie set her quilting hoop back in the basket by the chair. "Shall we have prayer before we go up?"

After Abram offered a prayer, they ascended the stairs. Annie had put Sarah in Katie's old room this time and

Martha in the spare bedroom. She bid them good night and followed Abram into the third bedroom.

Sarah set her bag on the chair, turned to the quilt on the bed, and examined it carefully. Her hunch had been right. Katie had painted the quilt block in the barn. It was similar to the center block on the quilt. She wished she could see the design again. Maybe in the morning she could find an excuse to go back into the barn. If Abram wasn't around, she would ask Annie about it.

She folded the quilt back and changed into her nightgown. She set her devotion book on the bed and plumped up the pillows. Settling back, she read about putting on the armor of God in Ephesians. Is that how the Amish felt? By wearing plain clothes they were arming themselves for God and against the world?

She glanced at Katie's clothing. A white apron hung on a nail. That must be Katie's church wear. From her brief research on the Amish with the kids, the apron signified that Katie was available to date. She also would've had a special apron made when she married. The white apron would then be put away until after she died and she would be buried with it.

What was Katie doing right now? Annie was probably lying in her bed thinking the same thing. Sarah's thoughts turned to her own daughter.

Was Jenna doing all right? She checked her cell phone but then remembered there wasn't any service in the house. She set it back down and turned off her lantern. The room was dark, the moon covered by a cloud. Sarah stared into the darkness and sighed. She wasn't going to be able to sleep until she checked her messages.

She pulled on her slacks and a sweater over her nightgown. She slid her feet into her sneakers and used the phone as a flashlight as she crept down the stairs. A step creaked underfoot and she paused, holding her breath. She didn't want to wake Annie or Abram. Nothing in the house stirred so she continued on to the door, unlocked it, and slipped out onto the porch.

The night smelled of damp earth and tiny plops of water dripped from the trees. Sarah's shoes crunched on the gravel as she made her way to the edge of the driveway, keeping a sharp look-out for any trespassers. She stayed in sight of the house. She held her phone up toward the cloud-covered sky until a bar popped up on her reception grid.

Missed call. Jenna?

Her heart thudded as she pushed one to access her voice mail. It was Liam asking if he could bring ice cream to go along with the huckleberry pie for their dinner date. His voice comforted her like a warm quilt.

She pushed her speed button for Jenna's house phone. David answered.

"It's Sarah. Sorry to bother you, but how's Jenna doing?"

"The doctor's said she's doing as well as can be expected. I'm starting to hate that phrase." David let out a rueful laugh.

"I can understand. I'm just relieved she's doing fine. I was a little worried since the last time I talked to Jenna, the doctor called her."

"He said that if it became necessary he could induce labor, but we're not there yet. They'll reassess next week if the baby doesn't arrive before then. They're thinking now that the ultrasound may have been a little off and this is just a big baby."

"Was Jenna relieved?"

"She'd have them start labor now if she could have her way and the baby was safe. She can't get comfortable," David said raising his voice above the sound of boys yelling.

"How are the boys doing?" Sarah asked with smile.

"It's after bedtime so of course they're full of energy and running all over," David said, a smile in his voice. "They can't wait to see their grandma."

"Well, I can't wait to see them," Sarah said. "They look like they're getting so big in their photos."

"Yeah, they're growing fast, and I'm starting to wonder how I'm going to feed these bottomless pits when they get to be teenagers."

"Keep lots of bread in the house," Sarah said. "Worked for Jason. He could polish off a loaf after school and not lose any of his appetite for supper."

"I'll keep that in mind," David said with a laugh. "Jenna went to bed early. I think she's asleep, but I can check to see if she's still awake if you want."

"No, let her rest. Can you tell her in the morning that I love her and am thinking about her?"

"Will do. And I'll give the boys a hug for you too," David said.

"Thanks, David," Sarah closed her phone and turned back to the house. At least Jenna must be relieved to know that the baby seems fine and there may be an option next week.

Sarah still wasn't sleepy and she wished she had the baby quilt to work on. She passed the barn and stopped, staring at the doors. She glanced up at the house. The windows were dark. Curiosity got the best of her. What would it hurt for her to take another look at the painted planks in the barn?

She crossed to the barn and pulled on the latch to slide the tall door back. The door was heavier than she had anticipated, so she settled for wedging her body through the crack. She stepped into blackness, listening. The horses moved in their stalls, but there were no other sounds. She pulled her phone out of her pocket and used the screen light to find her way.

Nell nickered softly as she passed the stall.

"It's okay," Sarah said softly. A hoof hit the stall wall. "Easy." Sarah pressed the cell phone against her leg to shadow the glow until the rustling noises eased. She cautiously stepped toward the back wall and bumped into the straw bale. She inhaled dust and sneezed. The horse shifted in the stall again.

"Sorry." She felt her way to the back of the stack. She tugged the board out to the end of the stack so she could examine it more easily. It was about four feet by four feet and made up of several planks. The design appeared to be a variation of an Evening Star with a unique design painted in the middle. Slightly different from the one upstairs but familiar in the details.

She wished she could use the phone to take a photo, but the flash might scare the horse even more. Maybe she could get the block outside. She pulled on the board again and it slid along the ground. Tugging harder with both hands, she made it out the door and leaned the board against the barn wall. Fishing her cell out of her back pocket, she took aim and got several shots.

The flash blurred the details some, but at least she could make out most of the block design. She tucked her phone away and pulled the board back inside the barn door.

"Sarah Hart!" a deep voice said. Sarah jerked as light from a lantern revealed her. Abram stood in the doorway clad in nightshirt and slacks. His feet were bare. The horses neighed and hooves banged against the stall walls again.

"Calm yourselves," Abram said to the horses. "Easy, easy." The rustling stopped. He turned back to Sarah. "What are you doing in here?"

Sarah put her hand on her chest and tried to recapture the air that had escaped her lungs. "I...um..."

Abram's lantern shifted to the board that had dropped against the stall. A strangling sound gurgled in his throat.

He lunged forward and snatched it up into his strong arms. He walked to the barn door and out into the night.

Sarah ran after him. He was heading to a burn pile, judging by the blackened rock and earth. Abram set his lantern on the ground, lifted the planks over his head and smashed them down on a boulder, splintering the wood into pieces.

Sarah gasped. How could he destroy something so beautiful? Something his daughter had made?

He picked up the large pieces and stomped on them until they broke. Sarah backed toward the house. When he turned to her, his chest heaved and his face glistened in the reflected light of the lantern. He wiped his forehead as he glared at her. "I know what you are doing here. I want you to stop."

"You mean you want me to stop looking for Katie? But why? Don't you want to know she's okay?"

"She is in God's hands."

"You mean she's …" Cold dread squeezed her heart. Did he mean Katie was dead?

"Katie chose her way. Do not meddle in things you can't understand."

"I'm trying to understand. As a mother, I can at least empathize with what your wife is going through."

"Leave in the morning and do not bother us again." He turned on his heel and disappeared into the night.

Sarah climbed the porch steps with shaky knees and went up the stairs. She dropped her phone into her purse and sat on the bed. A soft knock sounded on the door and the handle turned. Martha poked her head in.

"What's wrong?" she whispered.

"I went downstairs to phone Jenna."

"Is she okay? You were gone a long time."

Sarah nodded. "Jenna's fine. I was in the barn. Come on in." She explained to Martha about the quilt block painted on the wood and Abram smashing it.

Martha clutched Sarah's arm. "How sad. Do you think Abram's mad at you? Should we leave now?"

"No. He didn't threaten me. Just told us to leave in the morning and not bother them again."

Martha relaxed her grip. "I suppose I can understand his not wanting to talk about Katie because of the shunning, but what's with the painted board?"

"It's connected to the problem in some way. I just need to figure out how."

CHAPTER SEVEN

Sarah woke at dawn with gritty eyes and a headache. She had been plagued by bad dreams and a feeling of loss even though Martha had spent the night in Katie's room with her. They had talked for a while in the dark, just as they had as school kids, until they both drifted off to sleep.

Sarah stared at the ceiling, listening to Martha's even breathing. In the light of day, the incident with Abram didn't seem as ominous. Obviously Katie's absence must be upsetting Abram. But did he have something more to do with it? Did he know where she was? If so, why didn't he help Annie out of her misery? She would have some peace if she knew Katie was fine.

Pans clanged downstairs. Annie must in the kitchen. Maybe she could talk to her alone before they had to leave. She slipped out of bed and dressed as quietly as possible.

"Good morning, Sarah Hart," Annie said as Sarah entered the kitchen. "I hope I did not wake you making noise.

I was setting the cinnamon rolls out to rise and knocked some pots off the counter."

"Oh no, I was awake already. Martha's still asleep." Sarah joined Annie at the counter. "Can we talk about your daughter?"

Footsteps sounded on the wood floor and Abram came in from the living room. He glanced at Sarah, his expression stoic, and sat on a kitchen chair. Annie turned to her husband "You are done with chores already?"

"*Ja*, got an early start."

"The rolls still need more time. I will make scrambled eggs and potatoes, unless you would like something else." Annie looked at Sarah. "I can make pancakes."

"Eggs and potatoes will be great," Sarah said, turning her back to Abram. "Can I help with something? Peel the potatoes?"

Sarah peeled the potatoes and cut them into tiny chunks while Annie stoked the stove and started coffee. Abram had brought in a ledger book and was making notes in the columns.

Martha came into the kitchen. "Sorry I overslept." She shot a small grimace at Sarah. They would both still be in bed if they were in Maple Hill.

Annie shoved the tray of cinnamon rolls into the oven. "Breakfast will be ready in thirty minutes. I will go see if there are more eggs in the chicken coop."

"Mind if I tag along?" Sarah asked. "The girls had such fun gathering eggs."

Abram cleared his throat. "I already attended to the chickens. The eggs are in the refrigerator."

Annie shot a puzzled look at her husband. She opened the refrigerator door and took out a bowl of eggs. "Thank you, Abram."

"Since we have a little time, I think I'll freshen up and pack my bag," Martha said.

"I was hoping after breakfast we could do a bit of quilting before you go," Annie said.

Abram looked up from his accounting. "Have you forgotten that Mrs. Stoltz is in need of assistance with her children this morning?"

"*Ja*, I remember, Abram, but I do not have to be there until ten o'clock."

"I need the buggy this morning. I have to take a harness over to the Yoders and then go to the hardware store. I will take you to Mrs. Stoltz's on the way."

Annie stared at her husband for a few moments and then turned to Sarah and Martha. "I am sorry. There will not be time this morning. Will you be in Pleasant Valley later today?"

"No, we'll be heading home. It would've been fun. Maybe some other time." Sarah met Abram's steady gaze before following Martha up the stairs.

When they reached the room, Martha said, "Abram seems to be sticking to Annie like a bee to honey."

"He wants to make sure we don't get a chance to talk to her privately about Katie." Sarah grabbed her brush and ran it through her hair again before tucking it in her cosmetics bag.

"Is he protecting her or himself?" Martha asked.

"Probably both."

Sarah smoothed Katie's quilt on the bed and took photos with her phone. What was Katie thinking when she sewed this quilt? What was she feeling? And what about the painted quilt square Abram had destroyed last night? Had that been Katie's creation too? Sarah lined up the camera lens on the center square again and took several shots, hoping to get at least one that didn't blur.

"Did you get a good shot?" Martha asked from the doorway.

"I hope so. I need to be able to study Katie's quilt at home if Abram remains adamant that I stay away from Annie."

"Are you going to tell Annie what Abram said last night?"

"It'd probably just upset her and not accomplish anything right now. Besides, I don't think I'll get a chance to talk to her privately." Sarah certainly did not want to make the situation worse for Annie. She had already said yesterday that she had doubts now about asking Sarah to find Katie. But was she speaking out of guilt? Or had she really changed her mind?

Sarah picked up her devotion book and pushed it into the overnight bag.

Lord, I don't know what to do. Please guide me on how to help Annie and Katie.

The sun broke through the clouds, making Sarah squint against the dazzling wet landscape. She put her bag in the trunk and waited for Martha to bring her suitcase.

Breakfast had been pleasant on the surface, but the underlying tension radiating from Abram swelled as time passed until Sarah announced they needed to head home.

"Thank you for letting us stay over." Martha gave Annie a hug. "I will always remember this."

"Thank you too," Martha said to Abram who worked nearby with a hoe on the planters by the house.

Annie handed Martha a jar of jam. "It was nice to meet you. I hope we can visit again someday."

Annie returned to the porch, picked up a bundle of fabric and approached Sarah with a shy smile. "This is a sampler quilt I sewed when I was about seventeen."

"Annie, this is so sweet of you, but I can't take something so special," Sarah protested. This was something Annie should save for Katie.

"Please. I want you to have it." She placed the folded blanket in Sarah's hands. Something crinkled underneath the cloth, and Sarah hugged the bundle tighter. Annie stepped back and folded her arms over her chest. "Just remember

I was very young when I made that quilt and my stitches have improved over time."

Sarah looked at the neat, even stitching on the quilt. "You were an amazing sewer then as you are now." Sarah placed the quilt on the backseat and pulled out the gloves she had originally intended to give to Jenna. "Here, I want you to have something too. I didn't make these like your gift to me, but they came from the alpaca farm."

"They are so soft," Annie said, turning the gloves over and then rubbing them against her cheek. "I have wanted to try the alpaca wool. Thank you very much."

Sarah opened the car door and paused. "I might be heading out to Sunnyvale one of these days. Any Amish fabric or craft stores over there?"

Annie furrowed her brow at the strange question. "I do not think there are any Amish families near Sunnyvale. Do you, Abram?" she called over to him.

He dug his hoe deeper into the earth. "I have never visited anyone there."

"Well, thanks again for everything." Sarah smiled at Annie, wishing she could say more. Comfort her somehow with a promise she would still try to find Katie. She joined Martha in the car, and they headed toward town.

"Abram didn't exactly answer Annie's question," Martha observed after they had gone a couple of miles. "He just said that he had never visited anyone there."

"I noticed that too. Maybe Katie is in Sunnyvale after all," Sarah said as they drove through the downtown. But who would she be staying with? Where would a seventeen-year-old go?

"Do you mind if we stop at the art school?" Sarah asked. "Maybe Rachel knows of someone from that area who Katie could've hooked up with."

"Go for it. We have nothing to fear but fear itself," Martha said.

Sarah shot her a sideways glance.

Martha grinned. "Yup, that was the quote for today." They drove into the high school parking lot, which was jammed with cars since school was in full session. Sarah parked along the ball field in an unmarked spot hoping they would be quick enough that no one would notice.

The art room was empty, but a light shone from Rachel's small office. A young woman sat behind the desk. The red pencil she clutched in her hand matched the red feathers in her blonde hair. She stopped snapping her gum and adjusted her black glasses when she noticed Sarah in the doorway. "Yes?"

"I'm looking for Rachel Jackson."

"Rachel's at an art conference in Syracuse. I'm Charity, her TA." She raised her thinly plucked eyebrows. "Can I help you?"

"I'm Sarah Hart and this is Martha Maplethorpe. I spoke with Rachel about a former student here, Katie Fisher. We're trying to locate her. Do you know her?"

"Yeah, I knew Katie. Bummer there," the teaching assistant said.

"Did something bad happen?" Sarah asked.

"Depends on how you look at it. Rachel was working on getting Katie scholarships for some college-level classes. I told Rachel it was a waste of time. Katie's parents would never let her go."

"But if she had a scholarship, then she wouldn't need their permission, would she? At least not after she turned eighteen," Sarah said.

"She wasn't eighteen then, and without her parents' signatures on the applications, Rachel was having a difficult time getting any kind of financial aid."

"So you're saying Katie wanted to go away to school?" Martha asked, leaning against the doorjamb.

Charity shrugged. "Not sure if it was more Rachel's idea, but yeah."

"Where do you think she is?"

"I came in here one time, and Katie was crying and talking to one of the girls. If she didn't quit school, her father had threatened to send her away to relatives in an Ohio community."

"Why Ohio?" Martha asked.

"She said that the community there was even stricter than the one here, if you can imagine that. I just assumed that's where she ended up. Sorry I can't help you. I'll let Rachel know you stopped by."

"Thanks." Sarah turned to leave but then paused in the doorway.

"Would you happen to know the phone number of Katie's friend Kevin? He was a student here too."

"Kevin Sanders? Nope. He graduated, and I heard he left for college. Don't know which one."

"We need gas," Sarah said as they reached the outskirts of town. Her light had yet to go on, but the needle was getting precariously close to the red E.

Sarah was feeling down from their visit with Charity, although she had managed to get Kevin's last name. Had Abram sent Katie away but didn't tell Annie? It didn't feel right to her. And besides, if Katie was in Ohio, why would they have shunned her?

Martha pointed at a sign coming up on the right. "How about that one? It looks like it has a store with it."

Sarah turned the car into the station. The sign hanging over the building indicated the adjacent store was Lydia's Crafts. Martha went inside while Sarah filled the tank.

"Wash your windows?" a teenage boy asked. He was dressed sloppily in torn jeans and a greasy green shirt. Earphones hung around his neck and Sarah could hear the faint beat of rap music.

"Sure," Sarah said and gave him a tip when he finished. Martha was still inside so she moved the car closer to the door.

She went inside to pay and discovered Martha talking to a plump, middle-aged woman by the counter. Lots of bright red hair curled about her round, heavily made-up face. Martha smiled at Sarah as she approached. "Lydia was just telling me that she knows the Fishers."

The woman smiled and a gold cap on a bottom tooth winked at Sarah. "I know just about everyone around here. The pros and cons of living in a small rural community."

"Lydia says that Katie even sold a few art pieces in here," Martha said.

"Yep. I still have one left. Here, I'll show you." Lydia walked over to a glass shelf. "This is it." She pointed to a small watercolor of an Amish house, with a horse and plow in a nearby field. The washed texture of her brush strokes gave it an almost impressionist feel.

"She also had some clay tiles that sold well," Lydia said.

Sarah turned over the price tag on the painting. Fifty dollars. Not a lot for an original watercolor as good as this one, but it must've seemed a fortune to a teenager.

"I'm not surprised she didn't stick around," Lydia said. "She had a lot of talent. I couldn't keep her art in the store once Dean saw it."

"Dean?" Martha asked.

"Dean Warner Art Studios in New York City. Dean used to come by every six weeks or so looking for art. The Amish stuff sells well."

"Did Katie ever meet Mr. Warner?" Sarah asked.

"A couple of times here at the store. He's a handsome thing. A real charmer. Helps if you want to be successful in sales. I wouldn't be surprised if Katie didn't take him up on his scholarship offer to study art."

"Scholarship?"

"Oh, sure. Dean's a good guy and was always doing something kind like that. He has a small art school and studio. Very respected among the art crowd in the city. She would've been nuts not to take him up on it."

"Has he been in recently? Does he know if Katie's in New York?" Sarah said, feeling a little breathless.

"Didn't occur to me until later. He started coming around less after Katie left and I haven't seen him in about a year. I didn't even realize Katie had moved until I tried to call her about more stuff to sell." Lydia walked back to the cash register. "I just put two and two together. Did you find what you needed?" she asked Martha.

"I'm going to get a calendar and this soda," Martha said. Lydia rang up her purchases while Sarah looked about the store in a daze. Maybe Katie wasn't in Ohio as Charity had suggested. She could be in New York City at Dean Warner's school.

Sarah spied a basket of knitted booties and picked a cute pair for the new baby. And after a moment of hesitation, she grabbed Katie's painting and took both it and the booties to the counter.

"I'll wait for you outside," Martha said heading for the door.

"I'm kind of sad seeing the last of Katie's paintings go." Lydia added the cost of the painting and booties to Sarah's gas total.

"What's the best way to contact Dean Warner?" Sarah asked.

"He has a Web site. I think I have one of his business cards here someplace." Lydia pulled open a drawer and rummaged through it. Through the glass door, Sarah could see Martha talking to the teenager who had washed her car windows.

"Here you go." Lydia gave the card to Sarah. "Tell Dean 'hello' from Lydia White if you do talk to him and tell him to come around. I have some new stock to show him."

"I will." Sarah dropped the card into her purse and as she dragged her wallet out her fingers brushed her phone. She wondered if the photos she had snapped last night in the barn would come out.

Sarah handed a credit card to Lydia. "Did Katie ever do any painting on wood?"

"Not that I saw." Lydia ran the card through the reader and punched in numbers. "Why?"

"I saw something at the Fisher farm that—"

The screech of air brakes outside drew their attention. A tourist bus rolled to a stop. The doors swung open and people started descending the steps.

"This place is going to be swamped." Lydia placed the credit slip on the counter and handed Sarah a pen. "If you get a chance, let me know if you ever see Katie. I miss the girl."

Sarah quickly signed her name and bid Lydia good-bye. She squeezed past the crowd flowing inside the shop and hurried out to the car. Martha leaned against the trunk still talking to the young teenager.

"Sorry it took me so long," Sarah said reaching in her pocket for keys.

"No problem. I thought maybe Lydia would talk more freely with you one to one. Besides, Jesse and I were having a nice chat. Jesse knows Katie Fisher too," Martha said as Sarah unlocked the door.

"Well, I don't *know* her exactly, but I saw her around." Jesse adjusted the earphones on his neck. "The last time I saw her she was riding in a pickup with a dude."

Sarah nearly dropped her keys. "Do you know the dude?"

"Nope," he said, watching the people milling around the bus.

"What did he look like?"

He shrugged. "Didn't get a good look. I'd seen the truck around before. But it was a long time ago."

"And you're sure it was Katie Fisher?"

"Yeah."

"Did it look like she was in trouble?"

He squinted at Sarah. "Huh?"

"Like, was she scared?" Sarah asked.

"No way. She was laughing. I remember because I'd never seen her crack a smile before," Jesse said, his attention on a car rolling up to the pumps. "Gotta go."

"Here, take my business card. Please call if you see Katie again." Sarah passed him her card.

He looked at the card as if not sure what to do with it, and then crumpled it into his jeans pocket as he trotted to the pumps.

Sarah and Martha buckled up, and Sarah rolled the car onto the country highway. Since it was a Friday afternoon, a steady stream of cars was heading into town.

Martha picked up her crocheting. "So who do you think Katie was with in the truck? The Amish don't drive. Do you think it could've been that friend Katie met at art school?"

"Kevin? Possibly," Sarah said. "Though Lydia mentioned she wouldn't be surprised if Katie had taken an offer of a scholarship to study art in New York City. Dean Warner Art Studios."

"Oh, that worries me. Sweet, innocent girl in New York without her parents. People might take advantage of her," Martha said with shiver. "If she's there, I hope she has someone looking after her."

Sarah hoped so too. Although Lydia seemed to think Dean Warner was a great guy, she was going to get more information about him when she got home. "Charity also mentioned that Rachel wanted to help Katie get scholarships. Maybe Rachel helped Katie go to college so she could take more classes."

"Then why didn't Rachel just tell you that?"

"Maybe she worries Abram will find out and send Katie to relatives in Ohio anyway. Or he could have found out about the plans and sent her away before she could go to college."

"But then why the big secret? Why wouldn't he tell his wife or anyone else?" Martha asked, echoing Sarah's earlier thoughts.

"Good point." Sarah sighed. "This is all really puzzling. It isn't helping that Abram and most of the others in the community won't discuss it. Now even Annie is withdrawing."

They drove in silence for a while. Martha finished a row on the poncho and flipped the project over. "Did you get the impression that Annie might be afraid of Abram?"

Sarah glanced at her. "Like how?"

"I don't know," Martha looped her yarn over and started the needle down the next row. "Something seemed off."

"She was more subdued with him around," Sarah said. "Part of it may just be the culture. But ... he did lose his temper last night at the barn. You should've seen him smash the boards."

"Maybe Abram lost his temper with Katie and frightened her off," Martha speculated.

"I suppose anything is possible at this point."

Martha looked at Sarah. "You're going to keep searching for her despite Annie's doubts?"

Sarah nodded.

"That's what I thought. I want to help if I can."

"Thanks," Sarah said with a smile for her best friend.

Down near the floor, Sarah's phone gave out a beep.

"Want me to check it?" Martha asked.

"Please. It might be Jenna."

Martha set her crocheting in her lap and reached into Sarah's purse to get the cell phone. She held it up. "It's a text from Jenna."

Sarah gripped the steering wheel harder. Was the baby coming? "Go ahead and read it."

"Some contractions early this morning but baby a no-show. He/she is stubborn. Love you." Martha paused and then asked, "Want me to text her back?"

"Sure." Sarah let out a deep breath. "Tell her I love her too, and I'll talk to her soon."

Martha punched in the letters with her thumbs. "I'm so slow at this. You should see Lexie on her cell phone. She can type about as fast as she can talk. I guess you have to be a teenager to master these things."

"Audrey and Amy are pretty quick too." Sarah smiled. "Considering we're grandmothers, I think we do rather well."

"Yeah, we stay informed. We stay hip," Martha quipped.

Sarah laughed. "Do people still use the word 'hip'?"

"Oh, who knows?" Martha grinned. "But it sounded good."

"Hey, I'm impressed," Sarah teased.

They laughed and joked the rest of the way home, talking about old times and adventures. By the time Sarah dropped Martha off, she was feeling more lighthearted than she had in days. Her longtime best friend had that effect on her.

She tucked her packages and Annie's quilt under her arm and grabbed her suitcase. She unlocked her front door, and as she stepped inside, the quilt shifted under her arm. Something cascaded to the floor in a series of soft plops.

Sarah stepped back and stared at the envelopes. She picked one up. It was a letter addressed to Katie Fisher.

CHAPTER EIGHT

Sarah placed a container of frozen bowtie pasta and pesto sauce into the microwave and went back to the kitchen table where she had piled the letters. She reread Annie's note.

Dear Sarah,

I am giving you Katie's diary and letters from her friends and cousins with the hope you will find something useful in your search or at least come to know my daughter better through her friends. If it is not God's will that I find Katie, I will accept that. But if you are my answer to prayer and God brought you to me, I will trust that He will guide your way. Soon I will confess my actions to the bishop and my husband and ask for forgiveness.

> *God bless you and thank you,*
> *Annie Fisher*

Despite Annie being conflicted about her desire to obey the shunning, she was still leaving the door open for Sarah to continue to investigate. It must have been hard for Annie to part with Katie's things, and Sarah would make sure she returned the items even if Annie couldn't talk to her in the future.

Sarah set the note down on the table and picked up an envelope from Ruth Fisher, with an address in Ohio. Was this the stricter community that Abram wanted to send Katie to?

She examined the other envelopes. Most of the letters were from Ruth Fisher, but there were a few from Esther Yoder and Mary Grace Chupp. All were from the same town. She skimmed some of the letters before sorting them into piles by sender. All the letters appeared to be from girls around Katie's age.

The microwave dinged, and she got up to stir the pasta before putting it back in for another two minutes. Sarah toasted two slices of sourdough bread and poured the pesto pasta into a bowl. She placed everything on a tray and grabbed the diary before heading to the front porch. The sun was just starting to set and the air was crisp but not overly chilly. She buttoned up her sweater and settled in her rocking chair.

As she ate she read some pages from the diary. The black-and-white composition notebook dated back four years, and the beginning entries chronicled Katie's daily activities. Katie wrote of canning with her mother, working on her quilts, and wondering who would be at the singing Sunday night. Sarah flipped through the pages until she came upon an entry about starting art classes.

My dream has come true. Father has let me attend art classes at the high school as long as I do not fall behind on my chores and do not spend too much time with the Englishers. *I do not know what he is worried about since this is* Rumspringa. *S. is dressing in Englisher clothes when she is out at night and I heard D. tasted beer. Just because some have left the church doesn't mean I will. I am just learning how to draw better. I wish he would not worry so much. I am not going anywhere.*

Sarah gazed at the western horizon as the sun, a fiery orange ball, dipped behind the distant houses. Apparently Abram had had a right to worry, considering how things had turned out.

She read through the next couple of pages. Katie wrote about her art projects and how K. and M., whom Sarah assumed were Kevin and Madison, made her laugh. Sarah also noted Katie had started referring to people by first initials at this time. Was that just for convenience or was she hiding something from her parents?

I do not know what to do. Father is putting pressure on me to quit classes and work at home so I will be ready to get married. K. says that I should do the things I want to do first. Explore the world. That is what he wants to do.

Did Katie have a crush on Kevin Sanders after all? Could she have run off with him? He could have lied about not knowing where Katie was. He had no reason to trust Sarah. She read on.

A man from New York City is interested in buying my work, maybe others will be too. My father should be pleased that I have skills that can contribute money to the family.

Sarah flipped to the last few pages of the diary. The entries became sporadic, and the last one was dated about a year and a half ago, right before she left.

I do not know what to do. I love him. I love my art. I do not know how to choose. I pray and God does not answer.

Katie *was* in love. Was it with the person she referred to as K? She remembered how Kevin had referred to Katie as K in his e-mail. Maybe Abram had discovered she was in love with an *Englisher* and was going to send her to relatives. And then Katie ran away? Jesse at the gas station said she had been in a truck with a dude. But which dude?

Dusk crept up the lawn and onto the porch. The dampness in the air seeped through Sarah's sweater. She shivered as she picked up the tray and went back inside to her warm, cozy kitchen. She set the diary by the letters and put her dishes in the dishwasher. She was in the middle of wiping the counter when the phone rang.

"Sarah, you're home," Maggie said. "I didn't know whether you and Martha were going to be gone one night or two."

"Just one, but we did a lot," Sarah said and told Maggie about their shopping. "Martha was thrilled that we went to an alpaca farm. She came home with lots of yarn."

"That sounds like fun. The girls are still talking about their trip," Maggie said, a wistful note in her voice. "I've heard of a couple of interesting antique stores in Pleasant Valley."

"We should go together sometime. It's only two hours away. You might find some bargains for the store."

"We'll plan on it then. Just let me know when it's a good time for you," Maggie said. "Anyway, I was calling to see if you wanted to come over for Sunday lunch. Afterward, we were thinking of taking Leland for a drive, if he's up to it."

"That sounds like fun. Count me in if I'm not in Texas yet. I'm sure Leland will enjoy getting out and about," Sarah said. Leland Montgomery Mercer II lived in Bradford Manor. He had known Sarah's late father William from school and now had no family left. He was a grouchy old man, but he had a good heart. The Harts had made a special place for him in their family when William passed away, and although Leland didn't want to admit it, he sincerely needed and appreciated the attention the family gave him.

"Any news from Jenna?" Maggie asked.

"Only that the baby is being stubborn. If he or she doesn't make an appearance by next week, the doctor might induce labor."

"I hope she doesn't have to wait that long. Those last few days can be hard," Maggie said. "The girls are excited about having a new niece or nephew. I hope we can get down there to visit sometime this year."

"Jenna would love to see you all," Sarah said.

"I hope so," Maggie said with a laugh. "Jason still loves to tease her."

"And Jenna still tries to needle him every chance she gets." Sarah smiled, knowing the tormenting masked a deep and lasting bond between the two siblings.

"Well, I should go and make sure the girls have finished their homework and are getting ready for bed. Audrey was groaning about having to do a project from their Amish trip."

"I'll see you Sunday, if not before," Sarah said. "Oh, one question. Have you ever heard of Dean Warner Art Studios? It's based in New York City."

"Not that I recall," Maggie said. "I can check at work if they ever sent me any flyers or brochures."

"Thanks, but only if you have time. The owner of the studio was buying up art made by the daughter of the Amish family we stayed with, and I want to check him out. I'll look up his Web site."

Sarah finished cleaning the kitchen and then went to her desk and turned on her laptop. She gazed longingly at the strips of fabric stacked on the cutting mat and promised herself she would start sewing after she did a little research.

Warner Art Studios had an elaborate Web site. The home page featured new artists and announced an upcoming show. They carried a variety of artwork, unlike some galleries that liked to specialize.

Sarah studied the Americana art pages and spied some paintings that looked similar to the one she had bought at Lydia's.

She found the paper bag from Lydia's and unwrapped Katie's small painting. Sarah's art education consisted of only art appreciation class in college, but the years of making and restoring quilts had given her an eye for detail and color. The brush strokes and the way the artist applied color were similar in all the paintings. The paintings on the Web site looked to be of superior quality. If they were Katie's, she had become more skilled since painting Sarah's watercolor. No name was given for the artist, just a note to call if interested.

It was after business hours and too late to call the studio or the cell number on Dean Warner's business card. She would have to wait until the morning.

Now that she had Kevin's last name she did a search on "Sanders" and found a listing for Pleasant Valley. She got out her notebook and jotted down the number. She had all her newly gleaned information about Katie to add to the pages and the letters to read, but she would save that for morning too. She wanted to work on the baby quilt.

She turned on one of her favorite CDs and filled her office with uplifting worship music. Humming along with the songs, she pulled out her sewing machine and began sewing the strips together in groups of ten. As the pile grew, a feeling of calm slowly replaced the sense of urgency she had felt about finding Katie.

Tomorrow evening Liam was coming over for supper and on Sunday she would spend time with her family. It was going to be a great weekend. And any time now she would have a new grandchild. She had a lot to be thankful for.

She turned out the lights and picked up Katie's letters and the diary. She climbed the stairs to bed humming "Showers of Blessings."

Sarah awoke early Saturday morning to a world engulfed in thick fog. She padded downstairs to the kitchen and made coffee, then carried the mug back upstairs and crawled under her quilt. After plumping up the pillows against the headboard of her sleigh bed, she relaxed to enjoy her coffee while finishing Katie's letters.

They often contained reactions to things Katie must have written earlier. The girls were typical teenagers exchanging information about what the other kids were up to. The only difference from modern girls who might talk about the latest music gadgets, cars, fashion, and movies was that the letter writers referred to making quilts, going to singings, and long buggy rides with Amish gentlemen.

Sarah enjoyed the chatty letters but found nothing useful until she came across a letter from Ruth Fisher that was dated two years earlier.

I overheard Mother talking about you with Father on the porch. They did not know I was sitting behind the big oak tree in the front yard. Mother said that people were talking about you and that your parents were worried you were straying too far. And that there was an Englisher *boy you were friends with that they did not approve of. Is that true? I thought you were promised to someone. Don't worry. I have not told anyone. My mother also said that you might come here for a visit.*

I would love to see you. It has been a long time since you visited. I don't even know what you look like anymore. We will have fun. Rebecca's wedding is this fall.

The letter continued with talk about Ruth's sister's wedding plans and the food they would be preparing.

Sarah skimmed the next couple of letters. In the last one, Ruth had written that she was sorry Katie wasn't coming soon after all, and she hoped to convince her parents to let her visit Katie in Pleasant Valley.

Sarah sighed. So it did sound like Abram had been planning to send Katie to Ohio, but something had changed his mind. Or maybe she ran away before he could. Anyway, it explained why Annie hadn't mentioned that Katie could be with those relatives.

And who had Katie been promised to? Was that just girls' wishful talking?

Sarah drank her coffee, her finger tracing the pattern on her blue and green Log Cabin quilt as she rehashed the possibilities. When the mug was empty she got out of bed and chose some soft denim slacks and pulled a fuzzy gray sweater over a rose-colored short-sleeved shirt. The cozy feel of the sweater made her think of the alpaca gloves and the Friendship Quilt at Eva Miller's store. She wondered if Katie still quilted, which reminded her that the photo of the painted board was still on her phone.

She hurried downstairs and printed out the photos from her phone. They were quite dark, but she was able to compare the block from the barn to the center of Katie's quilt.

The patterns were very similar. Most likely Katie had done both.

After fixing scrambled eggs and toast, Sarah updated her notebook about what she had learned about Katie. She started a new page and wrote down clues to where Katie could have gone.

Sunnyvale-postmarked letter Eva received.

NYC to Dean Warner's art studios.

Ohio, in case Abram had sent her there after the letters from Ruth Fisher.

Somewhere with Kevin Sanders.

Somewhere else or with whomever she was "promised" to.

After some thought, she added,

Somewhere Rachel Jackson helped her to go. School?

Rachel Jackson seemed like a teacher who sincerely wanted what was best for her students. But had she crossed the line and actually assisted Katie in running away?

At ten o'clock Sarah set down her pencil and placed a call to New York City.

"Warner Art Studios. David speaking," a deep, male voice said.

"Hello, David. Is Dean Warner there?"

"May I ask what this is in regard to?"

"There's a painting on your Web site that I'm interested in."

"I can check on that for you if you'd like, Ms. …."

"Mrs. Hart."

"Which one are you referring to, Mrs. Hart?"

"It's on the Americana Art page. It looks like one a friend's daughter might've painted. Katie Fisher? Is she there by any chance?"

"I'll have to get Mr. Warner. Hold please."

Soft New-Age-type music filled her ear. She waited for so long she was starting to get a crick in her neck when the phone clicked.

"Mrs. Hart, this is Dean Warner," said a pleasant voice. "I'm sorry to keep you waiting. My assistant said you were interested in one of our paintings."

"Yes, I am if the artist is Katie Fisher."

"Yes, she is," he replied. "She was a minor when she did the paintings and it was requested we keep her name private."

"So these paintings aren't recent?"

"They are her latest. How do you know Katie?" His voice deepened.

"I know her parents. Katie left home over a year ago and her mother hasn't heard from her. I've been trying to locate her."

"Really? I'm sorry to hear that," Dean said. "I had assumed she got married as is the usual path of Amish women."

"I was in Lydia's Crafts yesterday. She said to say hello for her. She also mentioned that you had offered Katie a scholarship."

"That's correct. I offer scholarships to many promising young artists. I run a small art school which, by the way, is largely funded by grants and donations if you ever feel a need to support the arts. Katie has tremendous talent as you can see for yourself."

"What happened? Why did she turn it down?" When he didn't answer for a few moments, Sarah added. "I apologize for all the questions, but it's been so long since anyone at home has heard from her. It would really help if I had more information."

"Well, I guess it really doesn't matter at this point, but Katie said her father wouldn't allow it. She was underage at the time, but I hoped she'd change her mind when she turned eighteen. Like I said, I wasn't surprised considering she's Amish. It was just disappointing."

"Have you heard from her at all?"

"Sorry. I wish I could help."

"Thank you, Mr. Warner. If you do hear anything about Katie, could you please contact me?" Sarah rattled off her number. She set the phone down. Something was bugging her about the call.

She got her receipt from Lydia's Crafts out of her purse. Sure enough, the receipt identified the store and its phone number. She placed the call.

"Lydia's."

"Hi, Lydia, this is Sarah Hart. I was in your shop yesterday."

"Yes, you bought Katie's painting. Is there a problem with it?"

"Not at all. I just got off the phone with Dean Warner."

"How nice! How is he doing?"

"He seems fine. When did you say you last saw him?"

"About a year ago. Of course, he could've been in the area and just didn't stop by here since then."

"Did you ever talk about Katie running away?"

"I must've mentioned it, but I can't recall exactly what I said. The older one gets, the rustier the brain cells. I can't even remember where I leave my coffee cup half the time."

"I've experienced some of that," Sarah said with a smile. "How did Dean react when you told him about Katie leaving?"

"Took it in stride, though he was disappointed he wouldn't be able to get any more of her stuff."

"He acted surprised when I said she ran away."

"Maybe he forgot. It's been a while," Lydia said, but her tone sounded skeptical.

"He still has some of her paintings on his Web site," Sarah said. "I was wondering if they all came through your shop."

"I can check when I get a chance. Katie could've supplied him with the paintings on her own. I told him she was taking classes at the high school."

"Thanks, Lydia, for being patient with me and all my questions."

"No problem. I hope Katie turns up."

"One last question. What kind of car does Dean drive?"

"I don't know what make it is, but it's a real nice black pickup."

 CHAPTER NINE

S arah poked her fork in a mushroom and twirled it in the gravy of the beef Stroganoff, one of her mother's favorite recipes. She had also made garlic mashed potatoes and green beans with fennel.

It felt good to relax. She had spent her morning trying to find an address for Kevin Sanders and searching the Sunnyvale phone directory for anyone named Fisher. In the afternoon she had grocery shopped, cleaned house, and gotten ready for dinner with Liam.

She took another bite of Stroganoff and finished updating Liam on her trip and her efforts to find Katie. Liam had listened with avid interest.

Sarah thought he looked particularly handsome tonight seated at her kitchen table. His chambray dress shirt complemented his gray hair and green eyes. He had arrived with a pint of decadent vanilla ice cream in hand and a smile that warmed Sarah from the inside out like creamy hot cocoa.

Sarah had considered using the dining room, but tonight eating in the kitchen seemed to suit their comfortable relationship. Another spring storm was upon them. Rain dripped off the eaves and wind rattled the windowpanes, but the kitchen, with its cranberry walls and creamy cabinets, felt cozy and isolated from the rest of the world.

Liam took a sip of the peach cider Sarah had found at the market that afternoon. "So you think Katie may have gone off to New York City to study at Dean Warner's studio?"

"It's one possibility. He has a pickup truck and she was seen driving out of town in one."

"A lot of people have pickups. Including me!"

"I know." Sarah sighed. "Maybe it's silly, but I got the feeling he wasn't telling me everything he knew."

"I don't think it's silly," Liam said. "Your intuition has proven correct many times in the past."

Sarah smiled at him. Liam could be such a sweet and loyal friend. "Too bad it's not a hundred percent accurate."

Liam set his glass down. "So why did you think Dean was being evasive?"

"He acted surprised that Katie had run away, almost too surprised." Sarah's fork poised over a green bean. "But Lydia says she told him. And he didn't list Katie's name on the Web site. His excuse was that she was a minor."

"Sounds suspicious to me too." Liam leaned back in his chair.

"I wish I knew for sure. I wonder if I should go to the city and see if she's there. But with any luck I'll be leaving for Texas any day now."

"I might be able to help," Liam said. "I have a friend, Bernard Shaw, in Brooklyn who might be willing to check out the gallery."

"That would be great, but wouldn't it be a huge imposition on your friend?"

"Not for ol' Bernie. He's English and a huge Sherlock Holmes fan. He'd probably enjoy getting involved in a real-life mystery," Liam said with a smile. "What do you think? He could mosey on into the gallery and look around."

"It's worth a try," Sarah said. "Thank you, Liam."

"Anything to help. What other leads do you have?"

"I'm trying to find her friend, Kevin Sanders, the one who e-mailed me. I called the Pleasant Valley number I had for Sanders this morning, but it was disconnected with no forwarding number."

"Sanders sounds like a common name."

Sarah nodded. "It is. I ran a search on Kevin Sanders and over thirty numbers popped up. Only a couple were identified as being in their twenties, and I think Kevin could be even younger. I tried those but no luck. I don't know his parents' names."

Liam rubbed his chin with the back of his index finger. "You have his e-mail address though. Any way to tell from that?"

"Not that I know." Although maybe someone else would. She filed that spark of an idea in the back of her mind for later.

"I also checked out the town, Sunnyvale, where Katie mailed a letter to her friend Eva. No Fishers or Sanders there, but there was a bus terminal and a train station. Katie could've been passing through."

Sarah noticed that Liam's plate was empty and she pushed back from the table. "I've been doing so much talking, the time is flying by. Ready for pie?"

"I'm always ready for pie." Liam helped her clear the table while they waited for coffee to brew to go with the huckleberry pie and ice cream. Sarah brought out her laptop to show Liam the Warner Art Studios Web site and the page with the three paintings of Amish countryside. "Those are Katie's."

"The girl shows promise," Liam said. "I'll let Bernie know which ones are hers if he agrees to head on over there."

Sarah dished up the ice cream, and they took their plates and coffee into the living room. Liam had brought a DVD, an old mystery that he thought might be fun.

They settled back on the couch and had a great time trying to pick up clues and outguess the bungling detective. The movie was three quarters of the way though when Sarah's cell phone rang.

Her heart thumped. It was almost nine o'clock. She popped off the couch. "Sorry, I have to get that." Liam paused the movie while Sarah grabbed the phone.

The caller ID showed Jenna's cell phone number.

"Jenna?"

"No, I'm not in labor," Jenna said, "and everything's okay."

Sarah let out a shaky laugh. "Good to hear. The part about being okay, that is."

"Yeah, I know. I'm feeling pretty good tonight, but every-one is still tiptoeing around me. I guess I haven't been very pleasant to be around lately."

"I'm sure David and the kids understand." Sarah returned to the living room where Liam waited.

"Jenna, Can I call you back in a little—"

Liam stood and waved his hand. "No, you talk. I'll go."

"Hold on a sec." Sarah cupped her hand over the receiver. "You don't have to leave."

"I know, but I will. You need to talk with your daughter." Liam shrugged into his light jacket. "We can finish that movie later. My house next time, okay?"

Sarah smiled. "Thanks for being so accommodating."

"Anytime. Thanks for the great dinner and company." He leaned over and kissed her lightly on the cheek. "I'll talk to you tomorrow.

As Sarah walked him to the door, Jenna's voice could be heard rising from the phone. "Was that Liam's voice I heard? You're on a *date*, aren't you? I'll hang up. Call me later." The connection clicked off before Sarah could say anything.

She tapped in Jenna's number.

"That was quick," Jenna said when she answered.

"It's okay. Liam was just leaving."

"Oh man, why didn't you say something? I didn't want to interrupt your date."

Sarah chuckled. "It was just dinner and a video, and it was getting late anyway."

"I should've guessed you might be busy. Saturday night is still date night, right?" Jenna said with a sigh.

"I assume so." Sarah smiled at the thought. When Jason and Jenna still lived at home, Gerry would declare Saturday a date night and he would whisk Sarah out of the house. Sometimes it was dinner at the Old Mill; other dates were much more casual, like fast food and the hardware store, but it was the time alone together that counted. They hadn't gone out every week, but those moments provided bright spots in the mosaic of memories she had.

"I can hardly remember dating," Jenna said. "I feel like I've been married and pregnant for a hundred years. Not that I'm complaining. I have the best man in the whole world."

Sarah smiled. "David is pretty wonderful."

"Most of the time." Jenna laughed. "Are things getting more serious between you and Liam?"

"Define serious."

"Seems to me you've been going out with him more and more frequently."

"We enjoy each other's company."

"That's the way a relationship usually starts," Jenna teased. "Oh! Did I tell you the current names we've picked out for the baby?"

"As of when?" Sarah appreciated the change of direction in the conversation. She was still exploring how she felt about her growing relationship with Liam. He was a nice man and he made her laugh. They both had lost loves, so their feelings had grown from an emotional common ground.

"So what are they now?"

"Charlotte, if it's a girl or Hudson if it's a boy. What do you think?"

"Those are very nice," Sarah said, careful to sound neutral. Jenna had changed name choices at least five times over the last couple of months.

"Well, I still like Lily and Levi, but as a friend pointed out, there are a couple of kids with those names at church."

"You're going to run into that a lot. Turned out Jason became an extremely popular name, and when we named you Jenna we thought we'd chosen something more unique. But a few weeks after you were born, I heard a mother calling for a 'Jenna' at the park."

"That was probably Jenna Kudrow. She was a couple of grades ahead of me in school," Jenna said. "So . . . really, you're saying I should just go with whatever name I like the best, regardless."

"Sounds like a good plan to me."

"David said the same thing, but names are so important."

They discussed names for a while longer and the topic switched to Jenna's boys and what she had lined up for them for summer. Swimming lessons and soccer camp.

Sarah settled on the couch, and they talked until Jenna's voice started to drift away. They said good-night, and Jenna promised to let her know if anything changed with the baby.

Sarah leaned her head against the cushion. The scent of Liam's light cologne lingered, and the TV screen was still frozen on the movie scene. It had been such a pleasant evening.

Tomorrow was Sunday, and she was going to set her problems aside and enjoy a peaceful day with God and family.

She collected the plates and coffee cups to take to the kitchen. As she passed the answering machine she noticed the light blinking. She hadn't heard the phone ring. She glanced at the counter. The holder was empty. Where was the phone?

She looked around the kitchen and then remembered she had taken the house phone into her office when she had made calls earlier in the day. She pushed the button on the answering machine and Irene's voice said, "No luck on locating Katie Fisher, but I did find out some interesting things about Amish records that may help you. Call me back when you get a chance, and I'll explain."

Sarah's heart thumped as she wondered what Irene had found, but the kitchen clock indicated it was too late to call back. She would have to wait until tomorrow to call Irene. She grabbed her notebook and headed up the stairs.

"Grandma, catch!" Amy called. A blue Frisbee sailed across the Bradford Manor lawn. Sarah reached for it, but the disk bounced out her hands.

"Butterfingers," Leland commented from his lawn chair.

"Yes, that's me," Sarah said with a smile. She sent the Frisbee toward Audrey, but it winged off course, hitting a tree.

"Humph. Can't throw either. Didn't your father teach you how *not* to throw like a girl?"

"He tried but no such luck. I made up for it in other ways. Like cookies. He loved my cookies, just like you do," Sarah said as Leland reached for another oatmeal raisin.

"That's your fifth cookie, Leland," a stern female voice said behind them.

Leland yanked his hand back and his face flushed as he looked up at Tiffany Henderson, one of the nurses. "Nobody likes a spy."

"Just watching out for you as always." She pushed the plate of homemade cookies down the picnic table toward some other residents of Bradford Manor. "The doctor said not to overdo it with the sweets."

"What does he know? I'm so old it doesn't matter if I get fat now."

"Gaining more weight might make it harder for you to breathe, among other things." Tiffany patted him on the arm. "At least these are healthier than your usual chocolate chip."

"I'm sorry," Sarah said. "I didn't realize he needed to cut back on the sweets." She had gotten up early before church and baked cookies and brought a platter of cookies to share with the residents.

"No problem," Tiffany said. "He's only on a mild dietary restriction. He can still have cookies, just not too many. Four was pushing it."

"She hates me," Leland growled after the nurse walked away.

"She's just following orders."

"I'm sick and tired of having to depend on people to feed me, clothe me, and walk me. I can't have any privacy and now they're even counting how many cookies I eat. It's terrible growing old."

Sarah didn't know what to say. She would hate it too, but the reality was that Leland would never be able to live alone and care for himself again.

Maggie strolled up behind Leland. "Okay, I got it cleared. We can go for our drive now. Jason is bringing the car around." She waved at Amy and Audrey to come.

"You ready?" Sarah asked Leland and scooted his walker closer to him.

"Anything to get me out of here." With a groan he got to his feet. Maggie and Sarah got on each side of him in case he needed assistance. The girls trailed after them.

Jason parked Maggie's red Tahoe by the front door and helped Leland into the front passenger seat. Audrey and Amy scrambled into the rear seat. Sarah sat in the middle with Maggie. They had decided to take a drive into the nearby mountains and soon they were cruising on country roads.

"Any word from Jenna?" Maggie asked.

"I talked to her last night, and she seemed to be more relaxed," Sarah said. "She's been working on baby names again."

"I thought they had decided," Jason said.

"Now Charlotte and Hudson are in the running."

"I like Hudson," Amy said.

"Uh-uh," Audrey said. "Levi is much better."

"We don't even know yet if it will be a boy," Maggie interceded. "Besides, your aunt hasn't asked for your input. Aunt Jenna and Uncle David will pick the best name for the baby."

Audrey and Amy exchanged glances.

"In my day, the firstborn boy was usually named after the father," Leland said. "I was named after my father and my son was named after me."

"This is Jenna's third child," Sarah said.

"Not too late if they have a boy," Leland said, his voice growing more agitated. "It's important to be remembered by your children."

Maggie pressed her lips together and locked eyes with Jason in the rearview mirror. Leland had lost his son and daughter-in-law. There would be no grandchildren to carry on his memory.

"Friends can be as close as family," Sarah said with a sting in her throat. "But I'll mention the idea to Jenna if I get the chance."

Leland's shoulders relaxed against the seat. "Where are we going?"

"We thought we'd drive through the Berkshires since it's a nice day," Jason said. "Unless you'd like to go somewhere else. It's your choice."

Leland gazed out the window. "The mountains will be fine."

Sarah settled back in her seat as Jason, Maggie, and Leland discussed politics. Audrey was texting on her phone and Amy had her earphones plugged in, no doubt listening to a ball game while watching the scenery pass by.

The budding green of the forests and cascading waterfalls reminded her of the morning's sermon on time and renewal. Pastor John had pointed out that as spring brings fresh new life to the planet, people too can have a time of renewal. A chance to leave behind the things that have proved harmful or worthless and begin a new life. He had been talking mostly about spiritual renewal and how important it was to forgive and move on in a better way, but it could apply to all areas of one's life.

Sarah wondered if that was what Katie had wanted to do. Shed the past and start a new life. And if she had, did she have regrets? Did she want to go home again? But what kind of life would she have returning home after being shunned? Would she get the forgiveness and acceptance that she needed?

Jason turned onto the gravel road to Rainbow Lake. The Tahoe bumped over a few potholes as they climbed a rise. The deep blue of the mountain lake shimmered under the cloudless sky. Jason parked in the clearing with several other cars.

"Can we get out?" Amy asked.

"For a little while." Jason set the parking brake. He stepped outside and rounded the car to Leland's door.

"I'll stay here," Leland said. "I don't want to be a bother."

"You're not a bother. Just lean on me and we'll go down by the lake." Jason reached for his arm but then caught Sarah's eye. She gave a slight shake to her head, remembering what Leland had said earlier about having to rely on everyone.

Jason shrugged. "At least you have a great view of the lake from here. We won't go far."

The girls got out and ran down the bank to the lake's edge.

"Don't get your clothes wet," Maggie called.

"Ah, you're no fun," Jason teased, taking Maggie's hand. "Life's too short to worry about wet jeans. You'll regret it."

"You'll regret saying that when the car starts to smell like swamp again."

Sarah leaned against the car by the passenger door and inhaled the damp, pine-scented air. Amy tried skipping stones on the smooth glasslike lake and soon the rest of the family joined in. Cheers and laughter arose when Audrey managed to skip her rock five times.

"Why are you still here?" Leland asked. "Why aren't you with the rest of them skipping stones?"

"I thought I'd hang out with you. Besides, you said I throw like a girl," Sarah said in a teasing tone. "I might hit someone."

"Humph. I don't like you just standing here."

"If it bothers you so much, why don't we go over there and sit on the boulders in the shade? The ground's flat so you shouldn't have any trouble."

She went to the back of the car and brought around his walker, unfolding the metal supports as she walked. Leland muttered something about stubborn women but swung his legs out of the car. Sarah guided one foot to the footrest.

"Put your hand on the door and the other on the seat and just slide down."

"Need help?" Jason called, starting toward them.

Sarah waved. "Leland's got it." Wedged between the door and Sarah, Leland couldn't fall, and in one fluid movement he was standing on the ground.

"That wasn't hard," he said, sounding surprised.

Sarah placed his walker in front of him and they moved slowly to the edge of the parking lot where big boulders had been placed as a barrier to keep cars from the embankment. Several were flat and smooth on top, perfect to lounge on if one didn't mind a hard seat. Sarah led the way to a couple beside two tall pine trees.

Leland scooted back on the boulder and looked around. "I never thought I'd be someplace like this again."

"It's been a while since I've been up here too. It's pretty." Sarah surreptitiously studied Leland. His face was flushed and his breathing a little rough, but his eyes were bright as he surveyed his surroundings. He seemed fine, and she relaxed, enjoying the spring sunshine and the sound of the breeze in the tree.

She wondered what Liam was doing at this moment. She had invited him along, but he had mentioned a visit with his daughter today. Sarah adored Caitlin. She had gotten to know her a lot better when she had helped Caitlin connect with a long-lost aunt. Sarah made a mental note to give her a call soon to catch up.

"Do *you* have regrets?" Leland's voice startled Sarah out of her musing.

"About not wading in the lake?" Sarah asked, referring to Jason and Maggie's conversation.

"No, I mean real regrets. Things you wish you could do over."

"I think most people have some regrets. Life is just that way," Sarah said as Jason and Maggie shed their shoes and rolled up their jeans, so they could wade out farther with the girls.

"I'm asking *you*."

Sarah sighed. "Yes, I have a few."

"Like what?"

Sarah thought for a moment. What was Leland really asking?

"Well, I suppose I regret not telling my mother I loved her more when I was young. She knew, but I didn't say it enough. I regret that Gerry and I never got to travel more."

Leland continued to stare at her as if he expected more, so she continued, "Sometimes I wish I had spent more days like this. Days where we just relaxed and enjoyed being together. We were just so busy with raising kids, work, and church duties. Always thought there was more time. Then the kids were grown and Gerry got sick." Sarah placed her hand on Leland's arm. "Don't get me wrong. We had a wonderful life, and I'm so thankful for what I have now, but you asked what I might've done or wanted differently. It's not the same thing as true regret."

Leland turned to stare out at the water.

"Why are you asking, Leland? Are you having regrets?"

"Humph."

"You're the one who asked," Sarah said gently. "Regret can eat people up inside."

"It is what it is." His shoulders slumped. "Can't change things now."

"Fretting about something won't help either," Sarah said. "You might feel better if you talked to someone, like your doctor or pastor."

Leland's eyes narrowed as he looked at her. "I don't want to talk to anyone there. They'll write notes in my chart and talk about me in their meetings as if I were something to study. I'm talking to you."

"I'll listen, Leland, anytime you need me and pray with you if you want me to, but consider what I said about talking to someone trained to help in these types of situations. They can keep it strictly confidential if you want them to."

He shrugged and turned his attention back to the water. Apparently he was through talking at the moment, not that he had said much. She sent a prayer heavenward asking God to give Leland peace.

She gazed up at the mountaintop. Gerry would have loved being here today. He had enjoyed his grandchildren and would've been thrilled to know another one was on the way.

She smiled as she watched her family. Jason was so much like his father. If Gerry were here, he would be playing in the lake and flicking water on Sarah just as Jason was doing to Maggie right now.

Maggie shrieked and kicked a shower of water back at Jason.

"Hey, Mom, you said we weren't supposed to get wet," Amy said.

"Yeah, stop it, you two," Audrey said, standing ankle deep near the shore.

Maggie stared at her daughters, water dripping off her auburn hair and then looked at Jason. As if on cue, they both turned and splashed the girls.

The girls shrieked and splashed back.

"What are they doing?" Leland asked.

"Playing." Sarah laughed as Maggie chased the girls out of the lake.

Jason caught Maggie around the waist. "What was that all about? I thought you didn't want anyone to smell like swamp."

"Life's too short not to have fun, remember?" Maggie grinned. "No regrets."

CHAPTER TEN

Regrets about being wet and cold seemed to rule by the time they dropped Leland off and were heading to Jason and Maggie's house.

"My jeans are rubbing my legs sore." Audrey fussed as she tried to pull the fabric away from her calves.

"I'm sorry. I shouldn't have gotten you wet," Maggie said. "I just got caught up in the moment."

"I love it when you're spontaneous," Jason said with a wink for his wife.

Audrey rolled her eyes.

"I thought it was fun." Amy made a face at her sister.

"You would. You hardly got wet."

"That's because I was smart enough to get out of the way."

"Chicken."

"Girls—" Maggie admonished, followed by a huge sigh. "Don't start. We're almost home and we can all change."

Jason pulled into the driveway of their rambling old Victorian, and they all scrambled out of the car. Sarah's car was parked by the street, but Maggie had asked Sarah to stay for supper.

Sarah turned to Maggie as they walked up to the door. "Since I'm the only one who's dry, why don't I start supper while you all shower and change?"

"That would be great, thanks. I was thinking of something fun and easy like nachos, popcorn, and apples," Maggie said as Jason unlocked the back door.

"And cocoa," Audrey said with a shiver. She swiped back her bedraggled blonde bangs and followed Jason into the house. "I get the shower first," she called.

"Not if I get there first. You take too long," Amy yelled back. Feet pounded up the stairs.

"Don't leave your wet clothes on the floor," Maggie called.

"I'll run you a hot bath," Jason said to Maggie as he headed for the stairs too.

Maggie smiled. "Bless that man."

"Do you want me to start with the popcorn?" Sarah moved to the sink to wash her hands.

Maggie nodded. "Yes, please." She waddled down the hall in her stiff, mud-splattered jeans.

Sarah pulled the popcorn box out of the cupboard and tossed a bag into the microwave. She poured milk into a pan for Audrey's cocoa.

The homey sound of popping corn filled the kitchen as the buttery scent wafted through the room. As Sarah sliced apples, she thought about Leland. He had been quiet on the way back to Bradford Manor but seemed content. Before she had left the facility she had asked the nurse on duty if Leland had been feeling depressed lately. The nurse had replied that Leland had been down a bit, but it didn't seem anything to worry about. Sarah left feeling a little guilty and hoped she wasn't betraying Leland's confidence by talking to the nurse, but she was worried about him.

Sarah rummaged through the pantry again and found tortilla chips and salsa. She grated cheese over the top and set them aside to heat in the microwave when the family emerged.

Her cell phone rang and Sarah dug it out of her purse. It was Irene.

"I hope I'm not intruding on anything, but I'm leaving tomorrow with Chris out to a dig in Maine that he read about in one of his archaeology magazines. Sometimes I wish he had picked a hobby that kept us closer to home. Anyway, I thought maybe you wouldn't want to wait about the information I have."

Sarah sat down at the kitchen table and pulled her notebook out of her purse. "Oh yes, thank you. I meant to call you earlier, but we were in the mountains and I didn't have any coverage."

"Well, don't get too excited. I wasn't able to find a Katie Fisher who matched the age you gave me. The Amish do record births and deaths with the county like everyone else, but you'd have to wade through a lot of names if you go to the county. And the Amish don't have a lot of variety when it comes to naming their kids. By looking at the records you also can't be sure who is Amish and who isn't. So if you want to save time, you can find detailed information in the local Amish church directory. They keep track of births and deaths, and there should even be a map of the area with family names on it. You should be able to connect the dots on who Katie's relatives are."

"This is terrific, Irene! You're amazing. Where would I find the directory? Is it online?"

"Afraid not. The bishop in charge of the community keeps it. In this case it would be…hold on a sec. I wrote the name down." Paper rustled. "Here it is. Bishop Samuel Stoltzfus. He has a cabinet business in town on Main Street and here's his home address."

Sarah's heart sank as she copied down the address. It was on the same road as the Fishers, the farm she and the girls had visited with Abram. This was the bishop who'd had Katie shunned.

Eva had warned Sarah against talking to the bishop so as not to get Annie in trouble. But she could just tell the bishop she was doing research. Plus, Annie had mentioned in her note she was going to eventually confess to the bishop anyway.

"Are you still there?" Irene asked.

"Sorry. I was thinking. Would it seem strange for me, an outsider, to ask him to see the directory?"

"I don't think so. Apparently it's not unusual to request the book. A Web site on genealogy recommended the directory as a means of tracing family trees if you happened to have a relative who was in their community."

"Thanks so much, Irene. It's worth a try." Sarah said good-bye and dropped her phone back in her purse as Maggie padded into the kitchen dressed in soft denim slacks and a flowing floral blouse. Her damp hair curled around her pink face. "I didn't mean to be gone so long. I almost fell asleep in the tub." She poured a mug of coffee and slid it into the microwave. "I heard the girls talking, which means they're out of the shower. Jason should be done soon too."

"Everything's ready. Just need to pop the nachos into the microwave." Sarah looked down at her notebook again. "Maggie, you still interested in a trip to Pleasant Valley?"

The next morning, Sarah spread out the photos of Katie's quilt on her desk and compared them again to the quilt block in the barn. What had Katie been thinking when she designed the squares? Did the pattern mean something special?

She glanced at her watch. Nearly nine. Maggie had jumped at the chance to go to Pleasant Valley, but since she had a special customer coming in the morning, she couldn't go until eleven. Sarah had agreed to wait until then. She had spent the morning working on the baby quilt.

Her fingers itched to call Jenna, who hadn't called since Saturday night. The only message on the answering machine was from the woman who had e-mailed Sarah about restoring a quilt and now wanted an appointment to bring the quilt over. Sarah checked her cell phone. Nothing.

She went back to studying Katie's design and use of colors. Sarah was mostly intrigued by the center block. She had already decided she would like to put a similar one in the center of her Trip Around the World quilt. She had never seen anything like it. She got out her quilting books and leafed through them. Nothing matched.

Maybe Vanessa Sawyer could help. She needed more fabric anyway. She grabbed her notebook and photos and headed for Wild Goose Chase.

Thankfully the shop was quiet. Vanessa was behind the counter reading one of the historical romance novels she loved. She smiled when Sarah came in.

"Back so soon. Did you finish the baby's quilt?"

"Not yet. I need more of the green fabric," Sarah said, deciding not to mention how she had goofed up the cutting of the original yardage. "Also, I was wondering if you've ever seen a quilt block like this." She showed her the photograph.

"It's a variation of a Trip Around the World quilt, but I don't recognize what she did in the center. Where did you see this?"

She told Vanessa about her trip to the Fisher farm and the painting she had found in the barn.

Vanessa studied the pictures. "You said this was painted on planks?"

Sarah nodded. "Actually it was several planks joined together to make a square."

"Oh!" Vanessa tapped the edge of the photo. "You know what I think this is? A barn quilt block."

"Barn quilt?" Sarah asked.

Yeah. I just read about them," Vanessa said. "Hold on, I may still have the magazine somewhere."

She rummaged through a pile. "Here it is. I knew it wasn't that long ago." She held up an issue of *Rural Living* and flipped through it. "Here's the article." She turned the magazine around so Sarah could see the photos, which featured various types of barns with squares resembling quilt squares nailed to them.

Vanessa picked up her shears. "How much do you need of the fabric?"

"Half a yard," Sarah said, still skimming the article. Barn quilts could range from three feet by three feet to eight feet by eight feet. Katie's had been on the smaller side of the range. The quilts were actually single quilt blocks that were enlarged so they could be mounted on a structure like a barn or any other farm building. They could even simply be displayed in a yard. Barn quilts, the article reported, were quite popular, particularly in the Midwest. The photos in the article showed Iowa school kids painting one and other examples in Pennsylvania, Kentucky, and Ohio. There was a Web site address listed at the end.

"Aren't they fun?" Vanessa slid the green material into a bag. "I was thinking of making one someday, although it's going to have to be small since I don't have a whole lot of space to hang it. Now, how about some tea?"

When Sarah finally got back to the house, she looked up the Web site the article had listed and found a link to the Amish Trail, which went through another Amish area of New York. The farms and houses on the trail featured barn quilts. Had Katie ever visited there? Where had she gotten the idea to paint a quilt block?

Sarah looked up Rachel's phone number in her notebook. She called the school first, but no one answered the phone. She tried Rachel's cell, which went directly to voice mail. "Hello Rachael, this is Sarah Hart. I was wondering if Katie had worked on any barn quilt blocks while she was taking her class with you." Sarah left her phone number.

She got out her cutting mat again and her rotary cutter. If she cut more strips, the sewing part would be completed quickly. Then she could start the hand-quilting. Even if she didn't finish before the baby was born, she could finish the quilt in Texas.

The ding on her cell phone indicated an incoming text message.

In class watching art history video. Can't talk now, but no, Katie did not work on a barn quilt block while in art class, but she has a relative who makes them.

Sarah texted back, *Do you know the relative's name?*

Rachel answered immediately.

No, but she lives near Sunnyvale.

Sunnyvale again. Where Katie had been when she sent her letter to Eva. Sarah needed a name though if she was going to find this relative.

One more reason why she needed to see that Amish church directory.

Bishop Samuel Stoltzfus was an imposing man. Tall and broad with massive arms that bulged against his blue long-sleeved shirt as he fed a long four- by six-foot board through a giant spinning saw blade.

Sarah and Maggie stood in the entryway of Stoltzfus Cabinetry Shop located on Main Street in downtown Pleasant Valley. Display cabinets were arranged in the front of the store and beyond that was the workshop. Cabinets, shelving, and countertops in various stages of completion lined the walls. Saws and workbenches circled the interior. All the workers wore Amish attire.

Bishop Stoltzfus looked up and lifted a hand. "Be with you in a minute," he called.

Maggie stepped to an oak unit and ran her hands over the surface. "This is beautiful work," she said. "Look at the detail in the scrollwork, and the edges all line up tightly." She pulled open a door. "Feels very solid."

Sarah pulled on a drawer. It rolled smoothly. "Very nice."

"Thank you." The bishop had left the workshop and stood behind them. "We make all the cabinet units and guarantee quality. We also install countertops like you see here. We can do granite, ceramic tile, or marble."

"Where do you get the marble?" Maggie asked.

"We ship it in from a couple of very reliable suppliers located in the United States, but we can get almost anything a customer wants or is willing to pay for."

Maggie asked more specifics about the grades of wood which gave Sarah a chance to study the man. He was even taller up close. She guessed six foot four. Sawdust was sprinkled on his bushy gray beard, and when he tilted his head, more showered to his shoulders. His deeply tanned face proved he didn't spend all his time indoors at the shop.

"The reason I'm asking so many questions is that we've done some remodeling on our old house, and I'm always looking for new ideas," Maggie said. "And I have an antique shop and sometimes customers who are furnishing their homes ask me for referrals to people they might consult about remodeling. I like the quality I see here." Maggie pulled out a business card and handed it to the man. "I'm Maggie Hart."

"Thank you, Maggie Hart. My sons and I personally see that each cabinet is built to suit and every customer is satisfied."

"We're from Maple Hill, Massachusetts. Do you ever come out that far?"

"We've mostly stayed in New York State, but we would consider it," Samuel said. He picked up a postcard off one of the counters. "Here is our contact information. The number is for the hardware store down the street. If customers call, they can leave a message and we will get back to them."

"Do you have a Web site?" Maggie asked.

"We do not use the Internet, but the Chamber of Commerce Web site lists the shop and the phone number also."

Samuel turned to Sarah. "Are you two related?"

"This is my mother-in-law, Sarah," Maggie said.

"Your work is beautiful," Sarah said. She took a deep breath. "I was wondering if you could do me a favor. I'm here doing a bit of research, and I understand that there is a church directory that provides reliable genealogy. I was told that you keep it."

"Yes, I have that responsibility," Samuel's focus narrowed on her. "Please come with me. I keep the church directory in my office." He moved toward the back of the store.

Sarah turned to Maggie. "This may take a bit of time since I need to copy down names. Do you want to do some shopping?"

Maggie nodded. "If you're sure you don't want me to wait, I think I'll pop in on the store next door and go from there. I have my cell phone if you can't find me."

"Have fun." Sarah walked past the cabinet display into the workshop. The sawdust almost made her sneeze as she passed the golden pile by the saw. The rest of the shop was very organized. Two young men with facial features similar to Samuel's were measuring and marking wood with pencils. One of them looked up and watched her walk by. He was dressed like Samuel and he had his deep blue eyes, but he was clean shaven, which indicated he was single, and his sandy, sun-streaked hair hung over his forehead.

The office was built into the back of the building and a large plate glass window served as most of one wall. Notebooks were neatly stacked on a scarred, wooden desk, while filing shelves filled the opposite corner. A bulletin board occupied an entire wall. Sarah noticed the lack of computer equipment, copy machine, or anything else electronic.

"Please have a seat," Samuel said and gestured to one of the three wooden chairs in the room.

After she was seated, Samuel studied her for a long moment. "I know who you are, Sarah Hart. You stayed with Abram and Annie Fisher for the school children's visitation."

Sarah's stomach gave a little quiver. "Yes, that's correct. I was here with my grandchildren. The visit was very educational and a wonderful experience for them. I'd hate to see the program canceled."

"Why would you think that the program would be canceled?" the bishop asked. "Has someone conveyed my unease with the practice?"

Now why had she said that? Sarah hesitated, unsure how to answer without implicating someone. "I heard that we were lucky it was continued this year, and that it's a rare opportunity."

The bishop stroked his beard with one finger and tiny sawdust particles wafted to the floor.

"I do not wish to show you the church directory."

"I thought it was available to those wanting to do research."

"Under the circumstances you could do more harm with it."

Sarah looked the bishop in the eye. "What circumstances are you referring to?"

"You are interfering in private matters. Circumstances you cannot possibly understand."

Obviously, Abram or someone else had been talking to the bishop. Sarah kept herself from saying what was really on her mind, that the bishop and the circumstances he created were cruel to Annie and Katie. "I may not be able to fully understand your ways, but I do know when people are hurting. Is it wrong to try to help them?"

"Sometimes faith is to be tested. It makes us stronger people. I have a great responsibility to the people in this community. People choose to be sanctioned by their actions. We believe in the freedom to come to God by choice which is why we allow time for young people to experience the *Englisher* world if they choose to."

"I don't understand. Then why is Katie being shunned? I thought she was still in her *Rumspringa.*"

"When children choose to defy their parents and do not honor their wishes, they must be watched carefully. Sometimes children want independence and are granted that. But they must learn they cannot follow two paths. If they choose to experience life away from the community then their wishes are granted and they can return when they are ready to be baptized to follow *Ordnung.* And sometimes they must learn what it is like to live without the community."

"So Katie was shunned to let her experience what it would be like without her community?"

Samuel stood and towered over her. "As I said before, these are private matters. Please do not interfere in things you do not understand."

Sarah rose. "I will think about what you've said. Thank you for your time." She walked out, slightly confused. There had to be another reason why they had taken such a drastic action with Katie when they allowed other offspring to take their time before committing to the church and being baptized.

She strolled down the street, her thoughts troubled. After a quick look inside, she saw Maggie wasn't in the clothing shop next door. She must be on the next block by now. She stopped at the curb waiting for the light to turn.

"Ma'am? May I speak with you?" a voice said behind her. She turned and came face-to-face with the sandy-haired boy who had been measuring and marking wood in the cabinetry shop.

One of the bishop's sons.

CHAPTER ELEVEN

The young man glanced over his shoulder toward Stoltzfus Cabinetry and gestured for her to follow him up a side street, out of sight from his father's shop.

Intrigued, Sarah followed him into the shade of a brick building. "You want to talk to me?"

"I'm Abram Stoltzfus. Katie Fisher has been a good friend since before we started first grade together. I was wondering what you have learned. I have been trying to find Katie also."

Sarah studied the young man, something about his stance and the hat in the shadows seemed familiar. "You've been sneaking around the Fisher farm. You were in the barn when I got there."

His deep blush was her answer.

"Why? After all this time since Katie's been gone, why would you go there now?"

He gave her a shy smile. "Our farm is next to the Fishers, so I walk by there sometimes, hoping she has come home.

I heard you talking to my father. You have been looking for her?"

"Yes, but I haven't made much progress. Do you know where she might have gone?"

He shook his head.

"Perhaps we shouldn't be talking about this. I don't want to get you in trouble with your father," Sarah said.

"He never told me I could not speak of her."

"I don't understand. She's shunned. Why can you talk about Katie and others can't?"

"My father may not approve, but I am still in my *Rumspringa* and have not been baptized yet."

"So, technically, the shunning rule doesn't apply to you or anyone else not baptized in the church?" Sarah asked.

"Technically yes, although I do not want to disobey my father. But the shunning against Katie was unfair."

"How so?"

He nervously shifted his feet. "My father overreacted. Some bad things have happened and there have been several my age who have recently chosen to leave the community permanently. I think Katie's father was afraid she would too. She is their only child."

And now the Fishers still didn't have their daughter. Sarah just shook her head, still feeling there had to be more motive for Katie's shunning. "I think Katie may have headed to Sunnyvale initially, but I don't know where she went from there. Someone thought she might've gone to an Ohio community where she has relatives."

"She did not go to Ohio. I checked. I have relatives there too."

"What about Sunnyvale? Any family or friends?"

"Katie talked about a cousin named Hannah. She may be related to Katie's mother." He gave Sarah a rueful smile. "We are almost all related somehow."

"Hannah. Do you know her last name?"

"Katie just called her Hannah."

"If I could check the church directory I might find relatives who know something about her, assuming they would talk to me, but your father wouldn't let me look at it."

"You do not need his book," Abram said.

"I don't?"

"No. A copy is kept at the library in the genealogy section. I know because I have to take the directory over there when there are changes and wait for it to be copied."

"Thank you, Abram!" Sarah said, wanting to give him a hug but not daring to. "I'll check over there."

He pushed off the wall. "I must go back to work. If you find Katie, please let me know. I really need to talk to her soon." He turned and disappeared around the corner. Sarah stepped back to the crosswalk and saw Abram duck back into his father's store.

What did Abram need to talk to Katie about? He said they had been close friends, but Katie hadn't mentioned him in her diary. Sarah hoped she would find out soon when she talked to Katie herself.

She pulled out her cell phone and called Maggie.

"I'm at the antique store at the end of the street. Are you through?" Maggie asked.

"I need to go to the library to get the information. Do you want to come, or do you want to shop for a while longer?"

"I just got started in here," Maggie replied and then lowered her voice. "There are some great bargains that I may not be able to pass up."

"That's great. Okay, I'll head to the library and then pick you up after. Just call if you need me sooner." Sarah disconnected the call. Maggie had sounded happy and excited about her finds. Jason had been intuitive in nicknaming her Magpie. She did love to find things here and there and take them home, and her store benefited.

Sarah got the directions to the main library from a store owner and parked the car in front of the two story building. The reference section was actually in the basement. Sarah descended the stairs. A middle-aged woman sat behind a metal desk in front of the stacks.

"Can I help you?" she asked, peering over round spectacles.

"I'm looking for a copy of the Amish church directory." Sarah smiled.

The woman leaned back in her chair. "Which years? We have records that date back to 1890."

"I need more recent records," Sarah said. "Within the last twenty years."

"For which community? There are three in the county, each with their own bishop."

"I need the one with Bishop Samuel Stoltzfus."

"Ah yes, I'll be right back." She stood and disappeared into the depths of the stacks and emerged carrying a light blue bound notebook. "Here you go. It can't leave the premises."

"That's fine. I'll find a table."

"There's a copy machine if you need it," the librarian said.

Sarah found a small table tucked in between the stacks and opened the book to the scanned pages of the church directory. The records were handwritten. Luckily the printing was neat and, for the most part, Sarah could decipher the names and dates. It also recorded baptisms and marriages. She located Annie and Abram's marriage date and Annie's maiden name—Yoder. She got out her notebook and began a tree working from Annie Yoder's birth. She also wrote any names of community children around Katie's age.

Because of the limited variation in family names, the trail got confusing in places. It helped that some individuals were listed with their occupation, such as "John Miller, Blacksmith," or they had a middle initial.

A few families used the same middle name for each of their children, as was the case with the bishop's sons. Samuel Stoltzfus had married Sarah Kennel Miller and they had five children. Seth Kennel Stoltzfus, Daniel Kennel Stoltzfus, Abram Kennel Stoltzfus, Martha Kennel Stoltzfus, and Willis Kennel Stoltzfus. Sarah wondered about the significance of the Kennel name. Was it a family name of the bishop's wife? She didn't note any other Kennels in the community.

After an hour and a half, Sarah had a rudimentary family tree for Annie's family. Then she did the same for Abram. Judging from the marriages listed with addresses, it looked like most of the family had stayed in the area. She located a record of a Hannah Miller, who appeared to be Annie's second cousin. She was recorded as marrying a Samuel Yoder, with a note he was a woodworker from the Hilty settlement, but no address was listed.

This must be the Hannah that Abram Stoltzfus had mentioned. It looked like she had moved to a different church district. Sarah leaned back and rubbed the crick in her neck. At least now she had some names to work with. She carried the volume back to the desk.

"Are there computers available for the Internet?" she asked the librarian.

"Second floor."

She remembered what the bishop had said about businesses being listed on the Chamber of Commerce site, so she checked. "Yoder's Woodworking" had an address located just outside of Sunnyvale. Excellent.

Feeling satisfied with her findings, she called Maggie and brought the car around to meet her on Main Street. Maggie was sitting on the bench where Sarah had talked to Gertie the day she had visited the quilt shop. Piles of bags surrounded her feet, and she held a large cup with a straw. She smiled and waved.

Sarah parked in front of the bench and got out to pop the trunk. "I'm sorry it took me so long."

"Don't be. I had a great time," Maggie said as she loaded bags into Sarah's trunk. "I got the girls some pretty summer shirts and some trinkets for the store. I also found some furniture that'll be shipped later this week. How did you do at the library?"

"I think I may have located a cousin of Katie's. Do you mind driving out there? It's about ten miles."

"No problem at all. As long as I get off my feet and can drink my latte," she held up her cup, "I'll be happy to go anywhere."

Sarah followed the directions she had written down at the library and soon they were out on a country road surrounded by sprawling acreage and sporadic farmhouses. She updated Maggie on her conversations with the bishop and Abram Stoltzfus.

Maggie frowned. "It's such a shame they're having trouble. I was talking to one of the Amish women in the bargain store. She had little kids with her and she seemed so happy with her life. I was actually getting a little envious about all the time they spend together without the distractions we have."

"The Amish lifestyle does have its advantages. It's a simpler way of life," Sarah said.

"Yeah, but then it's hard to imagine life without my dishwasher or vacuum cleaner." Maggie laughed. "Or my cell phone."

Sarah laughed with her. "I understand. Things have gotten more complicated, but in some ways they've gotten easier. Like my sewing machine. Push a button and it instantly resets to a new stitch. My first machine was fine, but it didn't have the options the new ones do."

Sarah slowed the car when she got to an intersection with a flashing yellow light. She made a left. "Okay it should be up here on the right. Yoder's Woodworking."

"It's the next driveway," Maggie said.

Sarah turned and they drove a short distance to a white building. Unpainted park-style benches and picnic tables sat on the lawn. Sarah parked near the door. It appeared they were the only customers at the moment, which suited Sarah's purposes. They went through the door and the smell of cedar greeted them.

"These are beautiful." Maggie bent down to examine some hope chests. The sides had been created from strips of various shades of brown wood, which gave the chests a simple but pleasing design. Toy trains and other wooden toys lay on the floor. A set of beautiful wooden bowls and stirring spoons sat on a counter. But what made Sarah's heart rate jump was the row of barn quilt blocks on the wall. This had to be the right place.

A grizzled white-haired man sat at the back. He was whittling what appeared to be tiny ivy leaves and vines into the handle of a cane.

Sarah approached him with a smile. "Hello. Is Hannah here?"

The man nodded his head toward a back door. "*Ja.*
There."

Sarah opened the door to a large screened-in patio. A
woman in Amish garb knelt in front of a small coffee table
painting a clear gloss over the mahogany colored wood. The
fumes stung Sarah's nose, but the smell evoked a cherished
memory of Gerry working in his workshop.

"Hannah?"

The woman looked up. Sarah guessed her to be in her
early thirties. Freckles dusted her nose and cheeks. Her
smile grew wide and friendly. "Hello! I am Hannah."

She balanced her paintbrush on top of the can and wiped
her hands on a rag as she stood.

"I'm Sarah Hart, a friend of Annie Fisher's."

"Annie? I haven't seen her in ages, but we write occasionally. How is she?"

"She misses Katie."

The smile faltered. "Katie. Sweet girl. I miss her too."

"So ... you're Katie's cousin?"

"Third cousin, actually," Hannah said. "What is this all
about?"

"I'm trying to find Katie. Only I'm having a difficult
time since almost no one in Pleasant Valley will discuss
her."

Hannah stared at her for a few moments and then, as
if she had made up her mind, she nodded once. "Please,
join me up at the house? I made some lemonade this morning. My father can watch the store, and I could use a
break."

"I'd love a glass of lemonade. My daughter-in-law is with me too."

"She is also welcome, of course," Hannah glanced down at the table. "Let me finish with this and we can go on up. I am almost done." She swiped more gloss on the small table until the entire surface gleamed.

"You have many beautiful things," Sarah said.

"Thank you. My father-in-law is the real artist when it comes to making furniture, and I like to decorate with paint and stains, so it works out well."

While Hannah cleaned her brush, Sarah pried Maggie away from examining a carved chess set and they followed Hannah to the house. The wide porch held several chairs. Flowerpots with pansies adorned the steps on each side. "It is a nice morning. I will bring the lemonade to the porch. Please, make yourselves comfortable."

Hannah went inside, and Sarah and Maggie sat in the white rocking chairs that had probably been made in the shop below. Hannah reappeared in the doorway with a tray of glasses, a pitcher, and a plate of muffins. She set the tray on the small round table between the rocking chairs and poured them each a glass.

Maggie took a sip and then a longer drink. "This is wonderful."

"I used fresh squeezed lemons," Hannah said as she pulled up a wicker chair. "So how do you know Annie Fisher?"

Sarah explained about the class trip and Annie's tears over Katie.

"Without Katie, Annie needs the support of her community," Hannah said. "I am surprised she would risk shunning."

"She said she was going to talk to the bishop next week about it. However, the bishop already knows that I'm looking for Katie."

"There are few secrets in our communities," Hannah said. "I just hope the bishop does not try to make Annie an example."

"What about you? Will asking you questions get you in trouble?"

"No, I belong to a community under a different bishop. I am not bound by the same restrictions that Annie is."

"One of Katie's friends said she got a letter postmarked from Sunnyvale shortly after Katie disappeared."

"She must have written it while she was here. She came to visit every other month or so," Hannah said. "She stayed for about a week the last time, and then she returned home for a day or so before she went away."

"Do you know where she might have gone?" Maggie asked.

"If I did, I would have told Annie," Hannah said. "Katie did not confide in me about her plans. I should have tried to talk to her more. I was not too worried. She was enjoying herself with her art and her new friends, but I always assumed she would marry her childhood friend. She had been sweet on him for years."

"Who is that?" Sarah asked.

"Abram Stoltzfus."

Sarah gasped. "The bishop's son?" The young man who had followed her down the street. No wonder he wanted to talk with Katie.

"Katie used to have a pet name for him, although I do not remember what it was. She said she felt awkward calling him by the same name as her father." She chuckled and then sobered. "And of course the situation got tense between Katie and her father as she got older. She was very upset when he made her quit her art classes. He wanted her at home."

"Why was he so protective of her?" Sarah asked, setting her empty glass back on the tray. "Was she straying too far?"

"I don't think so, at least not compared to other children. *Rumspringa* can change people, sometimes for the worse but usually for the better. It is different for everyone. Most of our teenagers remain in Amish clothing and do not experiment too much with worldly ways. Others learn to drive and dance. A few go to the extreme and party, drink, and date worldly partners."

Hannah folded her hands together in her lap, her face softening. "You know, there was an accident involving some of the young people from the Pleasant Valley area. Drinking and driving. I think it was an *Englisher* driving, but they crashed. Two of the Amish died. They were several years older than Katie, but maybe that influenced Abram and caused the bishop to take a drastic measure. Shunning is not imposed around here much anymore, which is why it surprised me."

Maggie leaned forward. "Did Katie act like she was unhappy? Any clue this was coming?"

Hannah shrugged. "I know she liked her *Englisher* friends and was questioning why she could not continue her schooling. I tried to explain to her that because she was an only child, her father was being extra protective of her. Her role should be to get married and have children. Build a good life. She could still have her art on the side. I do."

Sarah smiled. "I saw your barn quilt blocks in the store. Did you teach Katie how do make them?"

"I did," Hannah said. "They are starting to become popular around here. If you look you can see one on our barn."

Sarah and Maggie stood and walked to the corner of the porch. On the side of a big white barn with a green roof was a large, colorful quilt block.

"A Bethlehem Star," Sarah said with delight.

Hannah came up behind her. "You are correct. You must be a quilter."

"I am. I also run a quilt restoration business," Sarah said as she returned to the rocking chair.

"Katie talked about seeing if people in Pleasant Valley might become interested in barn quilts," Hannah said. "She started one while she was visiting. I sent it home with her. It was quite good. I wonder if she ever finished it."

"I saw a quilt block in their barn but..." Sarah paused, not sure how to continue. "Abram must have been angry about my taking a photo of it and he broke it."

"What?" Hannah sat with a shocked expression on her face. "Why would he do that?"

"I suppose it's my fault. I think he sees me as a threat since I asked questions about Katie."

Hannah stared out across the yard. "That is no excuse. Poor Katie. What will she think when she comes home?"

Was Hannah not telling everything she knew? She seemed positive Katie would come back.

"Do you think Katie's father might know where she is?" Maggie asked and reached for one of the muffins on the tray.

"I would not be surprised if he did, but he is not going to share that with Annie or anyone if he thinks it is for Katie's own good," Hannah said. "In your world, you call it tough love."

Sarah sighed. "I just wish I could help ease Annie's heartache."

"I will speak to Annie soon. Being so far away and busy with my own family, I let time pass without thinking about how hard this still is for her. Of course no one expected Katie's absence to last this long. I wish I could be of more help."

"Maybe you can. One of the quilts Katie made has a center block with a unique design, and the design showed up on the barn quilt block too. Perhaps it has a special meaning." Sarah pulled out her photos and handed them to Hannah.

She studied them for a moment. "Yes, I think I understand what Katie was trying to convey. If you examine the border around the center block, part of the design represents the Amish school that Katie went to. See the stitched outline in the background? The rest of the design probably has to do with the world of her art classes."

"Like she's trying to reconcile her world with the outside world," Maggie said.

Hannah smiled at her. "*Ja*, I think that is right. She wants it all. This is a good sign."

"What about the quilting design?" Sarah asked. "The stitching looks like a flower but it's not, is it? The petals aren't complete."

Hannah peered at the photos.

"It's hard to see the details." Sarah dug into her purse and pulled out a pencil. "I'll see if I can sketch it."

Sarah drew the shape in her notebook.

"Oh!" Maggie said. "It's not a flower, but two Ks back-to-back and intertwined. Sort of a monogram. I think you can get the same shape by just drawing the two letters."

Sarah handed Maggie the pencil, and she drew one K with the ends looping to an almost closed circle and then she turned the page around and drew another K. The end result did resemble a flower, and Sarah could now make out the two Ks on the quilt.

"You're brilliant," Sarah said.

Maggie grinned. "I've seen initials worked into all sorts of designs—like on custom fabrics on lampshades, or on tablecloths, silverware, or wooden boxes and chests."

"It was clever of Katie to put her initial there," Hannah said. "And it makes sense since the block is about school."

"But there are two Ks. Why?" Sarah asked with a sinking feeling. "Did Katie mention to you a friend she had at art school. A Kevin Sanders?"

"*Ja*, I remember the *Englisher* boy. She talked about him," Hannah said.

"There was a young man at Lydia's Gas Station who said he thought he saw Katie driving away with a guy. Could Katie have fallen in love with Kevin?"

"You think the two Ks represent Katie and Kevin?" A flicker of emotions fluttered across Hannah's face. Shock? Dismay? Acceptance? She glanced down at the photo of the quilt block. "I do not know, but anything is possible."

CHAPTER TWELVE

Maggie seemed subdued for the first twenty miles on the journey home, her gaze focused out the passenger-side window. Her fingers toyed with the seat belt. Sarah glanced at her a few times and then finally asked, "Are you okay?"

Maggie gave her head a little shake and tucked a wayward auburn strand behind her ear. "I was just thinking about how I'd feel if Amy or Audrey were Katie's age and ran away. I don't know what I'd do."

Sarah sighed. "It'd be a very painful, difficult situation."

"Would I try to drag them back home? Accept their choice to leave? Do the tough love thing that Hannah mentioned?" Maggie asked. "What if they want to marry someone I can't stand?" She looked at Sarah. "Did you ever worry about Jason or Jenna marrying someone you didn't like?"

"Truthfully, it crossed my mind. When Jason told me all about his new girlfriend, you sounded wonderful, but how could I really know until I met you? I mean, it's a new member of the family being thrust upon you, and you have to make it work or suffer the consequences of maybe not seeing your child very often."

Sarah glanced at Maggie. "But you know what? When I met you the first time, all doubts vanished."

"Really? Mine too." Maggie laughed. "I was so nervous about meeting you and Gerry, but then I figured if you raised such a wonderful man as Jason, you couldn't be all that bad."

Sarah smiled. "Our family has been very blessed."

"Yep. I really feel sorry for the Fishers. Do you think the two 'Ks' ran off with each other?"

"It's becoming a strong possibility. I'm going to try to find out where Kevin Sanders is attending college. If he won't tell me, maybe Paul Barclay can help decipher something from his e-mail address."

"Good idea. If anyone can find something in cyberworld, it's him," Maggie said.

Sarah nodded, hoping Paul had time to help her. He used to work for the Chamber of Commerce but after getting fired, he had gotten his act together and started a Web design business. His hacking skills and Internet knowledge, derived from years of playing computer games, proved to be useful, and he had once helped Sarah track down an identity on the Web.

The conversation turned to more cheery topics, like the purchases Maggie had made for her store, the two hope chests from Hannah's store that she had bought for the twins, and her plans for a spring promotion and sale.

Sarah dropped Maggie off at her house and went straight home with thoughts of a hot bath and bed. She set her purchase down by the stairs, one of the beautiful carved canes the older man at the woodworking shop had lovingly carved. She planned to give it to Leland. He used a walker, but the cane would come in handy for very short distances and shifting positions on the couch.

She checked the answering machine. Liam had left a message. "Bernard is in. He found the whole idea of spying on the art studio intriguing. He's going to head over to the gallery first thing in the morning. Hope you had a great trip. I'll talk to you tomorrow."

No message from Jenna. Sarah went into her office and checked her e-mail. No message there either, but then Jenna had said she would call if there were any changes.

She quickly composed an e-mail message to Kevin saying that it was vital she talk with him about Katie. Would he please help her?

Feeling restless, she fixed herself some herbal tea and tried to concentrate on writing down everything she had learned that day in her notebook. Instead, she ended up doodling flowers. Sighing, she set the pen down. It was no use. She was tired and worried about Jenna and Katie. The future appeared so uncertain at the moment.

She closed the notebook and looked at the baby quilt lying on her table. The creation of the quilt was something she could control and make progress on. And it was something she could do for Jenna instead of just worrying.

She turned on the sewing machine and got to work. The feel of the fabric slipping under her fingers comforted her, and her tension seeped away as the pile of pieced strips grew.

By the time her eyelids began to droop, a peace had settled over Sarah. She imagined Jenna's face when she saw the quilt and how ecstatic Annie would be when she saw Katie. Keeping those happy images in her head, she trotted up the stairs to bed.

"How was your trip to Pleasant Valley yesterday? I wish I could've gone, but with two doctor appointments for Ernie, I needed to be here," Martha said, shedding her pink sweater and placing it on the back of the stool. The Spotted Dog hummed with activity at lunchtime. The only available seats were at the counter.

"I wish you could've come too." Sarah set her purse on the floor and hopped up onto the stool. "The trip went well. Maggie found some great bargains, and I learned some new things about Katie Fisher."

Karen Bancroft sidled up behind the counter. "The special today is cream of mushroom soup and basil, mozzarella, and sundried tomato sandwiches on focaccia bread."

"That sounds yummy. I'll try that," Martha said.

"Me too."

"And something to drink? Our special of the day is shaken lemonade iced tea. It's a bit tart, but some people find it refreshing."

Sarah and Martha both agreed to the tea and Karen hustled off to the kitchen.

Sarah looked around for Liam, but he wasn't in sight. She was anxious to hear if Bernard had checked in, but since it was barely eleven, she doubted it. The morning had flown by with recording details about Katie in her notebook, doing household chores, and her new customer dropping off a lovely old child's quilt to be cleaned and repaired.

Sarah had explained the job might take several weeks since she was planning a trip, but the woman said there was no hurry. The threads were coming loose along the border, so Sarah had put in some stitches and then set the quilt aside to be cleaned later.

Kevin still hadn't answered her e-mail so she had sent another one, gently pleading for some information. She hoped she hadn't crossed the line, but if Katie was with him, at least the knowledge would ease Annie's mind.

Martha propped her elbow on the counter and leaned her chin on her fist. "Okay, so tell me about Katie. Did you talk to the bishop?"

"Yes, but he wasn't much help. He wouldn't let me look at the church directory and told me not to meddle in things I don't understand."

"So what did you do?"

"I left, but his son followed me down the street and told me there was a copy of the directory in the library."

"Wait...the bishop's *son* helped you out? What am I missing?"

"Katie and he have been friends since childhood. He's worried about her too and wants to talk with her."

Martha's hand slapped the counter. "Well that might explain a lot."

Sarah raised her eyebrows. "As in?"

"Maybe the bishop saw Katie as a threat. Someone to lead his son astray. So he had more incentive to shun her, rather than just let Katie make her own way home."

Sarah thought about the possibility for a moment. "You might have something there. I didn't think of that motive. Great job, Sherlock," she teased.

"No, no, you're mistaken, my dear woman," Martha patted her round stomach. "I'm Watson, you're Sherlock."

"I don't think Watson and Sherlock Holmes could hold a candle to you two pretty ladies," Liam said, making his way behind the counter.

Martha laughed and Sarah smiled up at Liam, liking how his tousled hair made him seem young and boyish in jeans and blue T-shirt. "You've been outside."

"Been scraping old paint off the back door. The doors and window trims need a fresh coat." Liam glanced down at the dog at his feet. "And Murphy's been helping."

Sarah and Martha leaned forward to see over the counter. Murphy wagged his tail and grinned up at them. Flecks of paint dusted his coat. "Looking good, Murph," Sarah said.

"Luckily he doesn't chew on the paint chips, but he's still going to need a bath."

At the word bath, Murphy's tail dropped to the floor, and he slunk away.

"Spring cleaning must be catching like a head cold." Martha grinned. "Ernie's been talking about cleaning out the garage and painting it too, although you'd think we'd need a bulldozer to move all those years of stuff. Ernie never found a tool he didn't befriend. Course, I guess that could be said of me and yarn. I've already filled up one cupboard and I've been thinking of cleaning out others just to make more room." She laughed merrily again.

"I'm that way with books," Liam said with a glance toward his bookstore. "Good thing I can feed my obsession by having a store." He looked at Sarah with a twinkle in his green eyes. "What about you?"

Sarah smiled. "Fabrics, of course."

"Ladies, your order is up." Karen arrived carrying a tray laden with bowls of soup and sandwiches. Liam stepped back so she could move in front of Sarah and Martha.

Karen set down two tall glasses of a greenish liquid. "Sorry your drinks took so long. I had to brew more tea. The lemonade iced tea is getting popular."

Sarah took a sip. The sour taste hit her tongue and her lips puckered slightly, but it was, as Karen had said, refreshing. "I like it."

"Not bad," Martha conceded and added more sweetener to hers.

After Karen made sure they had everything they needed, Liam said, "I didn't want to interrupt your lunch, but Bernard called me from New York."

"Wow, that was quick." Sarah set down her sandwich. "Did he talk to Dean Warner?"

"No, but that may have turned out to be a good thing because his assistant was very talkative. I don't know if it's the British accent, his limp, or his basset hound looks, but Bernie inspires confidences from complete strangers."

"He sounds like a character out of a mystery book." Martha spooned up a sip of soup.

Liam grinned. "He's a good guy, and I'm hoping he'll come here to visit someday." He winked at Sarah. He knew she was dying to know what Bernie had discovered. "After they found that Katie's work sold fairly well, the assistant said Dean offered to fund Katie's initial expenses if she wanted to come to the city in exchange for a percentage of her sales. And he offered a scholarship for the art school. Then he lost contact with her, but Dean had gotten a few more pieces from a high school art teacher. The teacher said Katie had given her permission to sell them."

"That must be Rachel Jackson. She didn't mention she'd sold some of Katie's pieces." She wondered how Rachel got the money to Katie if, as she had said, she didn't know where Katie was. "How recent was this?"

"Well, apparently it was some time after she left home, because about a few months ago she wrote them a thank-you note, declining their scholarship offer. The assistant remembered it because she had drawn a picture on the front of the card."

Martha set her spoon down with a clink. "Where did the card come from?"

Liam shook his head slightly. "That he didn't know. No return address, and he didn't think to look at the postmark."

"But it's a relief to hear she's okay," Sarah said. "At least she was a few months ago." Now if only Sarah could find her. She smiled at Liam, gratitude filling her heart. "Thank you so much, Liam, and tell Bernard thanks too. If he's ever up in this area, I'd love to have him over for dinner."

"I'll let him know." Liam pushed away from the counter. "I better get back to work. Don't forget we need to find time to finish that movie. Dinner later this week at my place?"

"Sounds great." Sarah watched Liam walk to the kitchen.

"His place? Sounds like you two are getting mighty cozy," Martha said in a teasing tone.

"Cozy is for winter." Sarah picked up her sandwich. "This is more like spring can't-wait-to-barbecue."

Martha laughed. "As long as you're having fun." She glanced down at Sarah's untouched bowl. "The soup is delicious."

Sarah took a taste. The mushrooms gave the soup a nice earthy flavor, but there was a hint of something else. "Ginger?"

"I think so. It's good, whatever it is." Martha scraped the bottom of her bowl. "Are you going to tell Annie about Katie's note to Dean Warner?"

"Since Abram doesn't want me talking to Annie, and I can't call the neighborhood phone without everyone knowing, I'll probably have to drive there again and hope Abram is out working. But I'll wait until I know where Katie is before I do that."

"Good idea. Count me in again if you want company," Martha said. "I'll go unless Ernie needs me for something."

Sarah smiled. "Thanks."

Martha finished her sandwich and took a swig of tea. "So what else did you find out while in Pleasant Valley?"

"I haven't told you about Hannah and the Ks." Sarah reached back to pull her notebook out of her purse. "Wait until you see this."

Sarah burst through her kitchen door and rushed toward the ringing phone.

"Hello?" she said, panting.

The line had already disconnected. She peered at the caller ID. It had been Jenna. Her heart thumped. This could be it. She called the house and got a busy signal. She tried Jenna's cell, but it went directly to voice mail.

"Jenna, it's Mom. I'm returning your call."

Maybe Jenna was in the process of calling Sarah's cell. She pulled out her cell phone. Dead battery. She couldn't believe she had forgotten to plug it in last night. She redialed Jenna's house on the kitchen phone. Still busy.

She took several deep breaths and tried to stop pacing. Jenna or David would call back if it was urgent. She ran upstairs to get the charger for her phone. She was halfway back to the kitchen when the phone rang again. Sarah raced to get it before the answering machine.

"Hello."

"Mom, you sound out of breath. Are you okay?" Jenna asked. "I tried calling the house phone several times and then your cell phone, but when you didn't answer I got worried."

Jenna was worried? Sarah's heart still thumped madly. She collapsed on a kitchen chair and laughed. "I'm sorry to worry you, sweetheart. The cell battery was dead, and I couldn't get to the kitchen phone in time. How are you?"

"Better. I saw the doctor *again* this morning and he said that everything looks normal. Again. My blood tests came back fine *again* and the baby will come anytime. So...basically nothing new, but just getting out this morning on such a gorgeous day reenergized me. I stopped at the market, and I'm going to make David one of his favorite meals, lemon chicken and wild rice. And this afternoon I'm cleaning house and getting a mountain of laundry done. And I'm going to bake the boys' favorite cookies later this afternoon."

"That sounds good, Jenna sweetie, but please be careful and try not to overdo it," Sarah said before she could catch herself.

"I know, Mom. I'll be fine," Jenna said in an overly patient tone that sounded like the one Sarah had used on Jenna when she was younger. "You worry too much."

"You're right, but I can't help it."

"Anyway, I just wanted to check in and let you know we're still waiting for this little one to make up its mind when to be born. I better get to the kitchen and finish putting the groceries away. I'll talk to you soon. Love you."

Jenna hung up and Sarah stared at the phone. Was this the same daughter who had been so miserable only days before? All this energy and cleaning must be a good sign that the baby was coming really soon. Nesting, the pregnancy books called it.

She set the phone back on the counter, and a thrill of anticipation shot through her. It was even more important to hurry and find Katie before Sarah left for Texas.

Sarah went into the office and fired up her laptop. She was elated about what Liam's friend had discovered. And now a message from Kevin Sanders sat in her box. Sarah clicked it open.

Dear Sarah Hart,

This is Katie Fisher. I am fine, but I don't want to get my mother in trouble. So please don't talk to her about me.

Tears stung Sarah's eyes. *Thank You, Lord!* Katie was okay. Annie would be overjoyed. But as the adrenaline subsided and she stared at the words, a shimmer of doubt seeped in.

How did she know for certain that this was Katie? After all, Kevin had obviously lied to her about not knowing where Katie was. Would he fake an e-mail from Katie to get Sarah off his back?

Her fingers trembled slightly as she typed a message back.

I understand your concern, but your mother is very worried. Can you please tell me where you are? It would give her some peace.

Sarah sent the e-mail off and turned to organizing the pile of mail on her desk. Moments later, a response popped into her box.

Leave Katie alone.

Sarah leaned back in her chair. The message was clear, but why? What was the big secret? Katie was nineteen and it wasn't as if someone could legally drag her back to Pleasant Valley against her will.

In all her investigating, Sarah hadn't found any animosity between Annie and Katie. She wasn't so sure about Abram, as the image arose of him destroying Katie's barn quilt block. There had been great emotion involved.

But if Kevin and Katie weren't going to cooperate, then Sarah would have to try another way. She e-mailed Paul Barclay asking if he could find a street address or even identify the town or city from Kevin Sanders's e-mail address.

If they had a good reason to want to be left alone, Sarah could respect that, but she wanted to make sure that Annie knew for certain Katie was safe.

CHAPTER THIRTEEN

Sarah opened her eyes to sunlight dancing on her bedroom ceiling. She pushed herself up on her elbows to gaze out the window. Not a cloud in the sky. It was going to be a glorious morning.

She picked up her devotion book and turned to the day's lesson. It was a passage on perseverance found in Romans 2:7. If one persisted in doing good, then God would reward one.

Sarah got out of bed with a lighter heart and dressed in light blue slacks and a sunny, patterned blouse. "Happy colors," as Gerry used to say. She took a little extra time with her hair, checking to see if any more gray hairs were showing in her blonde strands, and added a swipe of mascara.

The baby quilt materials lay on the kitchen table. Last night she had sewn the remaining strips together and pressed the seams of all the strips to one side. Then she had carefully cut across the pieced strips to produce rows of squares, rows that would now have to be sewn together in the right order to produce the Trip Around the World pattern.

Sarah checked her e-mail. Nothing further from Kevin or Katie, but then again she didn't expect to hear back from them. No message from Paul yet either. She wasn't sure if he could do anything anyway, although he was a whiz with the computer.

She called Martha to see how she was doing. Martha suggested they meet up at the Spotted Dog to grab a sandwich. Sarah readily agreed. There were other diners and coffee places in town, but none that came with a handsome Irish owner who always managed to make her smile.

She decided to have a light breakfast of toast and coffee. While the whole grain bread was toasting, she got out her notebook. Starting a new page titled "Katie and Kevin," she listed possible places to check and people to call. She needed to try to contact Madison again since she was friends with both, and also their teacher Rachel.

The toast popped up and she spread peanut butter and strawberry jam on the slices and took the plate over to the table. After freshening up her coffee, she resumed pondering. At least she could cross some locations off her list. It didn't appear that Katie was in New York City, according to Bernie's report, nor was she anywhere in Pleasant Valley, or her mother or cousin would have found out. The relatives in Ohio were off the list too. She would contact them if she ran out of options. Right now, Sarah would go on the assumption that Katie was with Kevin.

She tried calling Madison, but her voice mail picked up. Sarah left a message asking Madison to return her call. Next she called Rachel, but again she got voice mail. She tapped her pencil on her notebook. She wasn't having much luck this morning. She was once again relegated to waiting.

The baby quilt beckoned. At least she could be productive there. She took her strips of squares out to the dining room table where she had lots of room to play with placing the squares. Once she was satisfied, she pinned them together. That just left the remaining block in the middle which she wanted to design herself.

The phone rang and she nearly tripped over a chair to get to it.

"Gram?"

"Audrey, why aren't you in school?" Sarah asked, her hand pressing over her heart. Had something happened to Jason or Maggie?

"I am. I'm calling on my cell phone. We're on a break, and my teacher gave me permission to call."

"Everything okay?"

"Well, yes and no," Audrey said. "We're supposed to do a project on something from our trip, and the teacher assigned Amy and me to do an Amish garden."

"That should be fun," Sarah said, wondering how this involved her.

"Yeah," Audrey said, not sounding enthusiastic. "We have to take photos and write a report. Only there isn't a lot of space at our house..."

"So you want to do it over here?" Sarah asked, finally getting a clue to the purpose of the call.

"Yeah, if we can. You know about gardening."

"How big does it have to be?" Sarah went to the window and looked at her backyard.

"Not very, but big enough to grow some corn and stuff. We have to plant it like the gardens we saw at Pleasant Valley, and we can only use hand tools."

"I've already turned the garden bed—"

"So we can't do it?" Audrey said quickly. "That's okay. I'll tell—"

"You didn't let me finish, sweetheart. There's plenty of room still, but you'll have to prepare more ground. That may be harder without a rototiller, but you can do it the old-fashioned way."

Audrey sighed. "Okay, I'll tell the teacher." She sighed again. "Thanks, Grandma. Can we come after school?"

"Sure, I'll be here." Sarah hung up the phone with a smile. Obviously, Audrey was hoping Sarah would get them off the hook by saying no. It didn't sound like a hard project. Amy might be more receptive to the work since she was more outdoorsy.

She returned to the quilt and considered the blank area in the middle. She studied Katie's block again for inspiration. She could quilt the edges with the state flowers of Massachusetts and Texas. An outline of a heart would cover the middle to represent the joining of two families and leave room for the baby's initials inside. She would twist the letters, once she knew what they were, as Katie had done with her Ks, to make something pretty and unique. And to make the quilt less feminine in case the baby was a boy, she would add some minicowboy boots and a hat.

Now for the border. She could try to match the color to the nursery. Or maybe she should call Jenna and ask what she preferred. Yes, that seemed the logical thing to do. She dialed Jenna's number and waited as it rang several times.

Jenna answered with "No, Mom, I'm not in labor yet." She was back to sounding tired again after her spurt of energy yesterday.

"Well, then, do you have a moment to tell me about the nursery theme? What did you finally decide on?"

"Wait until you see it, Mom." Jenna's voice brightened. "We went with a secret garden theme instead of the zoo and it turned out really nice. David painted the room a really soft yellow with green trim. There's a big tree on the wall in the corner and we stenciled on plants and flowers. I still want to add some bumblebees and a rabbit, and I think it will be fun for a girl or a boy."

"It sounds really nice," Sarah said, thankful some of the quilt fabric patterns had flowers and greenery. A soft forest pattern for the border would work fine and bring out the greenish hues in the rest of the quilt. They talked a little more about some of the shower gifts Jenna had received before Jenna said someone was at the door and hung up.

Sarah looked at her supply of fabrics, and although she had some green prints, nothing seemed quite right for the border. She would go to Wild Goose Chase after lunch and see if Vanessa had something that would work.

At eleven o'clock she drove downtown. She was a bit early and didn't see Martha's car, so she dropped in at Maggie's store. The store appeared empty and Maggie was in the back at a card table with tarnished silverware spread out in front of her.

"Look at this silver I got at an estate sale." Maggie held up a fork she had been polishing. "It's a hundred years old and beautiful. I didn't know what I had until I got the polish on it."

Sarah admired the intricate design on the handle. "That's a great find, but it looks like a lot of work to restore. Need some help? I only have about ten minutes right now, but I can come back after lunch."

"I think I've got it covered, but thanks. I don't want you to get your hands dirty. Bad enough I'll smell like polish the rest of the day. Besides, Jordan will be back from lunch soon," Maggie said referring to her assistant. "If we don't have any customers, she can work on this. Earn her paycheck."

Maggie picked up a spoon and rubbed it until a brilliant silver spot appeared. "All it needs is a little elbow grease. So what are you up to?"

"On my way to meet Martha for lunch and then this afternoon, Audrey and Amy are coming over about the garden project."

"Oh, they got you involved after all," Maggie said. "I think Audrey was trying to find a way out of it. She wanted to be on the 'cool' project."

"Which is the cool project?"

"Whatever project Mikayla is on. Instead she got stuck with Amy and Claire."

"They didn't mention Claire was going to be involved."

"Figures. I hope it won't be a problem. I told them we'd find a place for them to plant, although most of our yard is shaded. I was going to call Claire's mother and see if she had any room for a garden."

"No need. I'll be happy to help them. I have the space and I think it'll be fun."

"And you can keep most of the vegetables," Maggie said.

"Deal." Sarah laughed and headed for the door. "I'll be waiting for them after school." She closed the door and walked to the Spotted Dog.

Martha had arrived and was waiting for her under the café's awning. The slight breeze stirred her brown hair. Her lively hazel eyes sparkled. "Hey there, isn't this a gorgeous day?"

"Spectacular."

"Want to eat outside?" Martha asked. "I went by the historical society and they've got the park benches set up in the memory garden. We can surprise Irene and christen the benches."

Martha's enthusiasm was impossible to resist and Sarah agreed. They walked into the café. The lunch crowd hadn't descended yet and only a few tables were taken. The bookstore was empty, and Liam stood behind the counter, writing on a clipboard.

Murphy ran up to Sarah, his whole body wagging a greeting. He held a rubber ball in his mouth. "Hello, Murphy. I see you have a toy."

The corgi dropped the ball and it bounced over to Sarah's feet. She picked it up and rolled it across the floor into the book section. Murphy bounded after it.

"You just made his day. He was dying for someone to throw that ball," Liam said. Murphy trotted back with the toy and settled under the counter to chew on it.

"He's easy to please." *Like his owner*, Sarah thought. Both Murphy and Liam were generally happy and easy to be around.

Martha had moved to the counter and was perusing the menu. "I think I'll have turkey and Swiss on rye," she said to the waitress. "And a lemonade iced tea."

Sarah stepped closer to the lunch counter. "Make that two of them."

"Two please, and this will be to go," Martha added.

Sarah turned back to Liam. "We're going to eat outside."

"Great day for it," Liam said.

"Want to join us?" Martha asked.

"I would, but I need to finish this inventory before one o'clock so I can put in an order. Ask me again sometime." He leaned on the counter closer to Sarah and lowered his voice, "What about dinner and finishing that movie Saturday?" As Sarah opened her mouth to reply, he held up his hand. "That is, if you're not heading to Texas yet."

She smiled, remembering what Jenna had said. Maybe Saturday *was* becoming Sarah's date night. "I'll be there if I can. Much as I'd like dinner with you, I'm hoping to be with Jenna."

"Totally understood," Liam said. "This waiting is even getting to me."

"They just keep saying it'll be any time now." She grimaced. She was starting to hate the words as much Jenna did. "Of course, they've been saying that for the last two weeks."

Martha walked over, catching the last part of their conversation. "A watched pot never boils," she said merrily. "Of course, I have ten grandchildren so I've had lots of practice with hours in the delivery waiting room. But even so, with each baby, it's like experiencing it for the first time. The thrill never goes away."

"You're right about that," Sarah said. "I was on pins and needles waiting for the twins, then Jenna's boys, and here I have that feeling again."

"Any word about whether it's a boy or girl?" Liam asked.

"Jenna just had another sonogram and if she wanted to know, they'd tell her. It's still a surprise. This reminds me, I need to buy fabric."

"Order's up," the waitress called. She held up small white bags decorated with black spots. Sarah and Martha paid for their food and lemonade, bid good-bye to Liam with a promise from Sarah to join him for dinner if she was still in Maple Hill, and then headed for the historical society. As Martha had said, new park benches lined the space next to the building. The patio wasn't quite done, but some planters and a small fountain had been added. The sound of birds chirping overhead and the trickle of water from the fountain were soothing.

As they headed for a bench, Martha read some of the miniplaques on the bricks forming the patio. "I ordered one each for my parents and Ernie's."

"I did the same thing," Sarah said with a laugh. "And Gerry, of course."

Irene's face appeared in the window. She waved at them and then stepped away. Moments later she strode around the corner of the building.

"Isn't it turning out well?" Irene said, holding her arms out as if encompassing the entire area.

"I like it," Sarah said, sitting on a bench.

"Me too." Martha held up the spotted bag from the café. "Even brought our lunch. Thought we'd christen the benches."

"That's the idea. This is to be a place to sit and reflect," Irene said with a smile. "Nathaniel, you're looking regal today."

For a startled moment, Sarah didn't know who Irene was talking to and then she spied the statue of Nathaniel Bradford under the oak tree.

"He arrived day before yesterday," Irene told them and headed toward the statue. "My, my, you're covered in dust already. I'll have to get you cleaned up later."

Martha exchanged an amused look with Sarah.

Irene sighed and turned to Sarah. "How is the Amish research going?"

"The church directory really helped. Thank you. I found one of Katie's cousins who provided some useful information."

Irene beamed. "I'm glad. Let me know if there's anything else I can help you with."

Before Sarah could answer, a muffled ring sounded in the distance.

"Phone," Irene said. "I better get it. Enjoy your time here." She hurried back inside.

Martha's bag crinkled as she pulled out her sandwich. A corner of the bread fell to the ground. "Irene isn't watching, is she?" she asked good-naturedly and tossed the bread over her shoulder onto the grass toward a squirrel. The squirrel scampered over to retrieve it.

"The evidence is gone. You're safe now," Sarah said watching the little animal chew the bread.

"As long as Nathaniel doesn't tattle." Martha grinned at the statue.

Sarah bit into her own sandwich. The smoked turkey, cheese, and spicy mustard tasted extra good in the spring air. A bag of kettle-cooked potato chips and a pickle were included. She was almost done with her sandwich when her cell rang. The local number on the screen didn't look familiar.

"Mrs. Hart. Paul Barclay. I think I may have a lead for you on that e-mail you sent."

"Wow. That was quick."

"I'm between projects so I had the time. I haven't found an address yet, but Kevin Sanders is on Facebook."

"I looked, but there were dozens of Sanders."

"Under their information, some people list an e-mail contact address. I found a match for the e-mail address, but he doesn't list his current location. But there are photos that may be helpful. I e-mailed you the link. I'll keep running a search just in case."

"Paul, you're amazing. What do I owe you for your time?"

"Not a thing, but if you know of anyone needing Web design, I'd appreciate a recommendation."

"Anytime, Paul." Sarah hung up the phone.

"Good news," Martha stated.

"Yeah, let's see if Irene will let me use the computer."

They gathered up their paper and put it in the trash can as they went inside.

"Irene, I may have another lead on the Amish girl." Sarah explained what she had asked Paul to look for and asked to check her e-mail.

"Sure, the computer's online." Irene cleared some papers from the computer desk.

Sarah quickly hooked into her e-mail account and tapped the address link. Facebook flashed in front of her and Kevin Sanders's page popped up.

"Is that him?" Martha asked.

"I've never seen a photo of him." She clicked the info button. Minimal information was available since she wasn't "friends" with Kevin, but under contact info, the e-mail address matched the one he had used to e-mail her.

Irene and Martha peered over her shoulder. "He's kind of cute in a shaggy sort of way," Martha said after Sarah switched to the photos. "He needs a haircut and shave, but he has nice, blue eyes. They look kind. I can see why Katie might like him."

"I see what Paul means about the photos being helpful," Sarah said. "Some of these photos were taken at a school. Here's one where you can see part of the sign."

"Click on it," Martha suggested. Sarah ran the cursor on it and clicked the mouse. The photo filled most of the screen.

Kevin and a group of college-aged people stood on the steps of a stately looking brick building. Kevin was partially blocking a plaque with bronze lettering.

"w-l-e-r University," Irene said. "Try searching for universities. You can do it by state."

"He was living in Pleasant Valley, so he might be in New York." Sarah opened another computer window and typed in New York universities. She scrolled through the results.

"There!" Martha exclaimed. "Fowler University."

Sarah clicked the link and the school home page appeared. She scanned the information. "Looks like it's located in Brighton, near Syracuse."

Irene opened a drawer. "I have a New York map somewhere in here." Irene loved maps and had a great collection. "Here it is."

Irene's charm bracelet jangled as she unfolded the map on top of a short filing cabinet by the computer. She found

Syracuse and then ran her manicured fingernail north. "There's Brighton."

Sarah scrutinized the distance from Maple Hill. "It looks to be about an hour and a half drive."

"Hmm, could be a nice day trip," Martha said, standing behind Sarah.

Sarah smiled up at Martha. "Are you saying you'd like to go to Fowler University with me?"

"But of course, my dear Sherlock."

CHAPTER FOURTEEN

A my, stop throwing dirt on me!" Audrey stood in the middle of Sarah's backyard, hands on hips, glaring at her sister.

"Then move!" Amy lifted the hoe above her head and then took another whack at the grass as soil flew.

Audrey jumped back. "Gram—"

"Audrey, please go get the bucket by the back door, and we can put the grass in there to be dumped," Sarah said in an effort to put a buffer zone between the two.

As Audrey grumbled and walked away, Amy leaned on the hoe and rubbed her lower back. "This is hard. I wish we at least had horses and a plow."

Sarah grinned as she tried to imagine Abram's Belgian horses and plow in her yard. They would take only a few steps before having to turn around. "You're doing great. Just another foot and the garden should be wide enough."

After Martha and Sarah had made plans to go to Brighton the next day, Sarah had stopped at Wild Goose

Chase and picked out a lovely forest green print before hurrying home. She had changed into old jeans and a worn shirt before Audrey and Amy had arrived after school. Claire had come down with a fever and had gone home early, so it was just the twins working on the Amish garden today. They both seemed in a quarrelsome mood.

"If we get the soil prepared today, we can go pick out the seeds later this week. That'll be fun. Maybe Claire will be well by then." Since it was only April, northern New England could still get another hard frost, so there was no rush to plant seeds. The girls said their project wasn't due until the end of school.

Sarah picked up a grass clod and showed Audrey how to shake the soil clinging to the roots back into the garden before placing it in the bucket.

Audrey picked up a clod and then dropped it. "Oh, fail! I forgot to take a 'before' photo."

"It's not too late," Sarah said.

Audrey reached into her back pocket and extracted her cell phone. She took photos of the garden from different angles and of Amy working her way down the row.

"Can you take a picture of me, Grandma?" Audrey asked and gave Sarah the phone. "All you have to do is push this button."

Audrey grabbed the bucket and a handful of grass and posed by the strip of lawn they had cleared. Sarah snapped the photo.

"Done," Amy said. She sat on the lawn and watched as Sarah and Audrey finished picking up the grass clods.

"Next time we'll break up the big clumps of dirt and spread in fertilizer. Do you remember what the Amish used?" Sarah asked, knowing the girls were supposed to have researched the information.

"Manure from their horses, cows, or chickens, or they bought it," Amy said.

Audrey just wrinkled her nose. "Gross."

Sarah smiled. "Since we don't have any barnyard animals around here, we can buy a bag at the garden center. And we can work on a compost pile." She brushed the dirt off her jeans. "Does anyone want cookies and milk?"

"Me!" the twins said.

"Are you sure it won't spoil your dinner?" Sarah teased.

"No way." Amy ran toward the garage, dragging the hoe behind her.

Sarah took off her muddy shoes by the back door, instructing the girls to do the same. After washing her hands she put chocolate chip oatmeal cookies on a plate and poured three glasses of milk.

"Thanks, Gram." Amy took a big bite of cookie and washed it down with milk.

"Yeah, thanks for helping us with the garden too," Audrey said. "I still wish I could've been on Mikayla's team, but this will be good when we get done."

"At least we get to be outside, and we don't have to do a lot of writing," Amy added.

While they were eating, Sarah checked her messages and then went into the office to check e-mail. Nothing.

Audrey came into the office and looked at the quilt top. "This is pretty."

"Thanks. I just hope it's not *too* pretty if your cousin turns out to be a boy," Sarah said.

"Did you find any clues about Katie?" Amy asked from the doorway.

"Some. I think she may be living in Brighton, New York." Sarah told the girls about Kevin's e-mail and how Paul Barclay, Martha, and Irene had helped to locate where Kevin went to school.

Amy's eyes grew wide with her love for mysteries. "You think Katie is with Kevin? Like, *with* with?"

Sarah laughed. "If you mean do I think they're dating, possibly." Even if Kevin denied a relationship, he could just be trying to protect Katie. "Kevin and Katie might be the two Ks sewn into her quilt."

"That's cool." Her forehead furrowed with thought. "But the K could be someone else, right?"

"You're right. It could be," Sarah said. "But I can't find any other men with a name starting with K in her Amish community."

"Okay, so maybe she just liked Ks because of her name," Amy suggested. "Audrey is forever writing her name over and over in her sketch pad."

"I do not!" Audrey stepped away from the quilt.

"Yes, you do. I saw you," Amy shot back. "Show Grandma your sketchbook then."

"Okay, maybe I used to," Audrey conceded. "But not *all* the time."

Why hadn't Sarah thought about that? Why had she just assumed Katie had a crush on someone? Maybe Katie had just used her first initial to create a design. "You're an astute girl, Amy."

Amy smiled and Audrey rolled her eyes. "Katie could have a BFF with a name that starts with a K."

"Good idea, Audrey! I'll have to ask her mother if she has a best friend." Assuming she ever got to have a conversation with Annie again. She was so hoping that by the time she ventured to breech Abram's and the bishop's commands, she could tell Annie where her daughter was.

Sarah cleaned up the cookie mess and drove the girls home. Maggie was in the kitchen chopping basil, a casserole dish filled with chicken, vegetables, and penne noodles at her elbow. "How did the gardening go?"

"Good," Amy said as she pulled off her sweatshirt.

Maggie smiled. "Great, then you'll be able to help me with flowers in a couple of weeks."

Audrey groaned, falling onto a chair.

Jason strolled into the kitchen. He tossed his briefcase on the chair, grabbed his wife, and spun her around with a swift peck on the lips.

"*Da-ad!*" Audrey said.

"Hi, Mom," Jason winked at Sarah before turning to his daughter. "Hey Audrey, how was school?"

"Okay."

"Anything exciting?"

"Nope." Audrey slipped off the chair. "I'm going to change my clothes."

"Me too." Amy slung her sweatshirt over her shoulder and followed her sister to the stairs.

"What happened to giving us every little detail?" Jason asked. "I think I miss those days of hearing about who fell off the swing and skinned their knee or snorted milk through their nose at lunch."

"They're teenagers now," Maggie said with the laugh.

Sarah smiled at her son. "With you it was worse. I think you were eleven when you decided you didn't want to tell me everything that happened at school."

"That's just because I was saving all my stories up for my future wife," he teased.

Maggie rolled her eyes ceilingward and clasped her hands over her heart. "How did I get so blessed?"

"You love my stories, and you know it." He snitched an olive from the casserole dish, narrowly missing being swatted by Maggie. "How long until dinner?"

Maggie opened the oven door. "A half hour."

"You gonna stay, Mom?" he asked.

"There's plenty of casserole," Maggie added as she slid the dish in. "It's a new recipe. It's supposed to be very heart healthy. I just hope it tastes as good as it looks."

"Sure, I can stay," Sarah said, breathing in the enticing aromas.

Jason grabbed his briefcase and headed out the door. He spun in the doorway. "Almost forgot. Jenna called this afternoon."

"Was she in labor?" Maggie asked.

"Didn't say. She just wanted my legal opinion about setting up some tax-deferred college funds."

"Any news from her doctor?" Sarah asked, leaning back on the counter.

"She didn't say."

Maggie wiped her hands on a towel. "How are David and the boys?"

He shrugged. "We were talking *business*."

"And I bet you didn't ask." Maggie laughed. "Men! Everything has to be compartmentalized, even conversations."

"We're predictable." He grinned. "That's why you love us so much." He turned and strolled down the hallway.

Maggie shook her head, but love shone in her eyes as she watched him leave. "Have you heard anything new?" she asked Sarah.

"No, other than she could go into labor any minute."

"So it's still just a waiting game then."

"With a deadline, assuming the doc may induce labor." Sarah was glad to know her daughter still seemed okay but wished Jenna had called her. She wanted to hear her voice just for reassurance, just as Annie wanted to hear that her daughter was safe. She hoped that by tomorrow, when she and Martha went to the university to find Kevin, they would be closer to making that happen.

The house held a chill when Sarah got home after dinner with Jason's family. April weather could be unpredictable, and tonight temperatures were plunging into the thirties. Sarah built a cozy fire in the living room fireplace and relaxed on the couch with Katie's letters. She searched through them looking for any names starting with a K. Just as she remembered, there were none. Only the diary referred to a K.

She leafed through her notebook, trying to find inspiration on where to go next when the phone rang.

"Good evening," Liam said in his rich Irish brogue. "How was your day?"

A flood of warmth spread outward from Sarah's heart. "I'm going to college tomorrow."

"Aren't you too young for college?"

"Not for many years." Sarah laughed. "Martha and I are driving over to Fowler University in Brighton to find Kevin Sanders and, I hope, Katie Fisher." She updated him on what had transpired since she had picked up lunch at the Spotted Dog.

"I keep thinking about the entwined Ks on Katie's quilt," Sarah said. "The twins mentioned that it could be a girlfriend, or maybe Katie was just quilting her first initial."

"But?"

"But the Amish are very humble, self-effacing people and I don't think Katie would've put her initial on her quilt in reference only to herself. But a teenager in love?"

"She'd put both their initials on the quilt," Liam said.

"Exactly. But I can't find any other male friends of hers with names starting with K except for Kevin. So it's most likely him. Why else would he be so adamant about my leaving her alone? He's protecting her."

"Your intuition usually leads you in the right direction. I'd go with that for now, but please be careful. I know you usually are, but you don't know this young man and he might have his back up if he's fired up to protect someone."

Sarah's heart fluttered at the deep concern in his voice. "I'll be careful."

"Good."

Sarah listened to Liam tell her about his day for a few moments, comforted by having a male friend who cared so much for her well-being. "Amy and Audrey were over this afternoon getting the garden ready to plant." She told him about the Amish school project and talked about plans for the garden, which led to a discussion about the historical society's memory garden and then stories about their parents. Talking with Liam was so effortless; it shocked Sarah to realize an hour had slipped by. They said good-night with Liam setting an agreeable time for their dinner date, and Sarah headed up the stairs.

She plugged her cell phone in to charge and placed it on her nightstand, just in case Jenna called, and went to take a hot bath. After she had put on her soft flannel nightgown, she snuggled in her sleigh bed and pulled the quilt up to her arms.

Sarah prayed that the Lord would give Annie comfort as she missed her daughter and keep Katie safe. At least Jenna was just a phone call away, assured that she could call her mother anytime. Sarah fell asleep hoping Katie would soon have that assurance too.

CHAPTER FIFTEEN

Fowler University was located on the edge of historic downtown Brighton. Tall oaks towered over the campus's stately ivy-covered, stone buildings. From the Web site, Sarah had learned that the private college had been founded in 1883 and had an excellent liberal arts department. Some renowned artists had graduated from there, as well as some famous actors and musicians.

Martha held up the campus map. "I think if you turn left at the next corner we should find the visitors parking lot."

Sarah turned and drove into the parking lot at the end of the street. She had to circle several times in the full lot before a woman walked over and jumped into a Volkswagen. After she pulled out, Sarah maneuvered her car into the tight spot.

On the trip over, Martha and she had discussed strategy. They figured they would check the art department first and then the dorms, hoping to find someone who might know Katie or Kevin. They crossed the parking lot and paused by a large marble fountain while they got their bearing on the map.

The art department was halfway across campus, and they set off down the sidewalk. Students scurried by, heading in and out of the buildings. Squirrels scampered across the grass and darted under park benches, unafraid of the occupants slouched there, studying or staring at their cell phones.

"There it is," Sarah said as they approached a three story, gray stone mansion. Fowler Arts Building. The plaque on the brick archway indicated the house had once belonged to Clarence and Edith Fowler who had willed the land for the college.

Easels were set up along the railing on the wide porch. Several held canvases in various degrees of completion. A girl with paint-stained fingers looked up with a frown as they paused at the door.

Sarah smiled at her. "Hi! Where can we find the department office?"

"Down the hall on the right." She dabbed a white dot on her canvas. "But everyone will be gone to lunch until one."

"I like your landscape," Martha said.

She shrugged. "Thanks. I'm really more into abstracts. I just have to do this to pass the class."

"How long have you been studying here?" Sarah asked.

"I'm a sophomore."

"Maybe you can help us. We're looking for an art student you might know. Name is Kevin Sanders." Sarah pulled out the photo she had printed off of Facebook.

She glanced at it. "Maybe, I don't know."

"What about Katie Fisher? She paints too," Martha added.

"Nope." Her frown deepened as she swiped at a spot on her mountain, and then wiped her finger on her torn jeans.

"Thanks for your time," Sarah said. The girl didn't answer as Sarah followed Martha to the double-doored entrance.

"Can't hurt to look around." Martha pushed on the brass handle. Chances were the office wouldn't give them information on students anyway, seeing how they were no relation to Katie or Kevin. Maybe they would get lucky and find someone who knew them—and would admit it.

Despite the lunch hour, classes were being conducted in two of the rooms they passed. It appeared that some of the walls of the original mansion had been torn down to create larger spaces. Sarah inhaled the faint odors of paint, turpentine, and a flowery scent that reminded her of burning candles.

Sarah turned the corner to the right. A stairwell bisected the long hallway. A glassed-in directory that listed the classrooms and offices hung on the wall. Display cases lined both sides of the hallway. Sarah searched the name cards by the sculptures, paintings, and other artwork for Kevin Sanders. No luck.

She and Martha peered through the narrow window on one of the doors and could see students surrounding tables, their pens moving swiftly over their notebooks. A large screen with a PowerPoint projection of an Impressionist masterpiece dominated one wall.

Sarah glanced at her watch and as she was wondering how long before the class period would be over, a door opened and a girl in a janitor's uniform backed out, pulling a bucket on rollers and a mop.

"Hi there!" Martha said.

The girl glanced behind her and then at Martha as if trying to ascertain that Martha was actually talking to her. "Hi?"

Martha took a step closer to her. "Have you been working here long?"

"Um, just since school started. Why?"

"You probably see a lot of people coming through here. Maybe you can help us find someone," Martha said. "Do you know a Kevin Sanders?"

"Nope. Sorry." She backed away, tugging the bucket after her.

"I have a photo of him."

The girl stopped with a sigh and took the photo. "He looks familiar, but he doesn't hang out on this floor." She handed the photo back.

"But he does attend class in the building?" Sarah asked.

"Downstairs."

Sarah and Martha thanked the girl and they hurried down the staircase. On the wall opposite the stairwell a sign announced the "Commercial Art Department." Sarah looked in the first open door and saw a bank of computers lining the walls.

The room was bisected by a long table. A young woman with her hair pulled into a messy ponytail and dressed in worn jeans and a denim vest leaned over brightly colored poster boards arranging face shots. As Sarah got closer she realized the posters advertised an upcoming university play.

She straightened. "Hey."

"Hi!" Sarah said. "Is Kevin around?"

"Which Kevin? We have three."

"Sanders. Blond, longish hair."

"Oh, Kev! Sure, you just missed him. Are you his grandmother?"

"No. we're not related, but I do need to talk to him. Do you know where he was heading?"

"Didn't say. Although he usually hangs at the quad." Her smile lit up her lively, brown eyes. "Most of the art students do. Coffee bar."

"Would you have a cell number for him?" Martha asked. "We'd hate to miss him."

"Nope. We're not *that* friendly. I don't really hang out with the dude unless we're working on something together."

"Do you know Katie Fisher?" Sarah asked. "She's a friend of Kevin's from home."

Something on the poster caught the girl's eye and she tilted a photo to a more acute angle. "No, he's never mentioned a Katie, but maybe that's the girl he's been hanging with."

"Thanks. We'll head over to the quad then," Sarah said.

She nodded. "If he comes back, I can tell him you're looking for him."

"We were hoping to surprise him," Martha said.

"Gotcha."

Sarah and Martha went back upstairs and headed out the front door of the building, past the girl at the easel on the porch. She didn't even look up, but Sarah noted that she had made progress on her painting since they had been inside. Looked like she would be done soon after all.

According to the campus map, the quad was located in the middle of the campus between the administration building and the library. Sarah spotted the library first, an impressive stone building with large windows. In contrast, the quad was a squat, gray concrete structure that reminded Sarah of an old fort. She half expected to see cannons peeking out the narrow slits that served as windows.

"Kind of gloomy-looking compared to the other buildings," Martha said, "But it's probably cozy in the winter."

Sarah smiled. Martha was a glass half-full kind of person, seeing the bright side of things, even in ugly buildings.

They entered through the main door, and to their surprise, the entire center of the building was glassed in as an atrium. Plants, flowers, and trees bathed in sunlight from a domed ceiling and apparently thrived protected from the elements.

"It's like *The Secret Garden*," Sarah said, remembering Jenna's theme for the baby's nursery.

"I always loved that book," Martha said, holding open the door to the garden. A rush of warm, slightly humid air hit them.

Stone tables and benches were set along the cobblestone walkway. Most were full of students, some studying, others engaging in conversations. One young man was stretched out on a park bench, an open magazine on his face.

Martha's elbow nudged Sarah's arm. She nodded toward a couple sitting at a table tucked under a huge banana tree. Their heads were close together looking at a gadget on the table.

The boy lifted his head and Sarah's heart thumped. Kevin Sanders. The girl had a pretty heart-shaped face and long blonde hair, the tips of it brushing the tabletop. Was that Katie? Her coloring was similar to Annie's, but there wasn't as strong a resemblance as Sarah had expected.

She strolled up to them. "Kevin? Hi! We've been looking for you."

His brow furrowed and his gaze darted from Sarah to Martha.

"I'm Sarah Hart and this is Martha Maplethorpe," Sarah said in a breezy tone. "And are you Katie?"

The girl's eyes widened as she glared at Kevin. "Katie? Who's Katie?"

Kevin's face flushed. "Just a friend."

"Is that who you've been hanging with? You should've told me you had a girlfriend."

"There's nothing to tell."

"Right, I've heard that before." The girl picked up the MP3 player on the table and flounced off, her blonde hair swinging behind her.

"Marcy!" Kevin started to get up but then slumped back in his chair. He scowled at Sarah and Martha. "Thanks."

"Oops. We didn't mean to cause you problems with your girlfriend." Martha watched Marcy push open the door and disappear into the café.

"She's not my girlfriend. And now probably won't be, either." He narrowed his eyes at Sarah. "Why are you here? I told you to leave me alone."

Sarah sat on the bench opposite him. "I know, and I'm sorry to bother you, but you weren't straight with me about Katie. First you said you didn't know where she was, and then she supposedly e-mailed me from your e-mail address."

"I didn't lie. I didn't know where she was at that moment when you asked."

"Semantics," Sarah said with a slight shake of the head.

"Huh?"

"You twisted your words to imply something else," Martha said, sitting next to Sarah. "You knew what she meant."

"Whatever."

"Point is, if you had been straight with me, I wouldn't be here now," Sarah said in a gentle tone. "We're not trying to cause trouble for you. We're just checking on Katie. Her mother is very worried, and under the circumstances, she isn't free to look for Katie herself."

Kevin fidgeted on his bench. "Yeah, right."

"It's complicated. You should know that since you lived in Pleasant Valley."

"Still isn't right."

Sarah decided to change tactics. "What if Katie was in trouble?"

He glanced toward the door. "She's not. If she was, she's got me."

"So she lives here in town?"

"That would be a logical conclusion."

Sarah paused, letting the sarcastic remark dissipate for a moment. She leaned forward and lowered her voice. "Kevin, I understand your loyalty to your friend, but we're not going to do anything to hurt Katie."

"Look, I really don't know where Katie lives. If she wants to talk to me, she finds me," Kevin said. "Tell her mother she's fine and to stop trying to find her. I don't get it, but Katie says she doesn't want to get her mother in trouble."

"I'd feel better if I saw Katie and talked to her."

He shrugged. "Sometimes you don't get what you want."

"Now, listen here, young man," Martha said. "Someday you will understand what being a parent is all about. You *never* stop worrying or caring about your children, even when they insist they're okay."

Kevin scowled. "Why don't you tell that to Katie's father? Or the bishop?"

"But what about her mother?" Sarah said. "We may not understand why they went to such an extreme, but in their minds, they must have had a good reason. Meanwhile, we can try to make the situation a little more tolerable." Sarah took a deep breath, hoping she was getting through to him. "Is Katie happy?"

Kevin shrugged. "She's doing what she wants to do."

"Her art?"

"Not being at home."

"Does she go to school here?"

He shook his head and picked up an empty sugar wrapper and twisted it.

Sarah watched him for a beat. "If you have a change of heart and want to bring some peace to Katie's mother, here are my numbers." Sarah handed him her business card.

He stared at it as Sarah and Martha got up.

"Thanks for your time." Sarah turned to leave.

"Try Madison again. Tell her you talked to me," Kevin called after them.

Sarah looked over her shoulder and gave him a nod and followed Martha out the door into the crowded café.

"Whew! Talk about stubborn. Reminds me of my Duncan at his age. Good thing he outgrew it for his own sake." Martha grinned. "It was all I could do not to lecture Kevin about his manners. I wonder if his mother knows he talks to adults like that."

"Probably not." Sarah looked over at the line of students waiting to get to the counter where coffee, drinks, and sandwiches were sold. "Do you want to eat here?"

"It's pretty crowded. We could just grab something on the way home if you'd like.

"Good idea." Sarah trailed behind Martha through the milling students until they were outside the quad. "I want to try calling Madison and then see if I can find out if Katie is enrolled here. If she got her GED, I imagine she'd qualify for financial aid. I don't think Kevin would tell us the truth if she was here."

Once they were outside where it was quiet, Sarah called Madison. No answer, so Sarah left another message mentioning she had talked to Kevin. Then they headed to the administration building, which was near the parking lot.

A gray-haired woman with silver glasses sat behind the counter with her smile fixed in place until Sarah explained that she wanted to find out if Katie Fisher was enrolled.

Her smile tightened. "Our student enrollment is kept confidential unless a student wants to be listed in the directory," she said. "Is this an emergency?"

"Well…no," Sarah said. "But it's important that I find her. Personal reasons." When silence stretched, she continued. "She's been estranged from her mother, and we'd like to get in touch with Katie."

"Then why isn't her mother here?"

Sarah sighed. "It's complicated."

"Sorry. It's confidential unless the student wishes to make the information public."

"Can we please see a directory then?" Sarah asked.

The woman's steely gaze didn't waver from Sarah's face as she handed her a bound book with "Fowler Student Directory" listed on the front.

"Thank you. We'll bring the book back."

They stepped outside the office. Martha shivered and rubbed her arms. "Brr. That was a chilly reception. Of course if strangers came around college looking for my kids, I'd want that lady on my side."

"When you put it like that, so would I," Sarah said with a laugh. She and Martha settled on a bench near the fountain. The directory listed students and teachers alphabetically. Some had small photos next to their names.

No Katie Fishers were listed so they went page by page looking for any other Katies. They found two, but one looked to be of Indian descent and the other wore a lip ring and was listed as a senior. No one wore Amish attire, which Sarah had expected, and none of the other girls' faces jumped out at her as someone strongly looking like Annie. They searched for Madison, but she either didn't go to school here or she didn't want to be listed.

Sarah closed the book and turned to Martha. "Well, that was futile."

"Now what?" Martha asked.

"I doubt the staff in the dorms will confirm if Katie lives there, so no point in going over. Let's try the art department again. The office staff should be back from lunch."

They returned the book and walked to the art department. The office clerk was more accommodating, and although she couldn't look up Katie in the system for them, she did say that she hadn't come across any Katie Fishers in their department.

"Well, it was a long shot, but I feel better we checked," Sarah said as they set out for the parking lot. "And I'm glad we found Kevin. Maybe he'll change his mind and be more helpful."

Martha trudged alongside her, their pace slower than when they had first gotten there. "And maybe Madison will call back."

"I hope so," Sarah said, although she wouldn't hold her breath. She suspected Katie was indeed somewhere close, and her friends would keep diverting Sarah from ever getting close enough.

CHAPTER SIXTEEN

Sarah awoke with renewed determination and a cold room. She hastily dressed in slacks and a soft pink wool sweater that Martha had made for her one Christmas. She glanced out the window. Fog hugged the trees and drifted across the backyard. She hoped it would burn off by the afternoon when she was to take the girls to the garden center for seeds.

She ran a comb through her hair. The pink sweater cast a healthy hue on her cheeks. She added a dab of mascara and decided she looked okay for the day. After a hearty breakfast of oatmeal, boiled egg, and whole wheat toast, Sarah turned to her computer.

She ran Fisher though the online White Pages again, this time narrowing the address to Brighton. No Fishers in Brighton. She wanted to get an address for Madison, but she didn't have her last name. Remembering Paul's technique, she looked up Kevin on Facebook again and went through the list of his friends until she found a Madison Wells.

She tried Madison Wells in the online White Pages. An M. Wells popped up on the screen with a street address in Brighton. She copied the information in her notebook.

Sarah called the number for M. Wells and music blasted through the receiver. A groggy-sounding female voice said, "Hello?"

"Madison?"

"No, Madison is at work. I'm one of her roommates." The girl must have changed locations because the music grew louder.

"Is Katie there?"

"What?" She raised her voice. "Hold on." The music faded several decibels. "What did you say?"

"Is Katie there?" Sarah asked, keeping her fingers crossed.

"No, there's no Katie here. Just Madison, Jennifer, and me."

"Do you know how I can get in touch with her?"

The girl yawned noisily. "Who?"

"Katie."

"Right."

Sarah suppressed a sigh. "Do you know where she lives?"

"How would I know? She's a friend of Madison's. Who is this?"

"Sarah Hart. I talked to Madison last week about Katie. I'm still trying to track her down."

"Listen, I need to go. I have class. If you want to get hold of Madison, call her cell." The phone clicked off, but Sarah's ear still rang from the music onslaught.

Sarah circled Madison's address in her notebook. At least, after talking to Madison's roommate, Sarah had an even stronger sense that Katie was somewhere in Brighton. It was just a matter of finding out where.

She pulled up Brighton's commerce Web site and printed out the page of local businesses. If Katie was living in Brighton, she most likely had a job. In between emptying the dishwasher, wiping cabinets, and folding laundry she called several of the stores listed, including the two fabric shops and three of the restaurants.

No one had heard of a Katie Fisher. Sarah glanced at the clock. Almost noon. She set the phone down and stretched the knot in her neck caused by holding the phone between her shoulder and her ear.

She opened a can of chicken and wild rice soup and doctored it up some by adding some frozen mixed vegetables and dried herbs. As the soup heated, she looked up the Web site for Dean Warner Art Studios. She clicked the link to the Americana page and noted that one of Katie's paintings had the word SOLD typed over it.

She called the gallery and this time a woman answered the phone. "I was interested in the painting on the Americana Web page of a buggy beside a creek."

"I'm sorry. A gentleman bought that painting just this morning."

"That's too bad. Will the artist be providing anything similar in the future?"

"I couldn't say."

"Does the artist take requests on her subject matter?" Sarah asked.

"I don't deal directly with that artist. But if you'd like to send your request in, I can see if we can pass it along to the artist."

"Thank you." Sarah hung up and printed out the page with Katie's paintings. She added it to her notebook even though she wasn't sure yet if it would be useful.

She stared at the notebook as she ate her soup. The hours she had spent searching for Katie were not wasted. At least she knew where Katie was not.

She needed to pick up the girls after school and she decided to work on the baby quilt for a while. She longed to call Jenna, but she had promised herself she wouldn't bother her. If Jenna needed her and wanted to talk, she would call.

The rhythmic cycle of stitching once again soothed her, and she could let her mind wander again over everything she had learned about Katie Fisher. Length after length of fabric slowly turned into a quilt she would be happy to give her grandchild.

At two thirty, she set the quilt aside and grabbed her coat and purse. Outside, the air smelled fresh and damp. The fog had burned off and the sun seemed dazzling. Sarah pulled out her sunglasses and hopped in her car. The drive to the school took only about ten minutes, and she crept along with other parents picking up their children. School buses lined the parking lot, and boys and girls streamed into them.

Sarah spotted Amy seconds after she came down the school steps. She ran over to the car and got in the front seat, swinging her backpack down to the floor.

"Hey, Gram."

"Hi, sweetie. Where's Audrey?"

"She was talking to her friends. Look, there she is with Mikayla and Claire." Audrey descended the steps flanked by the two other girls. They paused on the sidewalk, their faces animated with whatever interesting discussion they were having. Then Mikayla peeled off and ran toward the buses and the other two came over to the car.

"Hi Claire," Sarah said. "Are you going to the garden store with us?"

"Yeah, I have a note from my mom." She handed over a standard consent form the school required whenever someone other than a family member picked a student up from school. It listed contact numbers and consent for emergency medical care if needed.

Claire slid into the backseat with Audrey.

"I'm glad you're feeling better," Sarah said as the girls fastened their seat belts.

"Thanks," Claire said. She and Audrey talked softly as Sarah drove across town.

The garden center was actually part of a home supply store, and it had a wide selection of garden plants and seeds. Sarah found a parking spot near the fenced garden area.

"Do you know what you need to get?" Sarah asked.

"I brought a list." Claire pulled a wrinkled paper out of her back pocket. "We need corn, carrots, squash, spinach, peas, and lettuce. The teacher said we could do more, but she only required six."

Sarah led the way inside to the tall rotating racks. The girls looked over the rows of seed packets. "Wow, how are we supposed to choose?" Amy asked.

"Since this is for school, you may want vegetables with a shorter growing period," Sarah suggested. "At least some might be ready to eat before you're out for the summer." She got them busy checking the backs of the seed packets, explaining what growing zone they were in and how to determine the harvest date, and then left them to look over tomato plants. It was probably still too early to put them outside in the garden, but she could keep them near the kitchen window until the frost danger was over.

She chose two cherry tomato plants, two Big Boys, and a six pack of Roma seedlings. The cherry tomatoes grew quickly, and she liked to pop them into summer salads. The Big Boys were great to slice for sandwiches, and Roma tomatoes made tasty spaghetti sauce. She placed them in the cart and rolled it back to the girls.

"Grandma, we can't decide," Audrey said, holding up two packets of carrots, one of a short variety that did better in heavy soil and the other the traditional long roots.

"Let's get both and experiment," Sarah said.

"Cool." Audrey tossed them in the cart and Claire and Amy added more seed packets.

Sarah looked over their choices and then picked out cucumbers, snap peas, and—for fun—sunflower seeds. "Is there anything else we need?"

"A bag of manure," Amy said.

Audrey glanced at Claire. "Ick."

"Glad you remembered." Sarah pushed the cart through the double doors to the outside section where bags of grass seed, fertilizer, and potting soil were stacked.

"Here it is." Sarah pointed to a white bag. "Be careful," she cautioned as the girls wrestled the big bag onto the rack on the bottom of the shopping cart. Amy tripped and landed on the bag, knocking the other two girls over. To Sarah's relief, the girls giggled as they managed to drag the bag onto the cart.

"Mom sent money," Audrey said. "It's in my backpack."

"Mine too," Claire said, her fingers digging in her jeans pocket.

"No need," Sarah said. "After all, you're doing all the work, and I get to eat your school project. I can at least pay for the seeds and supplies."

Claire grinned. "I'm glad I don't have to eat them. They're vegetables."

"I don't like squash, but we have to at least taste what we grow," Audrey said. "The assignment said we have to cook something too."

Claire made a face. "I wish we could grow fruit trees."

"I'm afraid the trees wouldn't be ready in time for your grade," Sarah said with a smile as they moved up to the cashier.

While the cashier rang up their purchases, Sarah noticed a magazine by the cash register. On the front cover was a serene farm setting with a farmhouse and barn behind white fencing. A painted quilt block decorated the barn. She picked up the magazine and flipped to the article.

The farm was in Vermont, but the article listed several crafts people in surrounding states who made the barn quilt blocks. One was Hannah Yoder. Sarah handed the magazine to the cashier and she bagged it with the seeds.

As they waited for the cashier to finish, Audrey said, "The teacher said something about checking the *Farmers'...* something."

"*Almanac?*"

"Yeah. I guess the Amish use the *Farmers' Almanac* to know when it's the right time to plant seeds."

"They may have one here." Sarah asked the cashier who pointed her to the bottom rack of gardening magazines and books. She found the almanac and added it to their purchases.

In the car, Audrey flipped through the paperbound book to the gardening section. "It says here that we can plant carrots and spinach now, and next week the peas. The corn, squash, and lettuce should wait until May. Some of them can be started indoors now."

"That's good. We can get the carrots and spinach seeds planted today after we work the ground some more," Sarah said cheerfully while casting a glance at the sky. Some wispy clouds had rolled over, but rays of sun still gallantly pushed their way through. More rain wasn't predicted until later in the week.

Sarah parked the car and let the girls into the house. The girls had brought extra clothes and shoes, and after they had changed, they all trooped outside. Sarah set them to work and returned to the house and checked the answering machine. Nothing.

She went into the office and grabbed her laptop, taking it back to the kitchen table so she could still see the girls through the window. She found two e-mails waiting for her. An online craft supplier announced its pre-summer sale and Martha had forwarded a joke. Sarah forwarded the joke to Jenna with a line "Thinking about you."

She glanced outside where the girls worked as a team. Audrey whacked the ground with a hoe this time, and Amy raked the dirt. Claire was picking up rocks and tossing them in a pile.

Sarah had kept a bigger garden when Jason and Jenna were their age. Jason hadn't been much interested in gardening, but Jenna'd had a green thumb. Her plants seemed to thrive and even now in the hot Texas climate, she and David managed to keep a lush landscape around their home.

Sarah brought up the Brighton Web site again and studied the town map. Where are you, Katie Fisher?

"Grandma, we're ready for the seeds," Amy called.

"Be right there." Sarah sorted through the packets and grabbed the spinach and the two packets of carrots.

The girls stood in the middle of the garden plot. Mud streaked their faces and clothes, but they wore big grins.

She surveyed the neatly turned soil free of large lumps and raked level. "You did a great job."

With Claire there, the twins were getting along fine and from their happy chatter, the garden seemed more like play than a school assignment. Soon they had the carrot and spinach seeds snug in their new homes. Sarah stuck sticks through the seed packets, and Amy put them at the ends of the rows.

"We need to water the seeds," Audrey said.

"Some Amish have soaker hoses that work with gravity," Amy said, obviously having done her homework on Amish life.

"We can water with a bucket, right?" Claire asked before Sarah suggested using the hose would be okay.

Audrey went to get the bucket, and as Sarah watched the girls cheerfully take turns getting water, she remembered something she had read about Amish farming. The hard work and long hours farming built strong bonds in Amish families, something that could be more difficult to achieve in families where everyone went their separate ways on a daily basis. Audrey and Amy might complain that working in Maggie's store was boring at times, but the time spent with their mother was priceless. Someday they would realize how

precious that time was and how it forged a strong bond between them and Maggie.

When the bucket brigade erupted into a water fight,
Sarah called the shivering girls inside. They took turns
changing in the laundry room, and Sarah popped their
clothes in the washing machine.

Sarah had already made arrangements for the girls to
have dinner with her. Claire called her mother, and she
agreed to let her daughter stay for dinner also. Sarah thawed
several pitas and used them for individual pizza crusts. She
spiced up tomato sauce with oregano and basil and grabbed
a bag of mozzarella cheese. She put out an assortment of top-
pings, and let the girls design their own pizzas with mushrooms, olives, green peppers, and onions. After the pizzas
were heating in the oven, Audrey and Claire went into the
living room to watch television. Amy lingered and offered
to set out plates and glasses.

"There's root beer in the pantry," Sarah said as she
cleared the counter. "You can move the laptop back to my
office if it's in the way."

Amy pulled the computer toward her. "Why are you
looking at Brighton?"

"I think Katie Fisher may be there. Her art friends both
live there and go to school, but so far I haven't been able to
find her."

"Can I help look online?"

"Sure," Sarah said with a smile. "You may have better luck
than I've had."

Amy took the computer into Sarah's office as Sarah checked the progress on their improvised pizzas. The cheese was just starting to melt.

Sarah washed a pint of strawberries, put them in a bowl, and whipped up a cream cheese dip. She checked the pizzas again and the mozzarella was bubbling now. She pulled the tray out.

"The pizzas are done," she called. "You're going to have to tell me whose pizza is whose."

Audrey and Claire came around the corner, still chattering away.

"This one's mine." Audrey pointed at a creation heavy on the olives. Sarah used a spatula to lift the pizza onto her plate. She did the same for Claire.

"Amy?" Sarah leaned into the office. "Ready to eat?"

"Yeah." She pushed back the chair and stood, still looking at the computer screen. "I can't find Katie on Twitter or Facebook." Amy sat down at the kitchen table. "Is there another college in Brighton?"

"That's a good question." Sarah wondered why she hadn't thought of that. "I'll check it out. Thanks for your help, Amy."

Amy smiled and took a big bite of her minipizza. "Anytime, Gram."

CHAPTER SEVENTEEN

After dropping the girls off at their homes, Sarah hurried back to the house. She wanted to work on the baby quilt, and also check to see if there was indeed another college or maybe an art school in Brighton.

The sun had set, and the office held a chill so Sarah took her laptop out to the kitchen table. Settling before the screen with a hot cup of tea, she typed in *Community Colleges, Brighton*, but the result indicated there wasn't another school in the town. Sarah tried Syracuse and several popped up. She checked their locations. The closest one to Brighton was a college about five miles away, near Colton, New York.

She clicked on its Web site. Colton Community College was a small school, but it did have an art department. A show was scheduled for Friday and Saturday featuring some of its young talent. There were photographs of several art pieces, mostly paintings, and an alphabetical listing of the participating student names. She skimmed the list. No Katie or Fisher, but there was a K. Visser.

The kitchen phone rang, and Sarah jumped up to answer it. Irene's anxious voice poured out of the receiver. "Sarah, I need some help."

"Sure, Irene. What's wrong?" Sarah's fingers tightened around the phone. "Is it an emergency?"

"No. Well, sort of," Irene said. "More urgent than an emergency. You have a laptop, don't you?"

"I do. Right here."

"I'm still at work, and I have someone here who's installing the new wireless system outside in the memory garden. We need to test it on a computer other than his. I don't have a laptop and Chris is at a meeting tonight with his. None of my staff is available. I know this is a *huge* imposition, but if you could bring your computer over, you'd help us out tremendously."

"Of course, Irene. I'll be right over. Anything for you. You've helped me out so much."

"Thank you. I hated to ask, but the handyman is volunteering his time so he can't come during business hours. We have lights outside. It'll only take a few minutes." Irene paused as if catching her breath. "And there's something I want to show you."

"I'll be there in ten minutes." Sarah closed the lid on the laptop and placed it in her computer bag, packing the AC cord in case this took longer than expected. She grabbed her coat and headed out to the car.

Night had descended by the time Sarah parked in front of the historical society. Lights shone from the windows and along the side of the building where the memory garden was located. Sarah walked across the lawn to find Irene standing at the foot of a ladder. A man dressed in gray coveralls stood on the ladder securing an antenna to the wall.

"Dave?" Sarah asked as she recognized the figure. Dave Diamond was a handyman who had worked on Maggie and Jason's home when they had first moved in. He had later gotten a job at the lumber store after his son was born.

"Hey, Mrs. Hart," Dave said as he cranked a screw into the wall.

"You're so multitalented. I didn't know you worked with electronics too."

"I don't, which is why Irene got me at slave wages." Dave grinned and pulled another screw out of his pocket. "Anyway, it doesn't take an engineering degree to install a wireless router. I have one in my home, although this one is a little trickier since it's outside. I have to install a waterproof cover on it."

"Sarah. Thanks again for coming," Irene said, clutching the ladder. "You're a lifesaver, or at least a job saver. I promised the board members the wireless would be installed by tomorrow morning because there's a reporter coming to write a piece on the garden, and they want to promote the wireless Internet feature."

Sarah nodded, although she sometimes wondered about this obsession about having Internet access everywhere. If people wanted to do research, they could go inside the building. Maybe the Amish rejection of technology was something to be admired. A memorial garden usually was intended as a peaceful retreat, an escape from everyday life, a place where one could remember the people who had come before. But Sarah supposed with all the electronic gadgets people carried these days, the wireless access might be a draw to those who wanted to be outside but still connected to the World Wide Web.

"Where do you want me?" Sarah asked.

"Try over on the bench, and see if you can log on," Dave said, coming down the ladder.

Sarah sat on the bench where Martha and she had had lunch and turned on the computer. She clicked the network button and found the historical society. "It won't let me connect. I need a security code."

"Dave, I thought we were going to disable that?" Irene said.

"Anything you want, Irene, but just remember, without the code, anyone can get on your network. You may want to control access. You could consider limited access. The first time people want to log on here at the garden, they can get the code from you or your staff, and then their computers should save it for future use."

"That's what they do at the library," Sarah said.

"Plus, this way you can keep track of how many people have actually used the wireless," Dave said.

"Okay, that makes sense. Let's keep the code for now. I can always take it off later if need be, right?"

Dave nodded. "Right."

Irene turned to Sarah. "The code is MapleHil1787."

Sarah typed it in. "Still won't connect."

"Hold on, let me reset the modem," Dave said and disappeared inside the building. Sarah shivered and buttoned up her coat.

"This shouldn't take long," Irene said, her fingers fiddling with the charms on her charm bracelet.

"It's okay," Sarah said, looking around. They had put a lot of hard work into the space. "The patio looks great."

"Most of the bricks are laid but not cemented in yet. As people donate money, we'll get the names added and then put the bricks in permanently. That reminds me, I have something to show you."

Irene walked over to a plastic covered pile and returned holding two bricks.

She handed the first one to Sarah. "Here's the one for your parents." The bronze lettering spelled out *William and Ruth Drayton*.

"This is so nice. How did you get this done so quickly?" Sarah asked. She had just sent in her donation earlier in the week.

"It doesn't take long. It's just a matter of affixing the lettering to the brick." Irene shifted her feet, acting nervous. "Now, if you don't like this one, I'll get you another. I know you sent the request for a brick for Gerry, and maybe I didn't explain well enough, but the memory garden isn't just for people who have passed on, so ..." She handed another brick to Sarah.

Sarah ran her finger over the names. *Gerry and Sarah Hart.* Sarah's heart squeezed. It had been a while since she had seen her late husband's name and hers linked together in printed form.

"If you just want Gerry Hart on there, I can change it."

Sarah looked up at Irene. "No, you don't have to. This was very thoughtful of you. It didn't occur to me to add my name."

"I'm glad you like it," Irene said, relief in her voice. "Anyway, I wanted to give you a chance to pick out where you'd like the bricks to be laid. Not everyone will get to do that, but since we're just starting, you can choose."

Sarah looked about the patio. "What about over by the oak tree between the bench and Nathaniel."

Irene beamed. "I would've chosen there too."

"Okay. Try again," Dave called.

This time the computer connected with the Internet. "It's working," Sarah called back.

Dave came around the corner carrying a laptop. "Okay, let me get online with my computer." He opened the lid and his screen lit up.

"Can you see me?" Dave said and then grinned at Irene's and Sarah's puzzled expressions. "Online. See if you can see my computer on your network."

Sarah clicked to the network window. "No, I don't think so."

"Good, I set it up that way. Better security." He snapped the computer lid down. "All set. I'll just go check to make

sure the cable is secure along the wall and I'm out of here."
He grabbed the ladder and tucked it under his arm.

"Thanks, Dave," Irene said.

"Say hi to Liz and the kids," Sarah added.

"Will do." He rounded the corner.

Irene sat on the bench beside Sarah and glanced at the computer screen where the art department Web page from the community college had stayed online. "Are you thinking of taking some art classes?"

"No, this is an art show over in Colton, New York. I'm still looking for the Amish girl and thought she might attend there. I was hoping she'd be listed under the art show."

Irene leaned closer to the screen studying the list of participants. "Katie Fisher, right?"

"Yes."

"You hit the jackpot then. Are you going to the show?"

Sarah blinked and scrutinized the screen. "I didn't see Katie on there."

Irene gave her a teasing smile. "But she's on the list."

"Where?"

She pointed to K. Visser. "I'm assuming the K stands for Katie."

Sarah's heart rate shot up. "But her last name is Fisher, F-i-s-h-e-r," she said and gasped. "Oh!"

Irene's grin widened and she nodded. "Visser is the Dutch translation of Fisher. When I was in high school, I took a little German, and the teacher was really enthusiastic about linguistics. Taught us way more than most teachers would about the origin of language. Dutch is said to be between English and German." Her grin widened. "You'd be surprised by the obscure things I know. Anyway, don't the Amish speak Pennsylvania Dutch?"

"Irene! I could hug you. Thank you!"

"I hope this made your trip out here tonight worth it."

Sarah laughed. "Oh, it has. You may have just solved the mystery."

Sarah leaned back against her plumped-up bed pillows, studying her notes on Katie. Outside, moonbeams bathed the backyard and the girls' garden. She had come back from the historical society feeling excited and hopeful. If Irene was correct about the name, and assuming the K stood for Katie, Annie would soon know where her daughter was.

So then why did she have a sense she was missing something important?

Assuming K. Visser was Katie Fisher, why hadn't she gone to Fowler University with Kevin? They had a great art department there. Surely she would qualify for federal funding. But, then, maybe she still couldn't get in. It was a private school and admission standards might be quite high.

Sarah tapped the pencil tip on the notebook. Of course, if Katie really was in love with Kevin, the community college wasn't that far away. Sarah made a note to check to see if there was bus service. Katie could've gotten a driver's license too.

Now, what if Kevin *was* just a friend, as he had implied when she had questioned him in the quad? Was there someone else in Katie's life? Hannah had said that Katie had been sweet on Abram Stoltzfus at one time. Maybe there had been other Amish suitors.

She flipped the pages and read through her lists, lingering for a time on the genealogy of the Amish community. She circled the names of relatives and children that would be about Katie's age. There were a dozen boys Katie's age, but again no one had a first name that started with a K. Maybe Amy's suggestion that the K had nothing to do with love was correct. The heart on the quilt could indicate friendship or family. Maybe even love for God.

She must have fallen asleep because the next thing she knew the phone was ringing. She jerked upward, the notebook falling to the floor.

"I'm sorry. Did I wake you? You answered before I remembered the time difference."

"Honey, you can call me anytime day or night." Sarah glanced at the clock. It was almost eleven thirty, which would be almost ten thirty in Texas.

"We went to bed early tonight, but I just can't sleep," Jenna's voice was low, almost a whisper. "David's asleep and I don't want to wake him."

Sarah pushed herself up against the headboard. "Are you feeling okay?"

"My back is achy and I can't get comfortable. And no, I don't think I'm in labor. Just tired. I moved the furniture around in the nursery this afternoon."

Sarah refrained from asking if that was wise.

"I have too much time on my hands," Jenna continued. "I worry about everything. Like if we should get a new minivan that might be safer for the baby, or if we should take out more life insurance. If the boys will accept the baby okay. They seem excited, but it's a big change. And they'll be quite a bit older than their new sibling."

"The boys will be thrilled with the baby."

"Jason wasn't when you brought me home from the hospital," Jenna said with giggle. "Dad said he wouldn't even look at me for an entire day."

"He was in a shy phase and didn't know what to think of you."

"Ha! Then he tried to drop me on my head."

"You were crying, and he was only trying to help," Sarah said, as she always did when the story came up in conversation.

"Likely story."

"He just picked you up at the wrong end is all." Sarah laughed, but a shiver ran through her at the memory. Jenna was crying and Sarah had stepped into the kitchen for a second to grab a blanket from the diaper bag. As Sarah was returning, Jenna stopped crying. Jason had Jenna's ankles in his little hands, dangling her head about a half inch above the carpet. Thankfully he didn't drop her as Sarah carefully approached him, trying not to startle him. From then on, they made sure the strap in the baby seat was securely fastened in case Jason wanted to "help" again.

Jenna yawned. "What's happening with that poor Amish girl you're looking for?"

"I think we may have found her. I'm going to go check it out tomorrow." She explained about the community college and Irene pointing out that Visser could be the same name as Fisher.

"That's great," Jenna said. "Her mother will be so happy when you tell her."

Sarah agreed, although an idea was forming in the back of her mind. Could she take Annie to see her daughter?

"Mom, do you remember when I went off to college?"

"Like it was yesterday."

"Was it hard to let me go?"

"One of the hardest things a mother has to do. I missed you every day. Still do." Although Sarah was proud of the life Jenna had built.

"That's what I thought," Jenna said. "I was thinking earlier tonight about when Jonathan and Thomas leave home someday."

"Sweetheart, you have over a decade to worry about that."

"I know, but I keep thinking I'm going to mess my kids up somehow."

Poor Jenna. Her normally independent, confident daughter was really letting her imagination run wild tonight. "Now, listen," Sarah said. "You are a terrific mom, and I'm not just saying this because you're my daughter.

Anyone who knows you and your kids realizes you are doing a wonderful job."

Sarah listened to Jenna's breathing for a few beats and then there was a sniff. Sarah decided to switch the topic. They chatted about some of Jenna's old friends around Maple Hill until Jenna sounded sleepy. They had a prayer together before hanging up.

Sarah leaned her head back and stared at the ceiling, wide awake again. She rubbed the ache in her chest with one hand, trying to release some of the worry she felt over being so far away from her daughter. She hoped Jenna would feel better in the morning. It was difficult to really discern if their talk had done any good since thousands of miles stretched between them. Sarah longed to speak face-to-face with her daughter and to see for herself that Jenna was coping.

Gerry would have told Sarah not to worry and would have reassured her she was a good parent, just as Sarah had done for Jenna. They had raised their children to be strong, capable individuals. Jenna would ask for help when she needed it.

Sarah turned off the lamp and closed her eyes, listening to the wind outside. She sighed. Sleep wasn't even on the horizon yet. She clicked the lamp back on and retrieved her notebook from the floor. If she was going to be awake, she might as well concentrate on whatever was bothering her about Katie's motivation to leave her family and community. Several minutes passed and nothing came to mind.

Her Bible lay on the bedside table. She picked it up and held it close.

Lord, I'm just a bundle of nerves tonight. I know You care about Jenna's and Katie's well-being. Please forgive me for my lack of faith and grant all of us peace, especially Annie. And guide me tomorrow in finding Katie and to make the right decisions for everyone involved.

She let out a deep breath and opened the Bible to Psalms. David's songs were a balm to her soul and she fell asleep reading the promise in Psalm 37 that no matter how they may stumble or fall, God holds His children by the hand.

CHAPTER EIGHTEEN

Martha leaned forward and adjusted the car's air vent to blow on her. The April morning had dawned surprisingly warm. "So Katie could've been within an hour of home all this time?"

"Assuming this is our Katie." Sarah tapped on the brake to allow a sports car to pass them on the highway toward Pleasant Valley. "K. Visser could be someone else. This could be a wild goose chase," she cautioned although her gut was telling her they were on the right track.

All the clues seemed to line up on the who and where, but Sarah still wanted to find out the why. Why did Katie really run away? Sarah felt a tingle of excitement. Today she might find out.

"I'm just glad I could come. Ernie has been feeling really great this week and his doctors seem pleased. I think working on the cars is very therapeutic for him."

"I'm glad," Sarah said as a sad twinge nudged her. They both knew that someday Ernie's Parkinson's could make it difficult for him to handle tools.

"So how are we going to do this?" Martha asked as the sign for Pleasant Valley loomed ahead. Forty miles to go.

"There's a fabric outlet on the way to Colton that I would love to stop at. I'll ask Annie if she'd be willing to help me pick out some fabric. We can stop off at the art show, and if Katie isn't there, we haven't gotten her hopes up for nothing. Then I'll tell her about Katie's e-mail and that she's probably living somewhere near Brighton. If she still wants me to keep looking, I will."

"What about Abram? Won't he be angry with us for talking to her?" Martha asked.

Sarah sighed. "I know it's not right, but I'm hoping he won't be home. He usually makes his business rounds in the afternoon."

"But what if he *is* there?" Martha asked again.

"Then I'll think of something."

Martha grinned. "Famous last words."

Sarah smiled at Martha's teasing, but her stomach quivered. She would confront Abram if she had to and try to convince him to let Annie go with her, but she was hoping that wouldn't be necessary.

"We could go look for Katie on our own, but I can't be a hundred percent sure I'd recognize her. It's not as though we have a picture to go by. I just know she favors her mother's looks. Annie's the only one who can tell us for sure whether it's Katie."

The last hour seemed to melt away, and Sarah took the turn by Lydia's Gas Station and Crafts. On a whim, she pulled off and parked. "I want to ask Lydia a quick question."

"No problem. I'll use the facilities while we're here."

They entered the back, and Martha headed for the restroom as Sarah approached the counter where Lydia rang up a customer's gas purchase.

She looked up as she handed over change and spied Sarah. "Hello there! I was wondering if I'd see you again. Did you find Katie Fisher?"

"Not yet. I was wondering if you'd had a chance to look at Warner Studios' Web site."

"I did, but I couldn't find your number. The paintings on the Web site didn't come from me. Is she studying in New York City?"

"No, she didn't take the scholarship, but she's been in contact with them. Anyway, I think we may know where she is," Sarah said as Martha joined her. They stepped aside to let another customer come up to the cash register.

"Great news! Let me know if you find her. Tell her I miss her if you get the chance and that I'd love to have more of her art to sell," Lydia said.

Sarah and Martha left the busy shop and resumed their journey to the Fisher farm. Sarah slowed as they approached the property.

"There are horses and a plow in the field. I think it's Abram," Martha said.

Sarah leaned forward to see around Martha. Since the Amish dressed alike, it was tough to be certain it was Abram Fisher. But since the field was close to his house, most likely it was him. She drove past the driveway. "It's still early yet. He may finish plowing and then go to work on his harness business. We can go back to town and get something to eat."

"Sounds good to me," Martha readily agreed.

Sarah pulled into the next farm's driveway and turned around. They passed the Fisher farm again and it looked like Abram was pointing the horses toward the barn. Good sign.

They drove into town and as they passed the high school, Sarah asked, "Do you mind if we pop in to see the art teacher? I have some questions for her."

"Sure. We need to burn some time anyway."

They made their way across the pavement and entered the art building. Rachel stood in the middle of the room, her gaze sweeping over her students, concentrating on their progress. She murmured a suggestion to one and then went on to the next pupil.

Sarah stepped farther into the room and a couple of students looked over at her. Rachel followed their gaze. She initially frowned, but then replaced her frown with a smile.

Rachel strode toward them. "Class, I'll be right outside the door, please stay in your seats and work." She gestured for Sarah and Martha to follow her, and they stepped into the parking area.

"Did you find Katie?" she asked, sounding a little breathless.

"Maybe," Sarah said. "We have a good idea where she might be. It would've been easier if you had been more honest."

Rachel let out a deep sigh. "I can't blame you for being angry with me. I should've told you everything."

"We're not angry," Sarah said, startled by the angst on the teacher's face. "But I must admit I'm now confused. If you sold her work to Dean Warner, you must have known where Katie was. Why didn't you just say so?"

"I didn't. I mean I don't. That's not what I meant," Rachel said, her face flooding with color. "Look, I just didn't want to jeopardize my job. People will think I helped a student run away from home. That wasn't my intention. I gave Katie the information, helped secure the proper financial aid forms, and established contacts for her in the art world. After that, I stepped away. I had no idea she'd be shunned."

"So you really don't know where she is?" Martha asked.

Rachel looked out over the parked cars to the baseball field. "No. Not now anyway and that's the truth," Rachel said. "I suspected she might be wherever Madison or Kevin was, but I didn't ask and they didn't tell, other than telling me she was okay. But I could have told you where to find Madison and Kevin."

"We found them anyway, and they're still being protective of her," Sarah said. "So if you truly don't know where

Katie is, how did you get her the payment for the pieces you sold to Dean Warner Art Studios?"

"I just deposited the money in Katie's bank account. She said it was okay to do that before she quit school. I suppose I should've told you all this before, although it would've done nothing to help you find her. I had no idea you'd be this determined."

Martha smiled. "That's because you don't know Sarah."

"So you still think she plans on coming back?" Sarah asked.

"I've always thought she would, but now," Rachel lifted her hands, "who knows? I can't help but think this is my fault because I encouraged her to continue school."

"You were just following your heart in trying to help a student," Sarah said. "As I've mentioned before, I was a teacher once too."

"Then you can understand," Rachel said with a wobbly smile. "I've been doing a lot of thinking about Katie, and I'm going to talk to the bishop. It may get me in trouble, but at least I'll have peace of mind. Probably won't do any good at this point, but I want him to understand how Katie came to take such drastic steps to leave. This wasn't a lack of faith or to purposely rebel against the *Ordnung,* but the desire to better herself."

"But don't you think the bishop already realizes that? Isn't tolerance something that goes along with the *Rumspringa?*" Sarah asked.

"Yes, it should," Rachel said.

"That's what has puzzled me most of all, and no one seems to have a really good reason for the bishop's drastic measure," Sarah said. "Why would he have Katie shunned when other Amish kids have done the same as she or worse? Until Amish adolescents are baptized they're granted leniency. I realize some of the Amish have been worried lately about youth leaving the church, but why use Katie as an example?" Sarah took a deep breath. The words had just rushed out of her.

"I don't know," Rachel said. "I've wondered that too. I should've spoken up and defended her sooner."

"Don't beat yourself up too much," Martha said to Rachel. "Your intentions were good."

"Thanks, but sometimes good intentions aren't enough," Rachel said, a sheen in her eyes. "Let me know if you find her, okay? I'm here if she needs me." She walked to the classroom and went in without looking back.

Sarah shook her head, as a wave of sadness hit her. "It's amazing how complicated people's lives can get even when their intentions are good."

Martha sighed. "I'll say."

"Good afternoon. You may take a seat wherever you like," the Amish hostess said at the Plain Pleasant Eating restaurant where Sarah had eaten with the class on the field trip. Martha and she had arrived at twelve thirty so the place was busy with a mix of tourists and Amish, but it was considerably quieter than when it had been crammed with twenty students.

Sarah surveyed the room with the long tables and family-style dining. "Over there okay with you?" Sarah asked Martha. She gestured to a table by the wall where four women sat at one end. They were dressed in bright pantsuits and walking shoes. Maps and brochures littered the table between them.

"Anywhere is fine by me," Martha said, her eyes bright with interest. They settled at the opposite end of the table from the women. The chalkboard on the table indicated today's lunch was chicken pot pie.

"They also offer sandwiches and hamburgers," Sarah said.

"The pot pie looks great," Martha said, looking over at their tablemates' generous servings.

"It is," the woman closest to Martha said. She gestured to her dish with her fork. "You can't find any better in northern New York." She turned back to the other women, and they continued their discussion about an Amish buggy tour they were going to take that afternoon.

"We have iced tea, milk, grape juice, or soft drinks," the pretty Amish waitress said. Her name tag indicated her name was Hannah M.

Martha and Sarah both decided on iced tea and the chicken pot pie. While they waited, Sarah pulled out her phone and checked to see if she had any messages. With phone service being so sketchy out in the country, Sarah wanted to make sure she didn't miss anything.

"Jenna call?" Martha asked as Hannah set a pitcher of iced tea, a bowl of lemon slices, and glasses with ice in front of them.

Sarah shook her head and stuck her cell back in her purse. "Last night she called me late, feeling uncomfortable after moving furniture around—"

"But you were thinking maybe she was going into labor?" Martha asked.

Sarah lifted a shoulder in a shrug. "I remember when Jason was born, it started with a backache."

Martha smiled and patted Sarah's hand. "This is still driving you nuts, isn't it?"

"Yes, and it's annoying. I'm usually less of a worrywart."

"This situation about trying to unite Katie with her mother doesn't help. It brings up all kinds of emotions."

Sarah smiled at Martha. "Don't worry. I'll survive, but thank you for understanding."

"Here you go." Hannah set down a steaming casserole dish in front of both of them.

Martha inhaled a deep breath. "This smells so good."

Sarah pushed her spoon through the golden brown crust which was molded over a deep dish of rich gravy full of vegetables, herbs, and chunks of white chicken.

"Careful, it's hot." Martha grabbed her glass and took a swig of ice tea. "But excellent."

Sarah blew on her spoonful and then nibbled the edge. It was indeed hot, but the heat didn't mar the exquisite flavor that hit her tongue. She sighed and took a bigger bite. It conjured up memories of her mother serving pot pie on a cold winter evening. A bittersweet feeling swamped her. The memories were good, but she still missed her mother after all these years. She imagined Katie probably sat at meals and felt that way too.

After they had made sizable inroads in their pies, Martha glanced at her watch. "It's almost two. Do you think we've let enough time go by?"

"I think so." If Abram was going out to make his work rounds, he would be gone now. If not, they would just have to take their chances that he wouldn't order them to leave. If Annie wouldn't go, they would see if they could find Katie on their own.

"I'm nearly stuffed, but I'm starting to feel hunger pangs again watching that apple pie," Martha said and looked over at the large portions of warm pie topped with vanilla ice cream that the ladies had ordered. The smell of cinnamon and apples wafted over the table. "I really don't need the calories though."

"The apple pie and the ice cream are homemade," Hannah said as she walked by.

"Oh, now that's just not fair." Martha grinned.

"I think we're going to order dessert," Sarah said.

"We're not ones to pass up a good opportunity, especially involving pie," Martha added, and they laughed. They decided to split a piece to ease their conscience and agreed that the pie and ice cream were worth every single calorie.

The ladies at the other end of the table were gathering up their things and one waved Hannah over. "Miss, we were wondering if someone around here made those quaint rocking chairs out of tree branches."

The waitress nodded. "You will want to see Jockey John out on Bernville Road just past its intersection with Potts Road. He usually has some sitting on the porch for sale."

"Jockey John?" Martha asked Sarah after the ladies had made their way out the door.

"With so many of the Amish names being similar, many use nicknames." Sarah smiled at Hannah who approached with their check. "Am I correct?"

She nodded, her eyes twinkling. "Some of our people are starting to use middle names, but nicknames are still more common."

"That sounds like it could be fun," Martha said.

"It is, unless you get named something you do not like. Piggy Abel, for one. How do you think he got his name?"

"He raises pigs?" Martha asked.

Hannah shook her head. "He once pretended to be a pig during recess at school. The name stuck."

Martha giggled. "I'd be afraid they'd call me that because of my appetite."

Hannah smiled. "Other nicknames might say something about where a person lives, like Dry Hill David, or what they do for a living, like Jockey John. He raises and trades horses. And then there is Sewer Sam. You can imagine how he got that name."

"Oh yeah," Martha said with a giggle.

As Sarah listened to Martha and Hannah chat about names, an idea begin to form in the back of her mind. All the tiny clues she had picked up came together. Could it be that simple?

She reached into her purse and pulled a sheet of paper out of her notebook. She quickly composed a note and turned to Hannah.

"Can you do me a favor?"

"What was that about the note back in the restaurant?" Martha asked as they neared the Fisher farm.

"Just a hunch," Sarah said, turning on the right turn blinker. "I'll tell you about it later."

The tires crunched on gravel as the car rolled up the driveway. Annie sat on the front porch, a quilt hoop in her lap.

As Sarah parked the car and set the brake, she scanned the barnyard and fields. No Abram.

Annie rose and came down the steps. "Sarah Hart and Martha Maplethorpe, how good to see you." Her gaze sought out Sarah's. "What brings you to visit?"

"I brought something to show you," Sarah said, opening the back door of the car and bringing out the baby quilt. She held it up for Annie to see. "This is the quilt for my grandbaby that we talked about."

"It is beautiful. Your daughter will be very pleased," Annie said taking the quilt in her hands.

"I'm afraid my stitching isn't as skilled as yours."

"You did a fine job," Annie insisted.

"I wanted to show what Katie's quilt inspired."

At the mention of Katie's name, Annie's smile faded. "I can see the similarity." She handed the quilt back.

"Annie—"

She held up a hand. "If you are here to discuss my daughter, I cannot, but please come sit with me. I was about to have some refreshment. I will be right back." Annie went into the house.

"Now what?" Martha whispered as they sat on the porch chairs.

"I'm not sure." Sarah shook her head. If Annie wouldn't even discuss Katie, then her decision not to tell Annie about the art show was probably a good one.

Annie came out the door with a pitcher of juice and cups. "Would you like to try some apple cider? I canned it last year."

"Yes, please." Sarah waited until they had all been served and seated and then said, "I was wondering if I could ask you for some help. There's a fabric shop near Syracuse I've been wanting to visit. I'm thinking of doing another quilt and I could use advice picking out fabric."

Annie stared at her for a moment. "You want me to go to the shop with you? *Ja?*"

"If you can. I would be much obliged."

"It'll be fun," Martha said. "A girls afternoon out."

"I do not know what a girls afternoon out means, but ... I would like to go."

"Go where?" a deep voice said and Sarah realized why Annie had not wanted to discuss Katie. Abram was home. He came around the corner of the house and stopped short when he spied Sarah and Martha on the porch. "What are you doing here? I told you to stay away."

Annie rose, her shoulders straight. She looked her husband in the eye. "Abram, we must be Christian to our guests."

Abram seemed taken aback by her boldness and was at a loss for words. His gaze shifted between the women.

"I have decided to go to a fabric store with Sarah and Martha. We will have a girls afternoon out." Annie held up a hand as Abram opened his mouth. "My chores are done for the afternoon. Dinner is prepared and just needs to be heated."

"But—"

"I have not been outside Pleasant Valley in two years, and it would be good for me," Annie added. She took a step closer to her husband and lowered her voice. "Abram, surely you would not stop me from helping my friend?"

Abram snapped his mouth shut and turned away. "As you wish, Annie."

"Thank you, Abram." Annie turned to Sarah. "Let me get my sweater and I will go with you." She turned and went into the house. Abram stared at Sarah and Martha for several moments. He appeared to want to say something, but in the end spun around and stomped off in the direction he had come from.

Martha whooshed out a big breath. "Talk about a tense moment."

Sarah nodded in agreement. Her chest hurt from holding her breath.

"Are we ready to go?" Annie asked, coming back out with a black bag.

"Yes, let's." Sarah rose hastily, worried that Abram might reappear. It was only after they had driven several miles that the tightness in Sarah's shoulders began to ease. Martha had insisted that Annie sit in the front passenger seat, and Annie watched the countryside go by with a stoical expression.

"I apologize for my husband's unfriendliness," Annie said.

Sarah glanced at her. "Well, it's hard to blame him after our last visit."

"The Bible teaches that we are to love our enemies and do good to them that persecute us," Annie said, and then a look of horror descended on her fine features. "I did not mean you are persecuting us or are the enemy."

Sarah laughed. "It's okay. We know what you mean. And I suppose Abram and the bishop might view us that way."

"I talked with Bishop Stoltzfus and told him how I felt about the shunning, and how I had asked you to look for Katie. He said that my sin was understandable and that he did sympathize with me. I told him that in every area of my life I have followed the *Ordnung* and the wishes of my elders, but in this case, I had to speak out."

Martha leaned forward in the backseat. "What did you say?"

"That Katie is not a baptized member of the church and that she is not bound by the *Ordnung* right now and I wished to challenge the shunning." She made a face. "I thought he would have a stroke when I said that, but he is a good man and he allowed me to speak. Then he said everything he had before about Katie being a bad influence on others her age, her disregard for our tradition, and her disobedience, but this time his arguments seemed weak. He admitted as much."

"So is he going to take the shunning away?" Martha asked.

"I do not know. He is going to pray about it and will tell me later."

"You took a big risk," Sarah said.

"If he decides to have me shunned for seeking my daughter, then I will accept his decision. I will be fine." She smiled at Sarah. "I am stronger than most people think."

Sarah reached over and squeezed Annie's hand. "I think you're brave. I haven't found Katie yet, but I think we're close."

Please, Lord, lead us to her.

They still had another hour until the art show opened, so Sarah opted to turn into the fabric store parking lot first. The shop turned out to be an outlet for excess stock that normally went to factories. Sarah was so delighted by the choices and discussing colors and textures with Annie that the time flew by. It also kept Annie occupied so she did not ask more questions. They all emerged pleased with their finds and happier than when they had gone in.

As Sarah fastened her seat belt her stomach twisted. What if she was wrong about Katie being at the show? "Annie, do you mind making a stop on the way back?"

"I do not mind. This has been a pleasant afternoon. Thank you, Sarah and Martha."

"You're welcome," Sarah said. "And I appreciated your help in the fabric shop. The new quilt will give me something to look forward to doing after I visit with Jenna in Texas."

Sarah spied the sign for Colton Community College ahead. She turned into the parking lot and wound around a building until she saw a banner strung across the entrance to the gym announcing the location of the art show. Sarah's hands were sweaty as she put the car in park. Annie glanced at her, her expression questioning, but she got out of the car without speaking.

Several heads turned their way as they made their way to the gym. Annie's Amish clothing was conspicuous, but she didn't appear to notice the attention she drew. Probably from a lifetime of having people stare, Sarah mused.

"I saw the art show advertised on the Internet," Sarah said by way of an explanation.

"This will be fun." Martha stood on tiptoe trying to see over the line of people in front of them. "They sure have a good turnout. Where have all these people come from?"

They inched forward until they were standing by a table. A young woman informed them that there was a small cover charge which was going to support the art department, and if they wanted to purchase any pieces of art there was information inside on how to do so.

Sarah insisted on paying for everyone's tickets, and her heart started to pound as they entered the large, brightly lit room. She stopped and stared with dismay. Finding out if Katie was there was going to be a difficult task. The gym had been set up with dozens of rows of art easels with paintings and tables covered with pottery and sculpture. It seemed as though hundreds of people milled about, making it difficult to distinguish guests from students. For a small community college, the art show had attracted quite a crowd.

They wandered down row after row. Annie appeared to be enjoying herself, although she kept shooting Sarah questioning glances. *She suspects something*, Sarah thought, feeling guilty. Maybe she should have leveled with Annie and told her why they were really there.

Some of the art students lingered by their work to answer questions and pose for photographs with eager friends and relatives. Sarah kept looking at the names on the paintings, searching for a K. Visser, but so far no luck.

As they rounded one end of a row, Martha suddenly veered off and disappeared into the crowd. A minute later she caught up with them.

"Look what I found. A map," Martha said waving a paper. "I saw people carrying these around, but they'd run out of them at the entrance. A guy just showed up with more copies." She grinned and handed one to Sarah and Annie.

Sarah scanned the sheet. Someone had drawn up a map of the room by rows and labeled areas with student names so you could find their work. Unfortunately, the names weren't in alphabetical order, but near the end of the gym, Visser was listed.

Sarah scanned the crowd in that direction, but it was impossible to tell if Katie was there. Annie stood near, studying a painting of flowers. "This is pretty. Very lifelike."

"It is," Sarah agreed and shuffled forward. It seemed an eternity before they made their way to the end of the row where walking would be easier.

"Look, Mommy, there's another lady in a funny dress," a young girl with pigtails said.

Her mother grabbed her hand and pulled her away. "Shush, Zoe, that's not polite."

Annie smiled at the departing child and looked beyond the girl and her mother, her eyes widening. She gasped and darted into the crowd.

CHAPTER NINETEEN

A nnie," Sarah called. She stood on her tiptoes, but she
had lost sight of her.

"What happened?" Martha asked, sticking close
to Sarah as they moved forward through a group of
teenagers.

"I don't know," Sarah said. "She took off." The crowd finally parted to reveal Annie standing near the gym wall,
hugging a girl with Annie's blonde hair and freckles. The girl
was dressed in the Amish style, a dark skirt and light blue
blouse draping her slim frame. Her hair was pulled up in
coiled braids instead of the traditional bun. Tears ran down
their cheeks.

Katie.

Sarah's eyes stung. Any doubt about bringing Annie here
evaporated.

"Wow," Martha whispered beside her, giving Sarah a
one-arm hug. "You found her."

"*We* found her." Sarah cleared the lump in her throat. "Let's let them be for a while." She started to back away, but Annie lifted her head and looked at Sarah. She smiled and waved them over.

Katie looked at them, a question in her blue eyes as they approached.

"Sarah and Martha, this is my Katie," Annie said with her arm around Katie's waist.

"Sarah Hart," Katie said slowly. "You were the one looking for me on Kevin's e-mail."

Sarah nodded. "Yes, that was me."

"I'm sorry that I was rude to you."

"What do you mean rude?" Annie asked, looking at her daughter.

"I wrote an e-mail to Mrs. Hart, I mean, Kevin sent an e-mail for me, and I asked her not to look for me."

"If we didn't find Katie today, I was going to tell you the whole story," Sarah said to Annie. "But I didn't want you to get your hopes up if we didn't find her here. And Katie, you have nothing to be sorry about. I understand what you were trying to do. I'm sorry if I made you feel uncomfortable. Your friend Kevin is very protective of you."

"Yes, he is," she said, a smile creeping to her lips.

"I asked Sarah Hart to look for you, Katie," Annie said.

Katie shook her head. "I didn't want you to be shunned too."

"I understand, but I wanted to know you were all right," Annie said.

"I didn't mean to be away so long." Katie looked about the room. "I just wanted ... I just wanted ..." Her words were hardly audible as the buzz of people in the room increased.

"Why don't we find a more private place to talk," Sarah suggested.

"There are some benches outside," Martha said, tugging at her collar. "It's getting hot in here."

They made their way outside, Annie keeping a protective hold on her daughter's arm. Benches were lined up along a walkway on the side of the gym. The cool air bathed Sarah's warm face as they sat down. She felt shaky inside, so thrilled they had found Katie.

Annie turned to Katie and clasped their hands together tightly. "Now, Katie Fisher, why did you not come home? The bishop might have lifted the shunning if you had gotten baptized. Is this life so much better, away from your family and friends? From your faith?"

Katie looked down at their entwined hands. "It's not better. It's ... just different. I wanted to paint. I wanted to take classes. I was angry that no one at home would listen to me."

"I tried to listen."

"You would have done whatever Father wanted you to do."

Annie sighed. "Yes, but I am here now. I am not trying to make you do anything you do not want to do. I just wish you to be happy and safe."

"I know, Mama. Some people, like Father and the bishop, think that my choice was a frivolous one. But I just wanted to try. Art is the only thing I'm good at."

"That is not true, my girl," Annie protested.

"I meant to be good at something other than keeping house, cooking, and growing a garden. Those are important, of course," she said hastily. "But I wanted to be different ... at least for a little while."

Annie stared at her daughter. "And did find what you were looking for?" she asked softly.

Katie nodded. "I did not mean to be gone so long. I just want to graduate and then I will decide."

"Your home is open to you."

"What about Father?"

"Your father will welcome you too," Annie said with strength in her voice. "He may not have shown much tolerance in the past, but he loves you very much."

"Maybe I will come in June," Katie said.

Martha learned close to Sarah and whispered. "What about Kevin?"

She lifted a shoulder indicating she didn't know. She scanned the parking lot. If her hunch was right, then Kevin really didn't factor into Katie's decision to return to her community.

Annie gave Katie another hug. "Are you going to show me what you made?"

"If you want to see it."

"I do." Annie rose. "I want to see it all."

"So do I," Martha said. They turned back to the entrance.

A man in an Amish hat and clothing stood by the gym door. He scanned the crowd until his eyes connected with Katie. "Katie!"

Katie froze. "Ken?"

He started toward her, and she ran to him. Sarah recognized Abram Stoltzfus as he gave Katie a quick hug and then stepped back, his face reddening.

"What are you doing here?" Katie asked. "How did you know where to find me?"

"I got a message you might be here," he said. "I have to talk to you." He looked at Annie, and she gave a slight nod. He drew Katie off the sidewalk and sat with her on a bench.

"So that's what you were doing in the restaurant." Martha grinned. "Your hunch."

"And it paid off," Sarah said softly, feeling tears rise again. "When I thought Katie might be here, I sent *Ken* a note."

"I'm sorry, who is Ken?" Martha asked.

"The bishop's son." Sarah nodded toward Abram.

"I thought he was Abram."

"Abram Kennel Stoltzfus," Annie said, her gaze never leaving her daughter. "Katie and Abram have been friends since childhood. I had hoped that someday they would be more than friends."

Apparently they were, Sarah thought as she looked at the couple sitting close enough their knees almost touched. They were still near enough to hear their voices.

Katie had crossed her arms over her chest. "Does your father know you're here?"

"Yes. I told him I needed to speak to you."

"I do not want you to get in trouble because of me," Katie said. "I do not want anybody to suffer for my decisions. What if they shun you? It would be my fault."

"No, you are wrong. Because of *me*, you were shunned."

Katie shook her head, looking confused. "No, I disobeyed. That was enough."

"I talked to my father until he admitted that he had guessed about our plans to be married someday. He had seen us talking. When you starting taking art classes and doing so well, he wanted to force you to make a decision. He wanted to see where your loyalty lay. He expected you to choose to be baptized. If you were not going to be a suitable Amish wife, he wanted you to stay away."

"But . . . my father agreed with him."

"I know. They thought they were doing what was right. I should have confronted my father earlier, but I was not ready to be a man."

"I do not want you to change because of me. That's why I never wrote. I know how important being Amish is for you," Katie said.

"And I *told* you I would wait, postpone baptism, until you made a decision. Did you not believe me?"

Katie's silence indicated she hadn't. "I am sorry I doubted you."

"I'm just glad to find you. Seeing you gives me hope."

"In what way?"

"You still dress Amish." He grinned.

She patted her hair. "Almost. I never stopped believing, but I did doubt some of our ways, the *Ordnung*. I still do, but maybe I can live with that if I can be with you."

Martha placed her hand on Sarah's shoulder and drew her back a few feet to talk to her privately. Her eyes were wet. "Let me sort this out. Katie calls Abram Ken?"

"Right. Hannah said that Katie had a secret nickname for Abram because he has the same name as her father, but it didn't click until this afternoon when you were talking about nicknames. When I was at the library I had seen that Abram's middle name was Kennel."

"Got it. So Ken is the other K in the quilt, not Kevin," Martha said and then giggled. "Oh boy. I guess we were pretty hard on Kevin, and he wasn't her boyfriend after all."

Sarah smiled. "Well, he shouldn't have gotten off too easy. After all, he did lie to me, and apparently he did help Katie run away. If he or Madison had told the truth, it would've saved us so much time and trouble."

"And to think, if Katie hadn't sewn the Ks on her quilt, you never would have found her," Martha said. "Even though it was the wrong K we were tracking."

Abram and Katie had stopped talking, and Abram came toward Sarah. "Thank you, Sarah Hart, for helping me find Katie again."

"You're welcome, Abram."

"I will take Mrs. Fisher home. She already agreed."

"How come you get to drive?" Martha asked. "I thought driving motor vehicles was prohibited."

He grinned sheepishly. "When I started *Rumspringa*, I wanted to learn. This is a friend's truck. My father does not know. Do not worry. I have a license, which I will not use after I am baptized."

Sarah smiled. Considering what she had learned about other Amish children's exploits like partying, learning to drive seemed a minor offense.

"Abram, did you drive Katie anywhere?" she asked thinking about Jesse at Lydia's Gas Station seeing someone who looked like Katie.

His face flushed again. "Yes. I took her to the bus stop in Sunnyvale."

"So you helped her leave?"

He nodded. "The Bible teaches that we must come to God with our free will. Katie has the right to choose her life. We all do. Many people do not understand the Amish. We live this way by choice. And I am going to make sure Katie can make a choice, free from pressure and guilt."

"Katie is lucky to have you," Sarah said sincerely.

"Thank you for everything you have done," Abram said as Katie walked up.

"Would you like to see my paintings?" Katie asked, shyness in her voice.

"We'd love to," Sarah said and the group headed inside. They offered well-deserved praise for Katie's paintings and later said good-bye to Katie and Annie in the parking lot with promises to stay in touch.

"Ken, or Abram, is such a nice young man," Martha said after they got in Sarah's car. "Do you think they're going to be okay?"

"Yes, I do, now that they're together again," Sarah said, her heart swelling as she looked in the rearview mirror at mother and daughter in another embrace. Abram stood protectively at their side.

Sarah turned out of the parking lot and drove the two hours back home, saying little, both she and Martha lost in their thoughts and as comfortable with the silence as two old friends could be. It had been a long day, full of emotion and satisfaction.

As they entered Maple Hill, Sarah sent up a silent prayer of thankfulness for a family on their way to being reunited and peace for everyone involved.

Sarah was turning into Martha's driveway when her phone rang, startling them both.

"Mom?" Jenna said, sounding excited and nervous. "It's time. Finally."

"I'm on my way, sweetheart. I can't wait to see you. I'll be praying."

"Me too," Martha said as Sarah clicked her phone shut. She reached over and squeezed Sarah's hand. "Congrats, Grandma. Safe trip." She hopped out of the car and watched as Sarah backed out of the driveway.

Sarah waved at Martha and pointed the car home, eager to start the journey that would reunite her with her own daughter and the newest member of their family.

ABOUT THE AUTHOR

From her first introduction to the beginner readers with Dick and Jane, award-winning author Kelly Ann Riley has wanted to be a writer. She started penning stories at an early age and received special recognition for her short stories. Later, she became a reporter and the editor for her high school newspaper.

Now Kelly Ann enjoys writing romantic suspense and cozy mysteries. Her past hobbies of quilting, cross-stitching, and crocheting make Patchwork Mysteries particularly fun to write. She loves watching fabric, string, and yarn transform into art. She is a member of American Christian Fiction Writers and Romance Writers of America, and lives in Alabama with her family. You can contact her through her Web site at KellyAnnRiley.com.

THE CALICO TRAIL

BY KRISTIN ECKHARDT

 CHAPTER ONE

Sarah Hart couldn't stop gazing at the beautiful photograph of her new granddaughter, Leah Nicole. She had flown down to Texas as soon as her daughter Jenna had called with the news that she was in labor. Sarah had arrived in Texas shortly after the newest member of their family had made her entrance into the world. Little Leah Nicole had stolen Sarah's heart the moment she had seen her in Jenna's arms.

After so many months of waiting, God had answered Sarah's prayers for a safe birth and a healthy grandchild. The last few weeks had been the most difficult, especially for Jenna. They had burned up the phone lines between Massachusetts and Texas, both of them impatient for the baby's arrival.

Now the waiting was over, and Sarah had returned from Texas the night before after spending a glorious week helping Jenna with the new baby. She had spent plenty of grandma-time with her two grandsons, Thomas and Jonathan, and did her best to keep the household running smoothly so Jenna and her husband David could get to know their new daughter.

Sarah breathed a happy sigh as she picked up the quilted picture frame that held Leah's photo. She had created the frame from the fabric remnants of the baby quilt she had made for her granddaughter. "Dear Lord, thank you for my beautiful grandchildren," she prayed softly, "for Amy and Audrey and Thomas and Jonathan. And thank you for the newest blessing in my life, little Leah Nicole. Give me the wisdom and guidance to be a blessing in all of their lives, Lord, and to be the best grandma I can be. Amen."

With a happy sigh, Sarah placed the picture frame back on her desk, next to the photos of her other grandchildren. Then she rose out of her chair, ready to do some spring cleaning now that May had finally arrived. And she knew just where to start.

Sarah walked over to the closet where she kept all of her fabric remnants, some piled almost as high as the ceiling. This time she was going to do it. She was going to go through her fabric stash and decide which fabrics to keep and which to clear out of her closet.

Like most quilters, Sarah found it difficult to give up any fabric in her stash. She wouldn't call herself a fabric hoarder, but there were some fabric remnants she would probably never use. Sometimes certain fabrics that had seemed perfect in the planning stage just didn't look quite right when it was time to add them to a quilt.

She placed several fabric remnants on her quilting table, wanting to see them side by side before she made any final decisions. Each remnant was wrapped around a nine-by-twelve-inch piece of cardboard she had cut from old cardboard boxes, the fabric end pinned down to keep it nice and neat. This made it easy to stack her remnants on the closet shelves and see what she had in stock with a quick glance.

Now she spread them out on the table, wanting to see them in the sunlight streaming in from the window. She arranged them according to color and soon had a rainbow of fabrics filling the large table.

Then she stood at the table for the next five minutes, trying to decide which fabric remnants she could live without.

"Just pick one," Sarah told herself.

But as she reached for a green cotton print with tiny horses on it, the telephone rang.

Grateful for the reprieve, Sarah walked into the kitchen and picked up the phone. "Hello?"

"Hi, Sarah, it's Maggie. How was your trip?"

"It was perfect." Sarah settled into a kitchen chair, in the mood for a long chat with her daughter-in-law. "Leah is so sweet, and I had so much fun with Thomas and Jonathan."

"We can't wait to meet her," Maggie said. "The girls loved the pictures Jenna posted on her Facebook page. It's so much fun to have a baby in the family again!"

"I know. I miss her already, but Jenna promised to keep sending pictures. And you should see the boys—they are such proud big brothers and so protective of her."

"Oh, I can just imagine," Maggie said, chuckling. "Jason and I are trying to figure out a good time to make a visit. The girls would leave tomorrow if we'd let them, but I told them we can't go anywhere while school is still in session. Only a few more weeks to go."

Sarah smiled, looking forward to spending extra time with her granddaughters this summer.

"Sarah, I was wondering…," Maggie began, her voice jumping a little, "I was wondering if you could come over to the house. Sooner rather than later."

Alarmed, Sarah sat up in the chair. "Is something wrong?"

"No, not at all," Maggie assured her. "I'm just so excited. My mom just sent me a whole bunch of wonderful antiques, including a nineteenth-century quilt that I'd love for you to see. Can you make it?"

"I'll be there in five minutes."

"Great," Maggie replied. "See you soon."

Sarah grabbed her purse. She felt a familiar thrill of excitement coursing through her as she made her way out the back door. There was nothing she liked better than examining an antique quilt and learning the history behind it. Sometimes it was easy to do and other times it took all her ingenuity to ferret out the secrets sewn into the vintage quilt blocks.

When she arrived at Maggie's house, the twins greeted her at the door, chattering with excitement.

"Hey, Grandma! How's Leah," Amy said, swinging the front door wide open. "Are her eyes really that blue?"

Sarah reached out to give both girls a hug. "They are blue, but most babies have blue eyes when they're born. They'll either stay blue or slowly change to a different color."

"Cool," Audrey said. "I wonder what color they'll be."

"I think I saw a little bit of green in them," Sarah said. "But we'll have to wait and see."

"We each got to buy her a present," Audrey told Sarah. "We just sent them yesterday. I got her a pink dress and bonnet."

"And I got her a stuffed, purple octopus. Each one of the eight arms has a rattle in it," Amy added. "It's so cute."

Sarah relished the twins' excitement about Leah and realized how much she had missed them in the week she had been gone.

"And guess what else?" Amy said. "Grammy sent us a whole bunch of cool stuff!"

"I got a new MP3 player." Audrey danced around the front hallway, pulling a pair of hot pink earbuds out of her pocket. "It holds over four thousand songs."

"You already have one that holds a thousand songs," Amy told her sister. "The camera she sent me is wicked cool." She dug a small blue camera, the size of a deck of cards, out of her pocket. "It will even do video-recording. I can't wait to record Leah on it."

Sarah could see a trail of boxes and packing paper leading from the front hall into the parlor. Patty's generosity was one of the things she liked best about Maggie's mother. Patty had other traits that sometimes rubbed Sarah the wrong way, but she tried not to let them bother her. Last Christmas, Patty had hatched a plan to entice Maggie and Jason to move back to California. Some of Patty's antics over the holiday had caused tension in the family, but it had been smoothed over by the time she and her husband Larry had headed home after the holidays.

"Hey, Amy, record me," Audrey said to her sister, putting her earbuds in and bopping to a beat that only she could hear. "I want to see what I look like when I dance."

"I don't think you do," Amy teased as she held the camera in front of Audrey.

Sarah ducked out of the view of the camera and followed the packing paper trail into the parlor. Maggie sat on the floor wearing a royal blue and white Hawthorne Middle School sweatshirt and a pair of blue jeans. Her auburn hair was pulled back in a messy ponytail.

"What's all this?" Sarah asked.

Maggie rose off the floor when she saw her. "My mom told me she had a surprise for me, but I never expected anything like this. There was a freight truck parked in our driveway when I got home from the shop and the driver kept unloading boxes until I thought we were going to run out of room. The big stuff is in the garage."

Sarah moved into the room, spotting some treasures among the packing materials strewn across the floor. She saw an antique butter crock, a copper teakettle, a vintage mantel clock, a crank-style phonograph, and other various collectibles. "Where did all of this come from?"

"My great-aunt Myrna. She passed away last week at the grand old age of ninety-eight." Maggie cleared off the sofa so they could sit down. "Do you remember her from our wedding?"

"I think so." Sarah thought about an older woman at the reception who had sought her out and told her how proud they were to add Jason to their family. "Did your great-aunt walk with an ebony cane?"

Maggie nodded as she plopped down on the sofa. "That was her. Aunt Myrna was an amazing woman and the self-proclaimed matriarch of my mom's side of the family. The Hollanders have a long and rich heritage, carefully chron-icled by Aunt Myrna. She was in charge of the Hollander family reunion, which was held every year. Family members would come from all over the country."

Sarah reached out to squeeze Maggie's hand. "It sounds like you're going to miss her."

Maggie nodded, tears shining in her green eyes. "I am. Her memorial service is scheduled for the end of the month in Willow Creek, Pennsylvania. That was the original set-tlement of the Hollanders before they migrated west. She's giving us all one more family reunion as her farewell gift."

"What a perfect way to honor her memory," Sarah said softly.

Maggie wiped a tear off her cheek. "She meant a lot to me." Then she looked out over the bounty on the parlor floor. "And she liked to collect antiques, as you can see. The family heirlooms were all divided between her nieces and nephews, but this is just some of what was left in her house." She picked up a small card from the end table. "Here's the note Mom included in one of the boxes."

Sarah took the card from her as she sat down on the sofa and began to read it to herself.

My dear Maggie,

As you know, your great-aunt Myrna was thrilled when she heard you had opened an antique store in Maple Hill. She wanted you to have the items that didn't have a Hollander family connection, so I'm fulfilling one of her last wishes. There is one item, however, that she specifically left to you in her will. It's the pioneer quilt that was made by the Hollander family as they made their way along the Oregon Trail in 1849. It has a few imperfections, but I know that Sarah likes to dabble in quilts so perhaps she can help you fix them. I think it would make a nice display piece in your shop and be a wonderful way to showcase the Hollander family history.

Love and kisses,
Mom

Sarah set the card back on the table, trying to ignore the jibe about *dabbling* in quilts. "Have you opened the box with the quilt yet?"

"I have," Maggie said, rising off the sofa. "It's in the dining room."

Sarah followed Maggie to the dining room, her curiosity putting a spring in her step. She had seen a few pioneer quilts before, mostly in magazines and at quilt shows, but they were all so unique that she didn't know what to expect.

Maggie stood in the doorway of the dining room and pointed to the table. "There it is."

Sarah approached it with a sense of awe, seeing such a smorgasbord of history spread out before her. She gently touched a corner edge of the quilt as her gaze took in each individual block. "Oh, Maggie, this is amazing."

"I've only seen it once before," Maggie said, "when I was a little girl. Aunt Myrna always kept it carefully packed away. I couldn't wait for you to see it."

Sarah could see the quilt was in good condition for its age. There were a few loose threads, some fraying and light stains, but nothing that couldn't be repaired. "Maggie, do you know what this quilt is telling us?"

A NOTE FROM THE EDITORS

We hope you enjoy Patchwork Mysteries, created by the Books and Inspirational Media Division of Guideposts, a nonprofit organization that touches millions of lives every day through products and services that inspire, encourage, help you grow in your faith, and celebrate God's love in every aspect of your daily life.

Thank you for making a difference with your purchase of this book, which helps fund our many outreach programs to military personnel, prisons, hospitals, nursing homes, and educational institutions. To learn more, visit GuidepostsFoundation.org.

We also maintain many useful and uplifting online resources. Visit Guideposts.org to read true stories of hope and inspiration, access OurPrayer network, sign up for free newsletters, download free e-books, join our Facebook community, and follow our stimulating blogs.

To learn about other Guideposts publications, including the best-selling devotional *Daily Guideposts*, go to ShopGuideposts.org, call (800) 932-2145, or write to Guideposts, PO Box 5815, Harlan, Iowa 51593.